# HARMONIOUS FIST

# By

# Elcid

D1641631

Visit:

Official TikTok: @elcidthewriter

Official Instagram: @mackadelcid

I say thanks to everybody.

*"Daruma had returned from his odyssey across the world, that did not surprise the people of the Sol Islands, they were seafaring people. Wondering about or lengthy adventures was a thing that flowed within their veins.*

*Nevertheless, they all gazed at him astonished, not by the stories of his voyage or the little he had brought. It was when he was challenged by the warriors of the islands that their gaze could not leave his effortless movements in neutralising his opponents at will, without harming any of them. Unless he wished to, going as far as breaking bones now and then, but rarely if not did he take away lives"-Ancient Tales of Daruma, The Wanderer.*

# PART ONE

# LEI TAI

# CHAPTER ONE-
# THE SEPARATISTS

Once upon a time, long before the birth of the universe, in the state of nothingness was wuji, which gave birth to taijitu, the two opposites that complemented each other, yin and yang. From these two arose the five elemental phases. Metal, water, wood, fire and earth and from the five, the myriads of things that make up the expansive universe.

These observations were made from the dawn of civilisation, by Daoist sages, who were hermits meditating in the high mountains, in an area known as the Dragon's Lair. Where it is believed dragons once resided (thus the name). The Daoist sages, observing nature made many discoveries.

They created meditative exercises, that increased longevity, amongst many other things. Their knowledge on the inner workings of nature also helped them create martial methods, all in the objective to adapt and survive all the changes that nature brought with it. They summed up their knowledge calling it the Dao, meaning the way.

Soon, their knowledge spread, reaching the rest of mankind. This knowledge was used for self-gain by some, leading to war and from this disease, came its many symptoms.

The world was engulfed in chaos, fathers and sons fought; brothers murdered brothers; for hundreds of years, the world experienced carnage. Moments of fragile peace were always broken by sporadic skirmishes amongst nations leading to calamity.

It was a young man, of a fiery nature, taught in the ancient traditions of the Water School of Daoism from the mountains of the Dragon's Lair, that brought peace to the world. His name was Fei Yue; he had a violent temper and was unbearable as a child. His mother, a single mom had him sent away as a last resort, to douse his flaming temper, once he was thirteen years of age.

He was sent to the Water School, where his strict teachers managed to extinguish these flames and bring balance to his heart. Within three years, the young Fei had finally found some form of inner peace. He was then taught all the secrets of the Water School. Training night and day, until he could not sweat any more. It was finally on the tenth year since his training had begun that he had mastered the hermits' teachings.

Given the very secretive nature of the Water School, compared to the other schools of thought in the area, the young Fei now at that time a twenty-six-year-old man, was their only disciple. Having passed all their trials, he was made a master of the Water School. It was now time for him to return to his mother. However, the Daoist hermits on the day of recognising his mastery in their sciences and arts told him that with the knowledge he now possessed it was his responsibility to cure the world and restore balance. Since he was not going to join them in living as a hermit. His contact with the outside world meant that he had to heal it. Fei honourably yielded to their demands.

Upon his return to his village, horror-struck him; the village was demolished and everything that once moved had lost their breaths to a violent death. A wasteland composed of decapitated heads and the corpses of people, their pets and livestock. Amongst the grim images was the mutilated body of his mother.

Head down and aimlessly strolling amongst what was left of the massacre with tears starting to streak down his cheeks. He spotted a short sword left by the murderers. Grabbing it, he firmly held it by the hilt as he sighed.

Gazing around him, anger long lost and now found, erupted and with brewing thoughts of revenge, he returned to the mountains.

The hermits from the Water School received a sobbing Fei, broken down and crawling on the floor holding the short sword on the other hand. Trickling tears and gasps of helplessness described him at that time. Days went by and Fei had calmed down and one day, after having finished a session of meditation, he approached the hermits, with the short sword he had brought from his village. There were only three sages in the Water School.

'We here at the school, have abilities that could have stopped what happened,' these were the first words spoken by Fei ever since his return. The Daoist blankly stared at him, Fei himself also looked detached. 'I know the teachings can be interpreted to teach one not to get involved in worldly affairs,' Fei paused and then continued, 'Regardless, the tragedy that has occurred could have been stopped, I blame myself. But I look at you lot!' his voice now rising in tone, 'calling yourselves servants of the Water School, when my village was in flames where was your WATER! I will save this world. But most important of all...I will also rid it of weakness and indecision.' By this time, he was pointing the short sword at the sages.

'You have already made your decision,' one of them said. 'You will save the world, for that we have no regrets for the full knowledge we have transmitted to you,' the other added. 'This is our end, and your beginning, although you will succeed in many battles that await you. Today is one war you have lost,' the third one concluded. 'Cowards!' snarled Fei, moving towards them like a swooping falcon with precision. He cut them down using techniques he was taught but most importantly had mastered. He then burned their bodies after the massacre, and now he was the sole lineage holder of the Water School.

Using his knowledge, Fei raised an army and started conquering parts of the world, marching through land and sailing by sea. Peace was brought to his conquered subjects and despite having become a king due to his conquests, Fei was simply known as General Fei.

His ambition was to have the whole world under his rule, after bringing peace and order in his kingdom, Fei set out to build an empire. His small kingdom soon had other dominions under its rule as kingdoms fell and he became an emperor becoming more powerful. With this rise in power, his fear that he would lose it all also grew. Birthing a paranoia within him, with this began his purge and tyranny.

Subjects, lieutenants, anyone he suspected to be against him, he killed. The more he killed the more the fears he felt grew. It was then that his eyes were set on the Dragons' Lair. Daoist sages still dwelled there, their knowledge he thought would stop his plans. At first, he brushed the thought of getting rid of them away. But it was during one of his campaigns in the Southern regions of the world, that he acted on those thoughts.

Here he struggled to conquer the small principality of Sud. A small city-state that was the home to the Loham Temple, where Buddhist adherents had fused their ways with Daoism, a synchronisation known as Chan Buddhism.

Sud was the home of the holy and the bravest of warriors; the warrior monks from the temple had shared their knowledge with the populace and its ruler, a lineage holder himself of Loham pugilism and all its other arts or sciences. The Sud ruler was more than a sore thorn in General Fei's passage. Unlike Fei, he was a sturdy short man, black-skinned with a thick black beard and thick black eyebrows that stuck out like flames. Prince Rey Sud was his name, a mighty warrior known for his hidden temper and conspicuous kindness. He had halted Fei's advance into the Southern lands (the world's only resistance to General Fei's ambitions of world conquest).

Prince Rey Sud managed to ally with all the nations of the Southern regions and with time began to push Fei's forces back. His end, however, came under the hands of Yu Guan, who was known as General Red Crow. He was a faithful lieutenant of Fei and one of his greatest students.

With Sud captured, Fei ordered the murder of all of Prince Rey Sud's sons. One managed to escape through the aid of loyalists and since the alliance was still intact, they held what remained of the South. While Prince Rey Sud's last son, Dos Sud made his way to the Dragons' Lair.

There he joined the school of Fire. This school was the opposite of the school of water in that it began its basic teachings with movements and ended it with stillness. The school of water did the opposite. Both, however, came to the same result and Dos Sud being the only one out of all of Prince Rey Sud's sons to have been trained in the ways of the Loham Temple, quickly grasped the concepts he was taught by the Daoist hermits.

Fei's spies finally had managed to gather information on Dos Sud's whereabouts and once the news passed the ears of Fei, he was furious. Not only was he going to kill Dos Sud, but he planned also killing all Daoist hermits at the Dragons' Lair. His enemies' plans were obvious (Dos Sud was to learn from the Fire School to stop Fei). Nevertheless, by the time Fei himself entered the mountains slaughtering the Daoist hermits. The news had reached him too late, years had already passed, a good ten years. The Southern lands still resisted and the alliance although now weaker, still held ground. Worse of all, he began to experience insubordination from his troops, who were tired, and the long wars cost him economically.

Dos Sud was back in the Southern lands and strengthened what was left of the alliance, winning various battles, he regained what was lost, including Sud. Where he was crowned prince the following day after its liberation.

Confused and disoriented from the tormenting fear he felt, one evening Fei resorted to the finest wines he could find from his imperial cellar, during an imperial banquet. It was then that his end came.

Seeing the degradation of his master become more visible, General Red Crow had enough as he glared at Fei (who was drunk beyond consciousness and thoughtlessly swinging his sword). Seizing the moment, General Red Crow drew out his sword, 'Your lordship this madness! Comes to an end tonight!' he said sternly as he rushed towards Fei. Fei beamed at his disciple chuckling as General Red Crow got closer, 'Even in my drunkenness, your no match for me.' Once he spoke those words Fei wasted no time and swung his sword at General Red Crow who dodged the blow. He was taken aback, feeling the power behind the blow; Fei was just toying with him. The confidence the general felt earlier quickly faded and astonished he awaited his death. Fei was now screaming, going frantic and saying words that could not be comprehended and with one wild swing heading for General Red Crow, he tripped losing his balance and fell. Somehow, he ended having his sword pierce his body.

His blood poured out and suddenly he remembered the words of one of his masters, *'This is our end, and your beginning, although you will succeed in many battles that await you. Today is one war you have lost.'* Fei then realised too late that he had forgotten the most basic of the teachings, inner peace. His worst enemy had been himself the whole time; the fear that he felt had given birth to his undoing. A sharp swing beheaded him, the cut coming from General Red Crow as he stood from the top, gazing at Fei's head, which had rolled to the side with its eyes wide open and the tongue rolled out.

The days that came after had the Fei Empire in a civil war, General Red Crow controlled parts of the empire and fought for what was left with the other generals. The alliance in the South was now known as the Sud Empire, with Dos Sud as emperor. There, there was peace and the decay of the Fei empire brought peace around the world.

Within the centuries that came by, to avoid losing many lives and instead of having nations have their troops engage one another in battle. Nations had their best champions fight each other, in one on one combat to the death on a raised platform, this way of conducting diplomatic disputes was to be known as the Lei Tai.

Then the Union of Nations was formed, and this global institution was the only one to have armed forces, known as the Union Guards. The Union Guards kept global peace and the world was divided into eight nations. The Northern Republics, the Nordic East, the Nordic West, the United West, Eastland, the Sud Republic, the East-South Union and the Sud-West Republics. The Union of Nations was run by the council of the eight permanent elders, each elder coming from the eight different nations. Their focus was on keeping world peace. Also, there was the annual Lei Tai fighting tournament, to commemorate the world's past.

Each nation of the world sent their best fighters to the Lei Tai, and the chosen fighters went through qualification by first competing in their regions' Sanshou competitions. The Sanshou was the name given to these qualification fights that also took place in a raised platform. The champions of these competitions were then sent to compete in the Lei Tai.

Years into the future and modern-day, in Main Central (Wobbleton City's high maximum-security prison) and isolated from the rest of the prison population, was a twenty-three-year-old man. His legs were chained and so were his hands. This did not stop him from training.

With most of his weight on his back right leg, he stepped slightly with his left foot and punched out simultaneously with his right foot following; landing the same time as whichever fist was in front.

The air was displaced like a gust of wind, with each punch as he stepped in a straight line, back and forth in his cell. His blue prison uniform's sleeves were rolled up, with sweat rolling down his black skin on both of his tattoos. Each one slightly below the shoulders of both arms, the tattoos being trigrams, the one on the right had two straight unbroken lines with one broken line split in two in between them. The tattoo on the left arm was the opposite of the latter. The one symbolised fire and the one on the left water. Daoist in nature, the tattoos were a representation of the union between fire and water.

This twenty-three-year-old man was Felix Sobek, jailed for manslaughter, he had been imprisoned since the age of sixteen. First to Wobbleton City's Juvenile Centre and then once he reached the age of eighteen, to Main Central. A prison housing the most dangerous criminals of the Sud-Republic.

A small spherical opening appeared on the cell door, with the gaze of one of the prison guards, 'It's time,' he said as he opened the cell door. It was time for Felix to take his last chi kung class (they were breathing exercises of a meditative nature for one's health, which he taught the prisoners). There were also martial methods of chi kung, used by martial artists.

That day was Felix Sobek's last day in prison, he was to be freed in the next few hours. After the class, he had the whole prison courtyard to himself. This time unchained, he strolled towards a boulder and the guards watched still flabbergasted by what was about to take place. Felix first began to slam his hands against the boulder looking calm and relaxed. It was then followed by a series of punches.

His hands were too conditioned to show any signs of damage and the boulder had indentations from years of abuse, by the hands of Felix.

Another prisoner stepped in the courtyard it was his time as well, a felon convicted for life and known to have killed five hundred people through deadly duels. He had grey hair, a flat snake-like nose and wolf-like small yellow eyes, that had no crease. They were monolid and his skin was like milk with a tinge of coffee. Silver Serpent was his name. He was an old man but with an upright posture of an adolescent and lean muscles and a body with barely an ounce of fat.

Belonging to an ancient clan believed to be extinct, Silver was thought to be the only one left. He was a lineage holder of the ancient martial art, Serpent Style. It was created by his clan known as the Slang Nyoka; one of his ancestors had transmitted bits of it to the Loham Monks who then created their style, calling it the Loham Snake.

'Hi Shirfu,' said Felix as he saluted Silver using the yin yang gesture (his left hand was open with the fingers pointed straight and on top of his right hand, which was closed into a fist). Chuckling, Silver replied with the less martial version of the gesture, (his left hand on top, wrapped on his right hand which was held as a fist). 'I am not your Shirfu, boy,' he said as he pulled out a vial from one of his pockets, which contained some red-brownish liquid and upon seeing the vial, a smile covered Felix's face. 'Here,' Silver handed the vial to Felix, who took it and quickly replied with, 'Thanks.' 'Anytime boy, you like family, do not forget to tell your uncle I send him my greetings,' began Silver and he continued, 'the dit da jow should help you heal after the bruising session you just had. Delivering before you bother me.' 'You make the best dit da jow Silver, really...thank you,' said Felix as he sprayed some of the liquid from the vial on both his hands and massaged them. It had an earth-like scent with a hint of alcohol. The dit da jow was a liniment used by martial artists to aid in healing, after the gruelling conditioning of their limbs. 'One more thing before I leave...just one technique,' said Felix. 'HA!' bellowed Silver, 'Your family's Harmonious Fist is good enough,' he concluded.

Waiting out of Main Central's main gate, Felix looked up at the clear skies and gazed directly at the sun. He did not mind its rays blinding him one bit. He closed his eyes and felt an exhilarating sensation rush throughout his body. And then screamed out loud with joy with his hands shooting up in the air, he was free.

After ten minutes of waiting outside, he suddenly heard the loud smooth roar of a car engine from a distance. The car was then within sight, red and fancy; it slowly slowed down in front of him. Both of its suicide doors smoothly flung open. And out of the driving seat stepped out a tall bald black man with a skilfully trimmed full beard, shorter than the thick trimmed beard Felix had across his face.

The man was neatly dressed in a black suit with a crimson necktie that had black polka dots. While his feet were adorned with polished maroon shoes. Tightening his tie as he beamed at Felix, it was Mr Carl Sobek, his father.

He was the last person Felix expected to pick him up. 'Where is Uncle Fred?' asked Felix. 'Wow,' frowned his father at the question. 'How about you greet me first, son!' he said. 'Sorry, how have you been?' asked Felix. 'Great!' laughing, Carl approached his son; once he was close, he grabbed his son by the shoulders as Felix gazed up at him. Beaming back at Felix, Carl said with a teasing tone in his voice, 'Hope they did not turn you into a bitch up in there.' Shrugging him off, Felix replied nonchalantly, 'Yea whatever…let's get out of this hell hole,' and then he headed for the car.

The engine roared as they drove off, and the moment of silence inside the car was broken by Carl as he said, 'Look you and I haven't seen eye to eye and we probably still would not, however, you will be staying with me. I may have not been the greatest of fathers even when your mom was alive, but I did and do my best. By the way, heard you studied while inside,' Carl glanced at his son and back at the road as he changed gears. 'Yea studied Biotechnology and got my honours last year,' answered Felix. 'Well done, your uncle mentioned it. Just did not know what exactly it was that you studied,' said Carl. 'You will be looking for a job?' he asked. 'Eddy has managed to get me a job at Gaia Corp,' answered Felix.

Eddy Sobek was Felix's cousin, they both were the same age, Felix being older by a few months. Eddy was a young executive working at Gaia Corp, unlike Felix, Eddy had never seen a prison cell and nor had his adolescences been as troubling.

Silence had fallen again in the car and Carl took a left turn and drove up on an incline as the road went up. Felix glanced around reminiscing younger days when he had crashed a few times riding down the sloping road with his bicycle. A smile painted itself on his face and then faded away. Driving up and then reaching level ground right in front stood big gates with dragon statues on each side, it was the Sobek residence.

Carl pressed a button from a miniature remote and the gates flung open. Even before heading to prison, Felix had left his house a year before after having a huge fight with his father. Now looking at the mansion, he saw nothing much had changed. Getting out of the car, they were received by a short and stocky old woman, in her black uniform. She was white and pale of complexion, with piercing sky-blue eyes and long grey hair; her name was Mrs Mary Witkins.

'Felix!' She exclaimed as she smiled. Felix smiled back as he opened his arms wide and hugged her, 'Been a long long time,' said Felix. Mrs Wilkins reached up for Felix's cheeks and squeezed them and said, 'You nearly gave me a heart attack! With your nonsense!' Then she slapped him, frowning and slightly shocked Felix massaged his cheeks and Mrs Wilkins added with a grin, 'Now we equal,' turning to Mr Sobek she then said, 'Okay I am going to get back to work.'

Mrs Wilkins was more than just the housekeeper; she was the de facto mother to Felix ever since his mother passed away when he was ten years old. She took care of him the best way she could. Now and then she would also be Mr Sobek's carer, he would seek her counsel when he was under the influence of alcohol and she would tuck him in. Despite the years of service, Mrs Wilkins a widow was still a mystery, she was one of the first female Union Guards in her younger days and despite her age, she was unusually strong.

Felix had gone to relax in his room, which he had not seen in eight years, everything seemed just like he had left it. Gazing around at the items in his room, brought in nostalgic emotions of his teenage years. They were posters of Lei Tai champions of old and one poster caught his eye, it was that of a bikini model. He smirked as he looked at it and then his eyes fell upon his computer. It had outdated software, he walked towards it anyway and switched it on. Felix was slightly surprised that it still worked. His computer looked dustless, the first thing that came to mind was Mrs Wilkins, she had cleaned up his room.

Opening a browser to browse the internet, he decided to take a quick peek at his social network. Felix went into the popular website known as Journal; it was not too popular when he went to prison. But had become the trend over the years with over a billion active users. The prison had facilities with computers for studying purposes, only in seldom occasions did he log in to his Journal account. Feeling a bit of excitement, he updated his status, writing in capital letters, "FREEDOM! I AM OUT!", and then logged out. Looking at his bed, he plunged in and sighed as he looked up at the ceiling.

What began as Felix slowly blinking, eventually led him to sleep. Lasting only a few minutes, it was suddenly broken. His bedroom door was suddenly opened; 'Felix!' Mrs Wilkins muttered briskly. Yawning as he looked at her and his torso and head rose with his legs still rested on the bed. 'Yes, Mrs Wilkins?' he said. 'Your parole officer is here, better not keep the officer waiting,' after those words,

Mrs Wilkins scurried away. He was a free man he thought, there was no need to be nervous. Brushing off the mild anxiety that he began to feel take presence, as he got out of his bed.

Realising Mrs Wilkins had not told him where the parole officer was in the mansion, Felix took his chances and went to the pool. There was his father dressed in a more relaxed attire; shorts and a golf shirt with flip-flops. Calmly puffing away as he smoked his cigar, he was seating on the poolside dining table near the fireplace that was used for barbecues. Next to him was a lady in a navy-blue suit and skirt. Felix felt an unexpected rush, as he glimpsed at the lady, scanning her up and down. His eyes falling on her gorgeous legs then sliding back up staring at her face. The lady looked young, about Felix's age. She was fair-skinned with blonde hair and dark blue eyes. Felix thought to himself to keep calm as he strolled towards his father doing his best to appear unperturbed.

When she looked back at Felix he nearly froze as he was now close and caught a glimpse of her full lips. 'Hi,' she said, as she got up; not waiting for Mr Sobek to introduce his son. She stretched her hand and Felix reacted only a few seconds later, shaking her hand as he kept looking straight into her eyes. His façade of confidence was broken at that moment.

After he shook her hand, she introduced herself, 'I am Claudia Fern.'

She was about Felix's height, as he noticed at that moment. As an attempt to control the situation, Mr Sobek who was still sitting down spoke, 'Yes Felix Mrs Wilkins probably told you, this is your parole officer.' Felix quickly glanced at his father who grinned at him and then glanced back at Claudia.

'We have little time, we will need to discuss a few things, let's sit,' said Claudia, as she sat back on the chair with Felix doing likewise. Once they sat down, he then noticed on the table was a folder, which Claudia began browsing through.

'Okay, look my job is too simply make sure you do not go back on the wrong track,' began Claudia, 'you were already briefed on me seeing you a few days before your release, now the crime you were convicted of was manslaughter, do not want to get into too much details. But simply it was a brawl between two people from opposing gangs. Has your former gang tried to make contact with you?' Felix sighed feeling like he was knocked back into reality, his head rocked slightly back and forth and then he responded, 'I was their leader I cut all ties and only spoke to a few of them, a year into my incarceration as I told one of the correctional service workers who visited before my release.' 'The last person you spoke to...' before Claudia could finish the question, Felix intercepting her thoughts answering abruptly, 'He died.'

Claudia asked him a few more mundane questions, which were answered quickly. Her job was to monitor Felix for a year, while he was rehabilitating back into society. She was then to write a report, which was then to be presented by the correctional services to the court. Should everything go according to plan, Felix would be completely free without having a parole officer supervising him. She was happy to have heard that Felix's cousin had gotten Felix a job. Everything looked great for him, he had just to keep himself out of trouble. Nevertheless, there was one more document she had forgotten to bring that Felix needed to sign. Claudia frantically searched her handbag and found nothing, exhaling deeply she then said, 'I will have a look in my car, will be right back!' Dashing away with her heels making sounds; Felix could not help but gaze at her posterior.

'Your day looking good, that is one hell of a beauty,' said Mr Sobek as he chuckled. Felix did not respond, nevertheless, he agreed with his father, Claudia was a stunner. 'Son if you land that, I will pay you a thousand Dinares,' continued Mr Sobek this time leaning towards his son. 'Whatever,' said Felix. 'No pressure,' replied Mr Sobek, sniggering.

Claudia reappeared rushing back towards them. 'Look! Um, we need to head back to my office, need to forward that document today with your signature,' she said. 'So, I must come with you...' before Felix finished his sentence Mr Sobek snapped, 'You heard the woman, you need to go with her! Hurry up, geez!' Felix then got up and Mr Sobek added, 'Excuse my son he is a tad bit slow.' He then walked off with a subtle smirk on his face. Felix just shook his head in retaliation.

During the drive in a chill of silence, Felix began to feel anxious as his heartbeat increased with pace. He hardened, feeling erect with every occasional glance at Claudia, who in that uncomfortable silence had noticed the glances and asked 'What?' mildly frowning. 'Nothing,' muttered Felix. It dawned on him that the scarcity of contact with women had left him unbalanced (He felt timid and childlike in front of Claudia).

The drive was still dictated by silence until Claudia finally arrived at the destination and parked her car. 'You feel safe around me?' Felix enquired. Claudia first smiled and then she answered, 'Well why not? Besides, I can defend myself and I have studied your case and files,' sighing as she peered around for something and continued, 'your psychological profile does not make you a threat. Okay, you wait here, I'm quickly going to go fetch the document, my office is not far.' Claudia hurried away after closing the door.

Felix wondered how Claudia was comfortable dealing with ex-prisoners. Nevertheless, if she left him alone in the car there must be a guarantee there was a tracking device or something. Locking his eyes on Claudia as her frame got smaller, he saw her head towards a tall brown building with the flag of the Sud Republic.

It was a red flag with a bright yellow rectangle in its centre and inside the rectangle, was an orange pentagon with a black trigram inside it, in the middle. The trigram was like Felix's tattoo on his right arm, which symbolised fire.

They were in town and Felix could recognise some of the imagery around him. On the other side of the brown building was a big shopping mall, that was new to Felix.

Glancing down for a second, an explosion sent a shockwave that shattered the parked cars' windscreens. Claudia's car was fine, but Felix felt tremors shake him up inside as he peered around, trying to gather back his senses. He quickly got out of the car hearing screams of fear coming from different directions. He looked ahead to see if it was perhaps the correctional services' building that blew up (the brown building Claudia had headed in); however, the explosion had come from the mall.

He crouched down and crawled back to the car as gunshots were being fired. He caught a glimpse of a small family, a father, mother and their toddler of a daughter whom the father carried as the daughter cried. 'GET DOWN!' bellowed Felix. The family managed to hide crouching down, next to a green car as the father did his best to calm down his daughter. The thought of if Claudia was alright surged around Felix's mind, he felt helpless and like a coward.

Five minutes after the explosion helicopters appeared in the sky heading for the mall with it rising smoke. They were gunmen in the helicopters firing shots. It seemed like they were aiming their shots at suspects. Within the chaos, Felix saw Claudia sprinting his direction, she was barefoot to ease her mobility. Once she was close, Felix grabbed her and asked, 'Are you alright?' as he looked at her shocked face. 'I am fine,' she quickly answered regaining some of her composure. She slightly pushed him away and Felix backed off astonished, she seemed fine with the whole ordeal.

'I do not know what is happening, but I need to get you back to your father in one piece,' began Claudia, 'seems like the police special forces have this under control,' gazing at the mall, she turned back to Felix. 'OK let's go,' she commanded. They hurried into the car and Claudia pressed her foot on the accelerator as they sped off.

On the road, Felix helped himself to increase the car radio's volume and Claudia did not object. Both were silent and attentive to everything that came out of the radio news. 'It seems there was an alleged terror attack happening as we speak, at the Westick Mall in town. The police's special forces unit is on the scene. No arrests have been made thus far and no deaths have been confirmed yet. No confirmation yet as to who is behind this, people at the scene have been filling social media with the news that it was an explosion inside one of the stores...' After the radio news, the latest pop song was being played.

Claudia sighed and then said, 'I will not be surprised if it's a terror attack. Must be the Separatist Group, anyway I assume so.' 'Who are they?' Felix quickly asked. 'Some crazy terror organisation, anyway crazy bunch.'

Felix signed the document Claudia had gotten from her office after she dropped him off. Receiving a call on her cell phone she quickly left. Felix heard her speak to what seemed to be another man on the other line. She mentioned the name, 'Richard,' letting this Richard know she was fine. Felix wondered if this Richard was her boyfriend.

# CHAPTER TWO-THE HARMONIOUS FIST

The news saturated its content confirming that it was a terror attack by the Separatists, as the days went by. But the most important thing to Felix was his training. He had not trained for a day and it felt like a year, his father was busy tending to his businesses and Felix not having a drivers' license nor a car, decided to head to his uncle's kwoon (martial arts school) by ordering a taxi. Fred Sobek was Carl Sobek's oldest brother and a retired Union Guard General. He was also the standard-bearer of the family's fighting system, the Harmonious Fist.

Felix felt an ambience of nostalgia creep in as he entered his uncle's kwoon, it was next to his uncle's house which looked modest in comparison to his father's mansion. It was a late afternoon and a class was in session. Twenty-odd people mostly young men were standing in a stance known as the horse stance. They were squatting at ninety degrees to the ground with their legs spread twice the widths of their shoulders. Their backs were straight, and their knees were bent with their buttocks tucked in. It was an intense exercise mastered only by masochists, however, the students seemed to be able to hold their own, as Felix peered at them.

'The waist is the commander, the general of the body!' barked the instructor as he strolled side to side sternly looking at his students. 'The power comes from the feet, travels up the legs and is amplified by the waist. Flowing up the arms and it exits through the fingers. This was well known by our martial forefathers,' he paused and stood still, having already noticed Felix. The instructor ignored his presence for the time being and continued, 'However the message that we send from our lower body sometimes is too strong for the upper body,' now with a sadistic smile he ended with, 'give me fifty push-ups, everybody down! I want you to start the first ten and then the counting moves on to the next person.' His eyes fell on one of the students, who were already in a push-up position like the rest and this student, immediately started to count the first ten repetitions.

The instructor wandered towards Felix; he was slightly taller than him. He had piercing blue eyes with a lean body and short blonde hair. The instructor was Eddy Sobek.

'Cousin,' said Felix smiling as they greeted each other, shaking hands and pulling close as their shoulders and chest areas touched. 'Wow, you are raising hell! Impressed,' said Felix as he looked at the obedient students counting loudly doing their push-ups. Eddy quickly glimpsed at the students with a sudden glare appearing on his face. His eyes inspecting to see if any of them were slacking, satisfied he turned back to Felix.

'You do not look too bad,' said Eddy. 'What you mean? I look great in fact last time we sparred...' cutting Felix sharply Eddy said, 'Last time we sparred was a loooong time ago. Yes, you made me kiss this floor, now at this moment in time it will be a different story if we sparred.' Felix chuckled, feeling his adrenalin pump, he did his best to control himself. Not intimidated by his cousin's eyes, he did, however, feel Eddy's air of confidence.

Eddy was the adoptive son of Fred Sobek, he was adopted when he was only five years old. Fred came across him when he was then appointed commander of Union Guard troops, sent in to quell a rebellion that occurred in the East-South Union. It was during an inspection to an area that had experienced heavy fighting that he found Eddy, who was hiding in an abandoned apartment building still alive and too shocked to cry. Not having any child of his own at that time, Fred decided to adopt Eddy.

Felix, Unlike Eddy, began his martial arts training under the tutelage of his uncle at the tender age of three years old and showed great natural talent. Eddy only started when he was ten years old, due to him being too sickly and feeble.

'Where is Uncle?' inquired Felix. 'His with mom and Charlie,' answered Eddy. Felix excited immediately responded, 'Charlie, shit how old is he now?' 'His seven-years-old,' replied Eddy. 'Follow me,' he added. Felix followed Eddy as they made their way to the front of the class. The students were done with the push-ups, each one looking exhausted. 'Everybody this is Felix! He is a senior student of this school and a lineage holder of the Harmonious Fist. I am sure some of you here have heard about him...his quiet a legend.' Felix was trying to hide the shyness that had been evoked from Eddy's last words. Smiling slightly, he nervously waved at the students. 'Anyway, time to close the class! Remember to train hard,' and after saying that Eddy did the martial yin-yang gesture to the class, who did it back to him.

Once the students had left the kwoon, Eddy and Felix made their way to the altar, which was behind them and in front as one entered the kwoon. The altar was to commemorate the ancestors of the Sobek family martial art. Displaying photos and painted portraits of former masters right up to the founder. With a lineage chart where the names of Felix and Eddy were also written. Even Carl Sobek's name was there. On the top of the altar written in ancient Daoist characters, it said, "*Sobek Harmonious Fist School.*" In the centre of the altar was a small jade statue of an ancient saint, with big eyes and thick eyebrows followed with a thick beard staring with a kind of glare, in standing meditation. The arms and hands of the statue stuck out as if it was holding a big ball. It was a statue of a man who in antiquity, had brought martial arts to the Loham Temple and had even travelled to the Dragon's Lair where he had martial exchanges with the Daoist hermits there. His name was Daruma, and it was said that he inspired some the Daoist hermits to create the Water School, based on Daruma's famed Standing Meditation, known as Zhan Zhuang.

Ancient myth has it that the martial arts he practised was the Harmonious Fist, the father of all martial art styles. Its focus was based on the essence of the lui he (the six harmonies or combinations).

'Ah…the boys, you should both light incense and bow to the ancestors and Daruma,' said a deep voice. It came from a bald black man who had thick eyebrows and a thick black beard with a stout physique. He was slightly shorter than Felix and his brown eyes had a hawkish gaze. The man was dressed casually as he wore flip-flops, turquoise shorts and a white vest. This man was Fred Sobek.

'Uncle Fred!' exclaimed Felix feeling a rush of joy. Both nephew and uncle hugged each other and then they greeted each other using the non-martial yin-yang gesture. 'Why did you not come and pick me up?' asked Felix. 'I thought it was more appropriate for you and your dad to spend some quality time… after all he did not visit you when you were in prison,' said Uncle Fred. Felix sighed, 'Oh well…' and then he was interrupted by Uncle Fred as he said, 'Enough! Enough!' He approached Felix, putting his hand around Felix's shoulder, 'You back! Time to step into the platform, hope you warmed up,' once he was done speaking Uncle Fred headed towards a raised platform, which stood in the corner of the kwoon. It was circular with a diameter of about seven meters and was raised a meter and a half off the ground. Felix was aware his uncle wanted to assess his skills by having a sparring session. They had chatted about it through the years during Uncle Fred's visits, while he was in prison. Felix exchanged glances with Eddy and then followed his uncle who had made his way to the platform.

'Father I think it's unfair, I should challenge him I mean...' Eddy's words were halted as Uncle Fred glared back at him. 'The time will come, however, his still your senior and you need to respect him,' he said, replacing his facial expression with a calmer demeanour. Felix feeling a bit uncomfortable as he looked at both Uncle Fred and Eddy kept his silence. Eddy did not reply, he simply sighed and walked away. 'Where are you going Eddy?' Felix suddenly asked him. 'Ah just heading to work, gonna shower and rush there,' answered Eddy. 'Hope to see you tomorrow, your first day is tomorrow you have not forgotten, right?' he said with a slight smirk on his face. 'Not at all, bro. It's an opportunity I cannot let pass,' said Felix.

Felix did not even get a chance to stretch, as he stepped in the platform, Uncle Fred made a sudden move. He deflected the attack and then launched his fist forward, however, at that instant in time he flew off the platform and fell on the ground. Uncle Fred had struck him with his right palm. He had just touched him and then a sudden current of electricity surged through his body not hurting him, but it made him lose his balance as he flew off.

Felix quickly got up; it was not the first time he had experienced his uncle's might. Regardless, just like the first time, he was shaken, and his heart pumped slightly as he looked at his uncle in awe, inspired to train harder.

'As you already experienced, being issued with power by your opponent with them using a minimum use...or no use of physical strength! You remember, don't you!? said Uncle Fred with an austere gaze. Felix answered his uncle, 'Of course.' 'Clearly, you have a lot of training to do,' said Uncle Fred as he hopped off the platform landing lightly on his feet. 'Follow me,' he said.

They both walked towards the altar, Uncle Fred lit incense and Felix followed suit as they both bowed and placed both incenses into an incense holder. The burning incenses quickly wrapped them in a sweet musk type of odour. 'See Felix,' began Uncle Fred, 'it is a great shame you went to prison very young, we would agree if it was not for your knowledge in the fighting arts that you would have ended up being killed or worse...only the gods know. The point is I know this would hurt but just like your father you did not pay great respect to our family art. Well to Carl it means really nothing, but to you, it was just a way to fight. The Harmonious Fist is about harmony! I will say it again and hope you chant this in your sleep! You know this already, but I will say it again! And again! There are three externals. The pairing of the feet with the hands, knees with the elbows, hips with the shoulders. Then comes the three internals, the pairing of your emotions with your mind, your mind with your energy and your energy with your physical body. You know the rest...However, this is what we call the six harmonies. And the bottom is slightly tucked in, and knees slightly bent.' Despite Uncle's Fred's lecture, Felix had always kept everything his uncle said in mind especially when he met Silver an old friend of Uncle Fred. Remembering a question, he had for his uncle, Felix asked, 'Uncle, Shirfu Silver did not teach me anything of his art, did you have anything to do with it?' 'Of course not,' chuckled Uncle Fred. 'That fucker did not even teach me anything! Ha!' he added.

'Before you leave, stand for an hour in a horse stance!' barked Uncle Fred as he left the kwoon. Felix got into the position obeying the order with immediate effect. An hour in the horse stance was a walk in the park for Felix.

# CHAPTER THREE- GAIA CORP AND THE NEW WORLD ORDER

Gaia Corp had become the biggest conglomerate in the world, there was no industry it did not have a hand in, originally a biotechnology company (which was one of its core businesses). It had branched off to everything from banking to selling hair products and automobiles; it owned various subsidiaries, even the media had fallen victim to its expansion. They were even companies that it owned that the common man or women in the street had no idea about.

The CEO of Gaia Corp was the richest man in the world; his name was Daniel Faris and he was the founder of the company. Originally born in the United West where he founded his company at the age of twenty-five. Daniel Faris was a college dropout and he started in the biotechnology field, where his company created simple diagnostic tools. Starting in the medical side of biotechnology, his dream was to replace ancient Daoist traditions, such as acupuncture and the various traditional medicinal practices that were around despite modern medicine. Those esoteric skills where too hard to learn in his vision and needed someone to be highly skilled. Thus, from that vision, Gaia Corp morphed into a monster with governments around the world failing to stop its monopolisation of different markets. Daniel Faris was highly regarded for his ability to adjust and adapt to an ever-changing business world.

Filled with excitement and mild tremors of nervousness was Felix. It was his first day at work, he tightened his red necktie as he beamed in the mirror, admiring his white shirt and black pants while he was in the men's toilet.

Despite his academics, the job Eddy had got for Felix was in Gaia Corp's contact centre. Having one of its largest office campuses in the world, in Wobbleton City. It was there that there was also one of the company's major R&D (research and development) offices. The contact centre in the campus however, provided services to clients who had purchased Gaia Corp's various medical equipment or tools, the clients being hospitals and clinics or private doctors. The contact centre at the Wobbleton City campus was the biggest in the world.

Stepping out of the men's toilet, Felix concealed his nerves with an air of confidence. He observed that his future colleagues were not all as formally dressed as he was; some were just completely casual in their dress code.

The contact centre was an open setting with two

floors, Felix was on the bottom floor. At twenty-three years of age, it was his first job and the more he observed the more the anxiety sunk in. Did they know he once was in prison? Different thoughts coasted inside his mind.

The office floor was noisy with different colleagues answering calls, some adjusting their headsets to hear the customers at the end of the other line. No screens divided the call centre agents and each one could communicate easily, without having to stand up from their seats.

Felix had just had his induction and was to start his training to prepare him for his job, he was to do a few tests which would determine if he finally got the job. 'So much for getting me a job,' Felix chuckled to himself as he thought of Eddy. He did not mind, at least knowing that he could fail from being hired, meant his hiring would not look like nepotism.

He was amongst fifteen other individuals who were being trained. Making a closer acquaintance with two, the one was fresh out of university and her name was Arrieta Long. A twenty-one-year-old brunette with emerald green eyes and wavy hair that stopped just past her shoulders. She had caught Felix ogling a few times, thinking he was weird. Regardless, she surprisingly made a bold choice to approach him first. The other acquaintance was the computer connoisseur Jim Coles, he had slightly large eyes with subtle mono eyelids, he was mildly dark-skinned, paler in comparison to Felix and chubby. He was chatty and full of energy; excited about the prospect of working for Gaia Corp. He mentioned to Felix how he planned to be part of the company's bioinformatics department. He also had studied biotechnology prior but now was continuing his studies in bioinformatics part-time. Jim was twenty-six years old.

The training took four weeks and Felix was then ready for the floor. His whole training school had made it. Figuring the best way to manage his fears, was to just plunge into the task at hand. Acing the mock calls during training, he ended up taking a real call. It was a doctor calling from Sud City, The Sud Republic's capital, he had an enquiry about his medical device and Felix although feeling very nervous, had managed to put the call through to support. Handling the call accordingly.

During the weekend and basked in motivation, Felix could not wait for the next week to begin. He sat at the poolside dining table having breakfast with his dad.

'So…' began Carl Sobek as he took a bite of his croissant and then a sip of his freshly squeezed orange juice, 'how excited are you about next week?' 'I am pretty keen, cannot wait,' replied Felix. He and Carl seemed to be talking to each other more frequently ever since his return. Although Felix was still reserved, 'It is good you have this thing going on…' Carl Sobek paused to sip more of his orange juice and said, 'however what are your goals it may be too soon, but you need to think of your future.' 'Well not going to work with you we know your business could put me right back in,' said Felix. Carl laughed and then his face lit with seriousness, 'look…' his words were cut as the figure of Claudia Fern came to sight. 'Oh, hi Miss Fern!' exclaimed Carl Sobek. 'Come join us for breakfast!' he added. 'Sorry to disturb, Mrs Wilkins, allowed me in...' Claudia said as she smiled nervously. 'No need to apologise,' said Carl Sobek as he stood up and then quickly muttered to Felix, 'See that...well if you want that you better be ambitious.' He then beamed at Claudia saying, 'I am going to leave, you two get on with your business,' and then he left.

'Hi,' said Claudia as she sat at the table. Felix cleared his throat and greeted her back, 'Hi, how you today?' 'All good and you?' Claudia quickly responded. 'I am doing well; life is very different I must say...' Felix pointed with his eyes at the food on the table and then took a sip of orange juice pleased by the refreshing taste. 'Well I am happy for you really, umm...the boy that you fought and killed...sorry if I put it that way...' Felix quickly responded as Claudia paused, 'It is okay,' and Claudia then continued, 'Well have you contacted his family or have they approached you...' Felix decided then to cut in, 'My father...my family sorted that out.' 'What do you mean?' asked Claudia as she subtly raised an eyebrow. 'They paid for the funeral; look he was a young thug just like me his family had disowned him. My father and uncle even attended the funeral. It is what it is! Do I regret killing that punk! Maybe...I do not know! A lot was happening back then and clearly, a lot is happening now.' 'Look I did not mean to upset you,' said Claudia. Felix smirked and said, 'I am a Sobek we have expressive personalities now and then, I am not upset.' With those words, he cast a gaze of appreciation at Claudia touching every inch of her skin with his eyes. 'Why are you looking at me like that?' Claudia responded to the gaze with a frown. 'Do not know what you talking about, look it is the weekend should you not be with your boyfriend...Richard,' said Felix. 'Richard...my colleague...his not my boyfriend,' Claudia looked confused. 'How do you know about my colleague?' she asked. 'Heard you mention his name the first day we met when he called you,' Felix answered. 'Okay...' began Claudia still frowning, and then she said, 'Anyway I have spoken to my superiors, I will only need to see you on a monthly basis from now on and given the fact that you have a job, living peacefully with your family ...we might not need see each other in the coming months.' 'That is a shame, I would really like to get to know you. Look it is not like I have friends,' said Felix. 'That's adorable, here is my card,' said Claudia as she took out her card from her handbag, Felix got out of his seat took it and then sat back down. 'Thanks,' he said as he looked at the card and then put it in his pocket. 'Felix, you never spoke about what happened, the attack. I have been seeing a shrink. Work has forced my hand on that case. Nevertheless, it helps, but I mean...have you spoken to your father or anyone?' 'Nope...no one really knows, well my dad knows we were there, but I did not speak about the attack though. Since those crazies did not touch me, I am fine. Besides that, I meditate...the counselling I only need is in my family's Harmonious Fist,' said Felix firmly and then he had a slight smirk on his face once he finished speaking.

'Okay well I have to go,' said Claudia as she got up and Felix followed suit and he said, 'You left too soon, it is a big mansion let me show you around, I am sure it will look good since you are my parole officer and all.' 'Thank you, Felix,' began Claudia as she politely beamed at him, 'however I have to decline,' after saying that she left. Felix stared at her posterior as he bit his bottom lip and slowly shook his head.

The first day of the next week came to shock Felix, his first call was from a livid sounding client, 'Your machine has not arrived!' Felix tried to control his nerves, he was not going to get angry, however, this did not seize the pumping adrenalin, 'I...um...' Felix was stammering and mumbling trying to maintain himself. 'LISTEN HERE! I Want what I ordered!' the client said and then hung up. Not letting that go easily, he used the details he had of the angry customer. Determined to find out what happened to the man's order. Nevertheless, he had another call to answer, which was luckily a general query. Felix then rushed to call the angry customer, and to his surprise, the client apologised to him for having gone off in a rant. The order was delivered; the delivery lady who delivered the item advised to the customer that she had driven twice past the location and was sort of lost. After the call, Felix took a deep breath. 'Wow,' he muttered to himself.

During lunch in the canteen, he sat with Jim and Arrieta. Jim enjoyed his sandwich and Arrieta her salad. Meanwhile, Felix was drinking his green tea.

'Felix...your surname is spelt S-o-b-e-k...right?' enquired Arrieta. 'Yea why?' Felix replied immediately frowning. 'Well one of the executives his name is Eddy Sobek, his quite handsome if you ask me,' said Arrieta. 'Oh...' begin Felix as he smiled, 'He's my cousin, the reason he looks different is that his adopted.' This time Jim joined the conversation, 'So why you in the contact centre then?' 'What do you mean?' asked Felix. 'Well, Eddy is known to be the youngest executive ever of Gaia Corp. He's considered a genius by some! Twenty-three years old!' said Jim sounding excited as he spoke. 'Tell me about it, I mean when we were younger and small, I thought I was the shit. However, Eddy was smarter...' Felix was cut by Jim who said, 'Smarter! He sold his first company to Gaia Corp at sixteen, the same year he started university.' 'Yea...yea... look I know his amazing, I could set up a date for the two of you,' joked Felix as he grinned back at Jim. 'Why did you not tell us, Felix?' asked Arrieta. 'Did not want my hiring to appear like nepotism, besides not a big deal,' said Felix as he took a final sip of his green tea. 'Wait...' began Jim and Felix's intuition knew what Jim was going to get at, 'The Sobek are renowned for their martial art, especially in martial circles,' said Jim. Felix thought he was going to mention his conviction. 'Oooh, so what martial art does your family do?' asked Arrieta as she looked interested and leaned in with her chin resting on her hand. 'The Harmonious Fist,' said Felix. 'Ummm yea, so you must be the one who ended up being locked up!' said Jim and Felix made a gesture for him to be quiet as he looked side to side. 'Dude if you are working here it's done and dusted, criminal record or not...' Arrieta interrupted Jim, 'What, wait...you were in prison.' 'Ok hold on guys wait,' began Felix as he explained and gave them a summary of the story.

'Do not know what to say, Felix, you full of surprises,' said Arrieta. 'Yea, oh well...' was Felix's response. 'So, dude you are taking part in the Sud Republic's Sanshou competition?' asked Jim. Felix just smiled and kept quiet. He had to get back to work and as he headed back to his desk. The answer to that rhetorical question was yes, Felix was thinking and preparing for the Sanshou competition; qualify for the Lei Tai and be crowned world champion.

The next two months of work felt like years for Felix and with the micromanaging and constant stress, he had enough of the job. To make matters worse one day he came across Eddy and his colleagues (they were all executives).

'Hi Eddy,' said Felix. 'Eddy is that perhaps a client?' asked one of Eddy's colleagues as he sized up Felix, who in return simply acknowledged him with a nod and turned back to Eddy. 'Hi,' said Eddy and then turned to his colleagues, 'This is my cousin,

Felix Sobek…he works in the contact centre department.' Once Eddy presented Felix, all of Eddy's colleagues greeted him and they all shook hands, the
one who had sized Felix up, made a smug comment,
'Why you dressed like that and working in the call
centre?' (Felix was suited up on the day). 'Well, one
always has to look good,' Felix answered calmly.
'Yea sure,' Eddy's colleague sniggered. Felix could
feel the upsurge of his blood as he told himself to
remain calm and Eddy could feel the temperature
was rising, 'That is unnecessary, there is nothing
wrong with dressing well when you working in the
contact centre,' he said coming to Felix's defence.
'If you say so,' his colleague said as he shrugged his
shoulders and at that moment in time decided to
cast another smug look Felix's direction, that was
the trigger. 'Buddy! Buddy! You might look good in
that suit…' Felix was cut as Eddy took him to the
side, Felix's body moved but his eyes were still zeroed in on the colleague. 'Hey!' grunted Eddy. 'Get
off me!' Felix grunted back as Eddy had his hands
on his chest. 'Dude, you do not want to get fired
over something stupid calm down,' Eddy muttered.
Eddy's colleague who was the trigger to Felix's frustration just smirked with the rest of the colleagues
and with some slightly shaking their heads. Felix
imagined how he could in a few seconds just knock
all of them out. 'Waste of my time,' he said calming down and turning to Eddy, 'hey look, see you for
dinner this weekend, Aunt Catherina sent me a text
this morning,' those where Felix's last words as he

walked away.

After being a few meters away, he turned and with an analysing glimpse, he looked at how Eddy talked to his colleagues. It seemed as if he was apologising to them; their gestures showed they were alright with him and they all broke into a burst of sudden laughter. Not trying to be paranoid, Felix brushed aside the feeling of betrayal he had suddenly begun to feel.

'Hey handsome,' said Arrieta beaming at Felix. 'Hi,' said Felix nonchalantly as he sat on his desk preparing for the incoming calls. Arrieta frowned back and asked, 'Hey what is wrong?' Remaining in her chair, she rolled herself closer to Felix and gently placed her hand on his knee. 'I am fine,' said Felix quickly glancing at her hand. 'Okay...so what you doing this weekend?' Arrieta asked as her hand remained on Felix's knee. Woman, are you going to keep your hand there? Thought Felix for a moment before he replied, 'Well I am having a family dinner and training...yea,' finishing his lasts words with a sigh. 'You still need to teach me some moves,' said Arrieta before she rolled herself back to her desk and Felix chuckled with a mild smile on his face. Opening his email inbox, he saw a message from Jim, he opened it, and this is what was written, *"Dude, she definitely wants you! When are you going to make a move?"* Felix turned to look at Jim who also did not seat far and was behind Felix, he was looking back and threw his thumbs up. Felix just laughed as he shook his head and turned back to his computer screen.

The weekend came, and Felix was dining at Uncle Fred's house, to his surprise Uncle Fred was missing. 'Frederick is behaving like Carl lately, I had invited your father regardless even though I knew he would be a no show!' those words came from a white woman with grey eyes, she was a brunette with short hair who was sitting at the head of the table, which hid her thin curvy figure. This was Catherina Sobek, a Chef and former model. Despite her mature look, time did not explicitly display her age, she was, however, younger than Fred Sobek. 'Well now you know how I felt most of my childhood years,' remarked Felix and Catherina giggled. Felix turned to wink at a small boy next to him, who was darker of complexion than Catherina yet lighter than Felix. It was Charles Sobek, Felix's young cousin. He had very dark brown eyes and black hair. In the other corner was Eddy who was quietly eating and enjoying his food. 'So…Felix, how has work been?' asked Aunt Catherina. 'Well…' Felix began with a momentary sigh and then he said, 'It is not too bad, it has its ups and downs.' 'Well you do not sound happy,' Aunt Catherina cast Felix a look of concern. 'Well my enthusiasm got the best of me; we get micromanaged and it can get pretty stressful.' Felix went on explaining his experience with his first call and how his team leader can be a pain, that the job did not fit his nature and he concluded with, 'I am not a doormat.' He did thank Eddy though, the job did put money in his pocket and for that, he was grateful.

Then he began to talk about some of his aspirations, 'Given my qualification, I would like to in the near future work in a lab, most importantly create my own business.' Eddy scoffed at him and then with a mild chuckle he sarcastically said, 'Yeah right.' 'Eddy!' snapped Aunt Catherina. 'It is okay,' said Felix remaining calm and then he continued as he looked at Eddy, 'look I have dreams and I am very ambitious; I rather die doing my best.' 'You go boy!' cheered Aunt Catherina. 'I want to be a fighter!' exclaimed Charles as he raised both his hands in the air with the outside of his mouth filled with sauce and bits of food. Everybody in the table roared with laughter and Felix took the liberty of wiping his cousin's mouth with a cloth. 'That reminds me,' began Felix, 'I want to take part in this year's Lei Tai.' 'Yes, Frederick told me. It is very dangerous, then again martial arts is in your blood,' said Aunt Catherina with a tone that objected, however, understood at the same time. 'It was cute hearing you say that when you were in prison, however, let's get real!' said Eddy. Felix simply rolled his eyes as he shook his head, then turned his attention to Charles and jokingly said, 'You will have to beat me first because I will be champion.' 'I can take you on,' said Charles as he slightly lifted his chin.

'Felix, can we have a chat about something, it will

be brief,' said Eddy as he got up, adding, 'let's head to the kwoon.' 'Hello! Who is going to help me pack all these plates and put them in the dishwasher?' asked Aunt Catherina as she looked at both Eddy and Felix. 'I will help,' said Charles. 'Come let's go,' said Eddy sounding a bit impatient. Felix quietly got up and followed Eddy as they left the dining table. Looking at Charles, Aunt Catherina said, 'Well come now. Let's pack up. We will save some food for your father geez, where is he? Let me give him a call.'

'So wasup?' asked Felix as they both entered the kwoon with Eddy leading the way. Eddy switched on the lights and did not answer. Once everything was lit, he walked to Felix. He looked angry and sighed before speaking, 'What is your problem man? Who do you think you are?' Felix frowned and although still looking calm he could begin to feel his heartbeat and responded to Eddy with a question, 'Dude? Hey? You Jealous or something?' 'Jealous of you!' snarled Eddy, 'You ain't! shit! I got you a job okay! You have these retard...' Felix cut his words as he spoke his, 'You have a lovely home and a mother and a father who love you, including a brother! A very good job! And when I found out you were done with university and you had jumped the first year to your third graduating early cause you smart! I cried tears of joy for you! So, you got me a job! Thank you!' 'You do not fucking get it! You just a fuck up, who ain't shit!' said Eddy, eyes wide and fuming, Felix looked back in disgust and then turned to walk away. 'You a disgrace to even be a lineage holder of our family art!' exclaimed Eddy. Felix having heard enough, turned back, 'I will give you what you always wanted, a fight between you and me! I am gonna knock your jealousy and cripple you when I am done! Fuck you and your damn job! Screw Gaia Corp!' he bellowed as he got into his fighting pose and as he did, Eddy charged forth leaping with a fly kick, which Felix dodged as he stepped aside. He then threw a punch aiming at the left side of Eddy's jaw. Eddy deflected it and as he did, Felix felt a weird shock-like electric sensation make him lose balance and he fell hard on the floor.

Sniggering, Eddy smiled with glee, he said as he stood beside a shocked and gasping Felix, 'I could squash you, we not on the same level. I should be the next standard-bearer of our art, not you. You are lower than me...PATHETIC!' Felix struggled to stand up, grimacing as he tried. The main door of the kwoon flung open and there stood the furious figure of Uncle Fred. 'Sweet Daruma! What the hell!' he barked.

'Look your rescuer has arrived,' muttered Eddy as he looked at Felix who was still on the floor. Uncle Fred rushed to Felix as he pushed Eddy who flew off the ground falling a few meters away. He slapped Felix on his shoulder with both his hands and Felix felt a mild warmth soothe his body starting from his shoulders and with every ticking second, he could manoeuvre his body properly again. Uncle

Fred helped him up and then turned his attention to Eddy, 'What is your problem! You guys are not just cousins, you like brothers.' Eddy who was back up sneered at Felix and then he said, 'I am over all of this, I am going to my apartment, tomorrow I will send for people to get all my stuff it is already packed anyway.' Eddy then made his way for the door and left.

Felix was slightly panting still recovering his breath, 'His...stronger than...me,' said Felix as he struggled to speak. 'Yes...he has been training hard. However, he has no harmony. He has chosen his path...oh well,' said Uncle Fred.

Felix explained everything that happened to his uncle, including the event at work. 'Do not worry Felix tomorrow is another day, I will drop you home,' said Uncle Fred.

That evening, Felix replayed the events in his mind of what had happened, his pride wanted him to train harder, so he could make Eddy pay, nevertheless, he was troubled by the hate he had felt from Eddy. He meditated to calm his nerves and restore his energy.

Eddy had moved to his apartment and despite Aunt Catherina's pleas he was not coming back. Uncle Fred did not bother, he simply gave his son a call to find out how he was doing. Felix began running the classes at the kwoon and training for the Sanshou. With work starting to become more of a strain, he felt nothing but hate for his job. What angered him more was Eddy, flashbacks of their argument infuriated him even more. Something else was creeping in his mind, it was the scarcity of Uncle Fred, he was rarely seen, and he would make casual appearances now and then. Felix was beginning to agree with Aunt Catherina, for a retired Union Guard general what was Uncle Fred up to?

At work, Felix had decided to warm up to Arrieta's advances, however, within weeks, there was a sudden change in her behaviour. She was a bit aloof, this caught Felix off guard. 'She says, you a bit too much,' said Jim who Felix had confided to. 'Too much?' Felix muttered to himself as he looked at Arrieta chatting to another female colleague from a different department, they were all in the main entrance of the Gaia Corp campus. Feeling mild tremors in his heart, Felix sighed. 'Anyway, I am heading to the other side,' he said having seen enough. As he turned, Jim quickly tapped him on his back and whispered, 'Hey check!' Felix quickly turned and looked, his eyes shot wide open and then he frowned. Eddy was chatting to Arrieta and the other female colleague, they giggled at something he had said. Each giggle deflating Felix's heart and then to stab it was what happened next. The female colleague left Eddy alone with Arrieta and within seconds, Eddy had his hands around her, slipping right down as he pinched her buttocks. She giggled and hit him as he laughed back. 'Fuck that! I am done!' scorned Felix as he marched away. Jim then hurriedly followed him, 'Relax Felix, that is your cousin, besides why you angry with her?' asked Jim. 'I am not angry with anyone! First thing! Sanshou! Second thing Lei Tai...to hell with anything else!' said Felix.

Before going live and answering calls the staff in the call centre, including most staff in the campus were glued to their computer screens watching a live web video announcement from the CEO. Daniel Faris was going to introduce a new product, it was already used by the military (Union Guard troops), the product was an advanced sophisticated medical equipment, known as the life tank.

Its purpose was to heal a person suffering from severe injuries quickly, within a matter of days. Burned victims with third-degree burns could be healed with a matter of weeks with no signs of scars as if the burns never occurred.

'The life tank cannot regenerate limbs, yet our R&D is busy working on that as we speak. Gaia Corp has the vision to revolutionise our world. The life tank would be part of the new world order. I cannot say for sure however I assume that in our near future such technologies as I have said before...will bring the end to ancient practices like acupuncture. The life tank makes life easier for everybody.' The voice came from Daniel Faris, seated with his hands clasped, he looked like he was in his mid-fifties. He had olive skin, a shark-like nose, beady dark brown eyes and had no hair on his head. Daniel Faris wore a navy-blue suit, with a crimson necktie. He then went on to talk about the life tank's basic functions and capabilities.

The life tank was a container like that stood vertically up and attached to it were different pipe-like structures. Its main healing element was a liquid in which someone will be submerged in while they healed. Felix had the suspicion as he smiled that the liquid surely must have derived from dit da jow.

A new month came, and Felix was to meet with Claudia Fern as per the new arrangement. Pulling a courting stunt, Felix decided that they meet up for breakfast in the morning at a restaurant. He wanted to then smooth his way to having dinner with her that evening. His father suspected what his son was planning to do, cheered him on and tried to give him some tips. But Carl's words fell before entering Felix's ears.

'Hi, so how have you been?' Claudia initiated the conversation as they sat down at a table. 'I am good! How you?' Felix responded. 'I am good, thanks for inviting me for breakfast,' said Claudia. 'Anytime,' said a beaming Felix, as he kept as much direct contact with her eyes. 'Look clearly your life seems to be getting on track and I am trying to push for them to take you off this supervision, so you can have your life completely on track,' said Claudia. 'Thanks,' said Felix as he gently put his hand on Claudia's hand and then removed it. 'Anyway,' he began, 'that is good news deserves some form of celebration, what are you doing this evening?' 'Um…nothing really why?' asked Claudia. 'Well, how about I really thank you with dinner, it is on me,' said Felix trying to sound as smooth as possible as his one hand which was laying on his leg shook uncontrollably. Claudia did her best to cloak her surprise as she drew herself back and said, 'oh… wow…um…look I will have to politely decline,' Felix by now knew what was coming next and he could feel his heart beat in his throat, 'to be straight with you it would be inappropriate, in other circumstances it would be okay, however sorry,' she concluded. 'No, it is not a problem,' said Felix trying to brush aside the anguish he felt. 'Anyway, thanks a lot just remembered I need to go do something, thank you very much,' said Claudia as she got up and left. 'Fuck!' Felix muttered as he watched Claudia walk away. It does not matter, was worth the try he thought.

Just before leaving the restaurant Felix received a call from Carl, he hesitated to pick up as he looked at his phone, 'Now you want to pretend to be a father…' sighing he then decided to answer. 'Hi,' he said with no ounce of emotion in his voice. 'How did it go?' asked Carl. 'She said no,' Felix answered directly. 'Don't worry these things happen,' said Carl trying to console his son, instead an irritated

Felix felt patronised. 'Cool, thanks anyway got to go,' said Felix sounding a bit sarcastic as he immediately hung up and left the restaurant.

That evening to drown his sorrows, Felix made his way to a bar in town at a five-star hotel. There he ordered a martini. As he peacefully drank contemplating resigning from his job the following week, so he could give everything to his training for the Lei Tai. A familiar voice coming from across the bar caught his attention. It came from a young man about Felix's age dressed in a white shirt and open collars and white pants; he wore spotless white shoes. He was white with curly black hair with trimmed facial hair, that looked like a shaven beard growing back after three days. 'Smokey,' Felix murmured, as he recognised the young man who was chatting up a group of ladies with a smirk attached to his face.

He was an old friend of Felix and part of Felix's former gang. The last time they spoke was just before Felix got convicted. Smokey was second in charge of the gang at that time. A lady's man, Smokey was not much of a fighter like Felix, however, his fist could do damage.

'SMOKEY!' exclaimed Felix. Smokey turned briefly and then turned back to the ladies he was chatting to and then turned back, his face painted with disbelief. 'FELIX!' he yelled back, he then made hand gestures for Felix to come his way. Felix got out of his seat feeling mildly dizzy as the effects of the alcohol subtly manifested itself.

'Hey buddy!' said Smokey as he hugged Felix. 'My man, been a while,' he added. 'If my parole officer was to catch me talking to you its overs,' said Felix as he beamed at Smokey. 'Who cares about that, a lot has changed my man…hey ladies this is my old friend Felix,' said Smokey as he presented Felix to the ladies he was chatting to.

The ladies then left later, and Felix said, 'Smokey why you let them leave?' 'Ah let them go, never be attached,' said Smokey, gesturing with his hands as he waved it down. 'My man!' he began, 'you have gotten laid when you came out of prison right?' Felix tipsiness brought him into a mild state of soberness, stumbling to reply. Smokey chuckled as he tapped Felix on the shoulder. 'Come let me take you to a place,' said Smokey as he walked, and Felix followed.

They walked out of the hotel and up the road, which was at an incline and then took a left turn to a road called, Lao Street. After a few more steps, there was a two-storey white building, which Smokey pointed to Felix, 'Remember that place?' he asked Felix. 'Umm…nah…' said, Felix, as he frowned. 'Come on let's get closer', said Smokey as they walked towards the building. There was a tower of a bouncer sitting on a stool next to the front door of the building. He was black, bald and was dressed in black with a leather jacket. Smokey nodded at him, with Felix doing the same as the bouncer got up rang the doorbell and the two were allowed in. The reception room of the building was dimly lit and by the front desk sat an elderly woman who wore glasses and smirked at both Felix and Smokey, 'Hi, see you brought a friend today,' she said. 'Yea,' chuckled Smokey, as he took out a roll of cash and handed it to the woman and said, 'that is nine hundred Dinares.' The old woman unrolled the cash and counted the money, smiling once she was done and then she said, 'Great, go in,' as she winked at both Smokey and Felix. Behind them was a door and as they strolled towards it Felix whispered to Smokey, 'Is this a brothel?' 'No shit, it a nursery,' replied Smokey sarcastically. Inside was another room sort of like a night club with a bevvy of beautiful women marauding around, dressed yet exposing their assets, Felix felt himself harden with his heartbeat thudding despite his apparent calm demeanour, whereas Smokey was completely the king of cool, externally and internally. There was a disco ball in the centre of the room, flickering light about.

Smokey and Felix headed for the bar, once they both sat on the bar stools, the bar lady who seemed to be herself a working girl made her way to them. 'So, what can I do for you boys?' she asked. While Smokey chatted to her, Felix's eyes further scanned the surroundings. They were the only customers in at that moment, and as his eyes fell on each of the ladies none failed to return a look.

'What you are drinking?' asked Smokey as he

turned to Felix. 'Um…well…what you are drinking?' Felix replied with a question. Smokey gave out a mild laugh and said, 'Nothing. Alcohol makes my dick soft.' Felix chuckled and then asked, 'Even red wine?' Smokey just replied with a laugh and then turned to the bar lady and said, 'We good for now.'

Felix glanced at an ebony goddess who sat enjoying her glass of red wine, she glanced back looking straight at his eyes. Her glowing black skin looked soft and her curves further aroused Felix whose eyes had dropped and were now fixated on her full lips, painted with crimson lipstick. He made his way to her and Smokey who was busy chatting up another girl turned and smiled and then turned back to the girl he was chatting up.

Felix sat beside the girl he had spotted, who looked at him as she took a sip from her glass. 'Hey,' said Felix sounding as smooth as possible. 'Hi,' she replied with a smile. 'You have nice lips, what is your name?' Felix asked. 'It is Naomi,' she said as she stretched out her hand and Felix shook it and said, 'I am Felix.'

After their introduction, Felix happy with his choice told Naomi, 'Come let's go.' Before leaving, Naomi pulled a serious face as she cautioned Felix, 'Look anything but anal.' Felix responded with a smile. Walking past Smokey, Felix nodded at him, they walked out of the room back into the reception area, where Naomi led him a the staircase.

She took him into one of the rooms, it was air-conditioned and dimly lit. The room had a king-size bed and a widescreen flat television on the corner of the room on mute showing different pornographic displays. An erect Felix started to rapidly take off his clothes. By the time, he was half-naked he commanded Naomi, 'Take off your clothes!' She frowned a little and said, 'Geez, why the rush, take it slow,' and then she slowly removed her clothes. Felix grinning approached her and removed her skirt and when she was completely naked. He first kissed her and slowly made his ways to her breast as she moaned biting her lip and closed her eyes.

Felix was in there with Naomi for close to two hours, when an already done Smokey waited for him. He came out with a smiling Naomi, by his side, who he then kissed. Claps and whistles came from downstairs as Smokey spotted them. 'See you,' whispered Felix as he kissed Naomi one more time. She replied with the same words as she watched him and Smokey leave.

'Thanks a lot, my man, that was a treat,' Felix said to Smokey once they were out of the brothel. 'Argh...you welcome...it is nothing,' Smokey replied. 'Where you get so much money? You sure came up compared to six years ago,' said Felix with a tone of admiration. 'We were thugs when we were adolescents...now I am bigger than that,' said Smokey as they both walked down the street.

'Okay…well…' as Felix spoke Smokey interrupted him, 'Felix I do a lot of things, I'm about that life, smuggling, contraband…you remember The Baron?' Felix's footsteps froze once he heard that name.

The Baron was considered Wobbleton City's biggest gangster. No one knew who he was or even believed he existed, his name was used to evoke fear in the underworld, but Felix's gang of misfits were known not to be afraid of The Baron. Felix always suspected Carl Sobek was The Baron, he just could never prove it and had forgotten about it over the years. Smokey, mentioning it, brought memories back to life and despite his suspicions, Felix never said anything to the guys in his former gang that he suspected The Baron to be his father.

'You remember, how you were the only one to actually not be scared of The Baron, we pretended but you, not an ounce of bone quivered in fear,' said Smokey. Felix brushed aside the thought of The Baron. He simply said, 'It is the past…fact you are an upcoming big shot. Anyway, once I am off this parole you and I should meet up! Until then we cannot be seen together.' With those final words, they both gave each other fist pumps and Felix headed for a parked taxi, in which he got in and left. Smokey waved and resumed strolling with a grin on his face, after a few more steps he noticed a hooded figure standing a few metres ahead of him.

On guard and feeling anxious Smokey screamed

at the guy, 'HEY! PUNK! Do we have a problem!' The hooded person stood firm and silent. Smokey took a few steps forward and in that sudden moment in time, he blacked out as another person hit him from the back propelling his body forward as he fell flat on his face, hitting the ground with a thud.

The following week at work Felix got out of his chair, he was done it was time to resign. He would let Claudia know as he needed to train full time for the Sanshou and the Lei Tai. Felix walked to one of his managers and in a few words, he simply said, 'I quit,' and before making his way out he headed to Jim. 'You are leaving, aren't you?' asked Jim. 'Yea... look was good meeting you see you around,' said Felix as he walked away. And as he walked Jim said, 'Hey you not going to say bye to Arrieta?' Felix stopped and turned and simply grunted in disapproval and then made his way out. He was done with Gaia Corp.

A surprised Mrs Wilkins saw Felix as he returned from work earlier than usual, 'And now?' she asked as she frowned in concern at Felix. 'I quit', answered Felix directly. Mrs Wilkins sighed as she shook her head, 'You young people take having a job for granted, in my days...oh well anyway got work to do,' once she was done she disappeared to tend to the different house chores. Felix then decided for some reason to check if his father was home. Even though it was not likely, however, he wanted to let Carl know that he was moving in with Uncle Fred to train for the Sanshou and then the Lei Tai. And to let his father know he had left his job. He made his way to his father's study and as he got close, he heard murmurs coming from inside. By the time, he was by the door which was a few millimetres wide open, he could make out what was said inside.

'You said Felix was with him!?' asked the voice that sounded like Carl Sobek. 'Yes, the punk was with your son, I waited for your son to leave before I could whack him from the back. I had one of my guys distract him from the front,' said another voice, sounding deep and coming from a man. Felix froze for a moment, did his father order a hit on Smokey? He thought, and then his thought where scattered away as he heard more from inside the study. 'So, you say he is dead this Smokey?' asked the voice that sounded like Carl. 'Yes, after I knocked him out, we took him to one of our dungeons where he was executed and then we dumped his body far away in a farm dam. Here is a picture,' said the deep voice coming from the stranger. 'Great. Good job. Next time bring me a real live finger. Regardless here is your money,' said the voice that sounded like Carl Sobek. 'Thank you, sir,' said the deep voice of the stranger. 'There is a great war to come, bigger than you and me,' said the voice that sounded like Carl. The stranger grunted in disbelief and then said, 'Even for the great Baron himself, doubt it.' 'Argh get out,' said Carl annoyed.

Hearing all of this made Felix feel a different emotion, he heard the confirmation itself. Something he always knew was true that Carl Sobek was The Baron the most feared gangster in Wobbleton City. Nevertheless, he also felt rage toward his father. Why did his father send people to follow him and why did Smokey need to die? These thoughts all rushed through his head and at that moment of thought Felix impulsively stormed in the study. Furious, he glared at his father and the stranger. Carl Sobek sat on his desk, and the man whom he spoke to before Felix stormed in was standing up in front of Carl. Felix sized up the stranger moving his eyes up and down. The stranger was as tall as Carl Sobek with a very dominating muscular figure. He was white and bald with a thick long black beard and thick intimidating eyebrows.

'What you doing here Felix?' asked Carl Sobek. 'I heard everything you idiot!' snarled Felix and then he turned his eyes towards the stranger, 'and you fuck face! Oooh, I am going to make you pay.' As he said that, Felix made a move towards the man, who tried to stop Felix with both hands stretched out. Felix stepped to the side, threw a fury of punches and then stepped into the man's centre line finishing him off with an uppercut. The stranger's head tilted back as he stumbled and crumbled down to a fall.

'Impressive, Felix,' said Carl as he pulled out a cigar from one of his desks cut it and lit it, then took a puff. 'We definitely would have made a great team working together,' he added as he grinned and took another puff of his cigar. 'Fuck you! Dad!' was Felix first words as he brewed with hate and continued, 'so you have this punk follow me and then you killed Smokey...Why!? Is this your sick way of trying to protect me?' 'First of all,' began Carl in a calm voice as his face got very serious, 'you have to learn to respect ME! I do not give a damn about your friend. As for you, you can protect yourself. Your friend was stealing from me! Fuck you lucky you are my son. Oh, boy I swear on your dead mother's name if you were somebody else, I would have killed you!' Carl was now also angry as he glared back at his son. 'What you think I did not know about your stupid gang harassing my business when you were an idiot adolescent! A rebel without a cause!' said Carl. Felix was silent, out of fuel to respond verbally but his fighting engine was on full and in that silence, Carl continued, 'What! You think it was your Uncle Fred that only took care of you when you in prison, with his friend Silver... NO! My boy I also played my part. Him and I, we have our differences, but we always come together because that is family! You, on the other hand, disowned me your own father before going to jail, I had the power to make sure you did not go in. Look at you now! You ruined your own FUCKING LIFE!' Felix's rage cooled and was about to be manifested into tears, but he held them firm and at that moment, he spoke, 'I did not want your help back then! And fuck it now! This is what is going to happen I am moving to Uncle Fred I am done with you. My life will be perfect, and I will be champion…in case you did not know I am going to train for the Lei Tai. Like I told mom when she was alive and promised her on her death bed when she died. I will be a champion for me and most importantly for her!' Once he was done with his words Felix marched away and Carl sighed relaxing a little, took a puff of his cigar and looking at his knocked-out henchman grinned and then he muttered, 'My boy,' chuckling afterwards.

Having left his home Felix packed what he could and headed to Uncle Fred's place. He told his uncle everything that had happened and to Aunt Catherina a modified version that omitted the death of his friend and the fact that Felix had visited a brothel. As far a she was concerned it all came down to Felix having a disagreement with his father. 'You and your father need to get along sooner than later. At least in the memory of your sweet mom Virginia may she rest in peace,' said Aunt Catherina once she heard what had happened.

# CHAPTER FOUR-
# A PHONEY
# CHAMPION

'Now, you nearly there, however, you need to go back to the basics,' said Uncle Fred. Him and Felix where at the kwoon and for months he was teaching Felix how to issue power with minimum to no muscular effort. They were doing an exercise with both their hands touching and they both had the same back foot at a forty-five-degree angle while the other foot was placed in the front-facing forward. With the distance between their feet being the width of their shoulder. Both knees of both their legs were bent with their hips square as they faced each other. Their upper bodies were relaxed, concentrating all their mass down to the ground and rooting themselves. Every movement was controlled by their lower parts of their bodies, without them stepping forward or backwards. The exercise was called, push hands. Their hands would move in a circular like motion with their elbows dropped down and when Uncle Fred moved forward in a slow constant speed (this was an initiated attack) Felix would respond using the same pace as he shifted his body weight and deflected whatever the attack was. One of the essences of the push hand exercise was sensitivity.

'It all comes back to listening, understanding, neutralising and attacking!' with his last words Uncle Fred sensed an opening and in an abrupt second, before Felix knew it, he flew off his feet landing hard on the ground. He slowly got up brushing himself off as he sighed. 'That is enough for today go meditate,' said Uncle Fred as he walked away and left the kwoon.

Despite the hard training in the following months, Felix felt emotionally overwhelmed, with everything that happened and to his surprise, Claudia had not made any contact, he did not bother calling her to find out. After all, she was his parole officer. However, the main thing in his mind was the Lei Tai. All the hard training he did in prison felt worthless, Eddy was always in his mind, Eddy surpassing him troubled him. Sometimes it motivated him to push or sometimes it just crushed him down into contemplation or a moment of procrastination. However, he knew he had to push.

Felix received a visit from Richard, who had replaced Claudia; Felix remembered who he was. He was about Felix's height and looked like he was in his mid-thirties. His hair was partially grey, and he was white with icy blue eyes. Richard was clean-shaven, and he was dressed in a black suit with a navy-blue necktie.

'Well your kind aunt said I would find you here,' said Richard looking around, (They were inside the kwoon). Aunt Catherina had guided Richard there where he found Felix training. 'How is Claudia?' Felix asked. 'Well she is good,' Richard first answered and then continued, 'look just to get to the point. By the look on your face, I am assuming you know I have replaced Claudia. Well I got good news for you,' Richard cleared his throat and then continued, while Felix remained silent, 'an order has come through from the judge, surprisingly your parole is over.' Felix smiled at the news, 'Sounds perfect,' he said. 'It does,' agreed Richard and then he added, 'your aunt said you training for the Sanshou and you have aspirations to then make it to the Lei Tai.' 'Make it? My man, I am winning the Lei Tai,' said Felix. Richard chuckled at the response and then said, 'Well I wish you the best Felix.' He then left, and Felix resumed his training.

While on Journal Felix was just randomly going through different pics and statuses of the people he was connected with on journal. He then came across a video post, it was from the Separatists. The video began showing different images, the first was the denunciation of Daniel Faris and Gaia Corp, this further intrigued Felix to watch more. The narrator of the video was a male and he said, 'Daniel Faris, rich billionaire, this man is cancer, he and our beloved whole system of the Union of Nations are liars. The eight big nations of the world should govern themselves. We shifting to a one-world government and that is nonsense. Our freedoms and even our beloved Lei Tai a world tradition is being bastardised...' Felix had stopped watching the video. He had seen enough Separatist propaganda, the video reminded him of the attack at the mall and then his thoughts floated towards Claudia. He then decided to train, he had to maintain his focus.

Now and then Felix in his hour of boredom would do some internet research about the Separatist movement. This group had appeared out of nowhere and authorities around the world had no idea who they were exactly. Felix decided to go to their website, which the authorities had not managed to bring down despite several attempts, they also had a group on Journal. Based on what they claimed the group is composed of the remnants of a failed rebellion that happened in the East-South Union.

The rebellion in the East-South Union had begun with peaceful marches organised by Cole Sud a direct descendant of Prince Rey Sud. Cole Sud was from a very wealthy family given his family's imperial history in the southern regions of the world. He and his followers first began protesting the East-South Union government's relationship with the rapidly growing company Gaia Corp. He alleged the government was corrupted by Gaia Corp's money and headed peaceful marches in Easex, the capital city of the East-South Union.

The allegation started with the Sanshou competition in that country. Given the global popularity of the Lei Tai, it had commercial potential, however, this was limited as not to ruin tradition and to uphold the symbol of what the Sanshou trials and Lei Tai meant, that they were a symbol of peace. A way for mankind to avoid major conflict and if not to reduce it to champions battling it out. It represented martial art in its true and traditional sense.

There were never any adverts, and companies were not allowed to show off their brands. Regardless, in the Lei Tai or Sanshou, champions won big prizes and with their titles came fame and glory, many dreamed about, and a few achieved.

In modern times things like endorsements were ways the corporates managed to cash in on the competition, they endorsed the individual contenders. But when Gaia Corp started to operate in the East-South Union, they slowly with time directly find ways to endorse the Sanshou.

This was one of the cornerstone themes of the protest, himself Cole Sud came from an illustrious martial arts fraternity (his family). He was eventually gunned down, during one of the protests. The East-South Union authorities had riot police try and arrest him. Cole Sud, it is said, took down twenty riot police officers by himself and then he was shot. The bullet was suspected to have come from a sniper and the uncertainty to his murder generated many conspiracy theories. But his death is what triggered the rebellion and within a year the rebels consisted of different groups. All originally former supporters of Cole Sud and now they all had their different agendas. However, they managed to overrun the East-South Union's government which like the other seven nations only had police forces to fight the rebels. Union troops were soon called in and within two years they crushed the rebellion and ended the civil war.

The Separatists' manifesto was that they wanted to end the Union of Nations. Restore the Lei Tai as it was in antiquity, the modern times had removed things like the use of weapons, although opponents sometimes still fought to their deaths.

But the Separatists saw the increase in restrictions turn the symbolic duel into nothing but an entertaining sport.

A federal type government is what the Separatists wanted, they saw the Union of Nations as an increasingly centralised form of world governance.

There were no rules in the Sanshou and Lei Tai competition, it was no hold bars fighting. The Lei Tai and Sanshou qualifications event also had no restriction on who entered man or woman could fight each other. People could forfeit if they feared for their lives or could not fight any longer.

The Sanshou was about four months away and a sweating Felix who was done teaching a class at the kwoon was busy doing push-ups. Once he was done, he started stretching, unwinding his locked-up thoughts about his uncle who had been missing in action. Felix was not too bothered about training himself, it was a way of life, but he felt it would help if his uncle around more, so he could demonstrate the hidden jewels of the Harmonious Fist.

'Felix,' said Uncle Fred as he came in the kwoon. 'Good stretch, it is all about flexibility, being supple and agile. Everything that aids mobility,' he added. 'I have been thinking of asking…for a retired man you sure look like you have a job,' said Felix. Uncle Fred stared at him not responding. 'Look Uncle Fred at least show me all the family secrets you clearly showed Eddy and…' 'I did not show him shit!' Uncle Fred fired back before Felix could finish his words and continued, 'That ingrate used to go through the manuals and train really hard…You, on the other hand, know the essence of the art, your arrogance in the past is what has held you back, you thought you knew it all. Until your cousin used the Harmonious Fist to a high potential. My advice to you,' speaking in a serious tone, Uncle Fred got closer, 'is that you do not get fixated on the one technique we have used on you…masters in ancient times did more powerful feats. Although I would knock the teeth out! Of the punk, you once were…that Felix at least was sure of himself.' Felix chuckled and said, 'I am pretty confident of myself.' 'No, you not,' said Uncle Fred as he put both hands firmly on Felix's shoulders.

Then he turned, as he began to walk away Felix said, 'Let's spar now uncle, come let's see if I am not sure of myself.' Felix began bouncing up and down on both his feet as Uncle Fred turned back and strolled towards him.

Felix settled down and then in that sudden moment he made his move. He threw a feint jab with his left hand and then launched a punch with his right. Uncle Fred did not fall for the fake left and grabbed hold of Felix right wrist and with his other hand, he held Felix's elbow. Felix relaxed his right arm and moved his right fist towards him; bending his elbow. Spiralling to the left, his left palm hit his right fist with his elbow facing Uncle Fred's centre line. Feeling the motion internally, a wild surge of a current flowed from his feet, with the turning of the waist and like a shockwave fired out from his elbow. Uncle Fred stumbled backwards, beaming at his nephew as he immediately regained balance. 'Not bad,' he said as he charged forth. A sidekick from Felix tried to stop him and he dodged it and stepped on the outside and then grabbed Felix's leg. While his arm hit Felix's torso with his leg sweeping Felix's other leg that was rooted on the ground. Felix went off the ground and landed a metre away. He quickly got up smiling while Uncle Fred gave him a serious stare and said, 'Great! You proved me wrong...however, you could not possibly think that I am at the same level as my son. You both still have not only a lot to improve on, but many more lives to live.'

'I am just happy! Got you there with my elbow, it's just a simple more refined way of issuing power,' said Felix sounding excited. 'Exactly!' replied Uncle Fred. 'Maybe I should find Eddy and teach him a lesson!' exclaimed Felix, 'that chop!' he added. 'No, no, no!' began Uncle Fred in a cautionary tone, 'I still want my son back, he might not be my biological son. However, we all sharing the knowledge of our ancestors makes us family regardless of blood.' Uncle Fred looked mildly sad at that moment. Felix could see in that flicker of time that his uncle was missing Eddy.

'Felix there is something else I need to tell you... it is very important, and it has just come to mind,' Uncle Fred spoke with a sombre tone. Felix did not ask anything instead he concentrated everything on listening. 'I am one of the leaders of the Separatists movement,' said Uncle Fred.

Felix looked shocked and confused, the revelation mentally punched his mind into disarray. He began pacing himself around and then said, 'A former commander of the Union Guards...What the hell?' 'Is that so much of a surprise?' asked Uncle Fred. 'A surprise! Uncle...what about Aunt Catherina, what about Charles! Hell! You put, everybody in jeopardy!' exclaimed Felix. 'Listen to me carefully! I know what I have sacrificed! This goes beyond me or you! It is bigger than everything!' Uncle Fred shot back. 'Uncle...look...' Felix words were drowned by

Uncle Fred's words, 'You never asked me if I was joking…deep down inside I am assuming you somehow suspected or you not that surprised with my revelation. You just shocked that it is true.' 'Well…you always missing, and you are a traditionalist when it comes to martial arts and the Lei Tai, so you would be a candidate to be part of the Separatist. But it is still a surprise…You were involved in the war in the East-South Union…' Felix paused; he was still in shock, and his uncle had made the wrong assumption. As far as Felix was concerned he wanted to find, the perfect time to confront his uncle to find out about his whereabouts. Nevertheless, the fact that Uncle Fred was part of the Separatists cleared a lot of things.

'Have you told Aunt Catherina?' asked Felix. 'I did before coming here she is bewildered by the news; however, she took it far better than you. She thought I was cheating on her,' once saying that Uncle Fred broke into laughter and then said, 'Look, Felix, I want to give you the honour of joining the cause.' 'Joining the what…the cause! Uncle no thank you! I am focusing on the Lei Tai! That's my cause! I promised my mother. I did not lose my confidence, those first few years in prison made me realise I had failed myself. I need to redeem myself. I just hope you protect our family which you hold so dearly to heart,' said Felix sounding a bit upset as he rushed off. Uncle Fred sighed and tilted his head down as he muttered, 'You will join the cause, it is just a matter of time.'

As the day went by, Felix felt his emotions rise transforming from sadness to anger, he felt like Uncle Fred was ruining his only dream. To keep himself focused he headed to the cemetery where his mother was buried. Casting his eyes at her tombstone with facial expressions of joy and sadness.

Virginia Sobek his mother had died from a sickness that the doctors could not cure at the time. Her death had caused a rift between Felix and Carl changing them both.

'What a surprise!' exclaimed Carl who had appeared and was walking towards his wife's tombstone. Felix kept quiet. 'I sometimes spend a whole day here...I really miss your mother...oh Virginia,' he said as he kneeled rubbing the tombstone and getting back up. Felix did not look at his father, his eyes were fixated on the tombstone. 'Son...' Carls' words were abruptly halted as Felix said, 'Save it pops...I just need some time to myself.' Felix abruptly walked away as Carl yelled a few times, 'Felix! Felix!' He ignored Carl and continued walking.

With too much pant up emotion, Felix wanting to let loose and blow some steam. He headed to a bar in town. Felix drank peacefully by the bar staring into blank space when out of nowhere somebody spilt their drink on him. He calmly stood up and shook the spillage off him as the man who spilt the drink snapped at him, 'I just fucking bought that! You buying me and my boys more rounds or you going to get it!' as he said this his friends stood beside him. Before one of the bouncers in the bar could make their way to the commotion, Felix threw his drink at the man and his friends. They then all went for him at the same time.

Seated not too far and watching the events un-ravel live in front of him was a tall and largely built man. He had light cold blue eyes that watched Felix in awe as Felix fought off the men who came at him. The man who watched was white, bald and he had a thick trimmed black beard. He wore white pants and a crimson buttoned-up shirt, with pol-ished black shoes. 'Hey!' He snarled at the approach-ing bouncers as they were about to close in on Felix who was fending off and beating his attackers. The bouncers looked at the seated man who signalled them to stop. Twenty seconds into the brawl, Felix had the guy who had spilt the drink on him on the floor and before he could finish him off, the seated man signalled at the bouncers and they moved in. One of them using a short baton that had electrical sparks shooting out of it, zapped Felix from behind till he was out cold.

Felix woke up to a splash of water on his face, he shook his head as he blinked and was slightly pant-ing. His eyes moving anxiously around and then he caught a glimpse of the man who had signalled the order to the bouncers. His face looked familiar to

Felix and in a couple of seconds, it clicked who the man was.

'I am assuming you know who I am...' began the man calmly, 'you Felix Sobek, Carl's son...aren't you?' Felix kept quiet, realising that he was handcuffed with his hands in front as he was seating on a chair with his legs tied up. He was in what seemed to be an underground cellar in the bar, it had one glaring light, shining from the ceiling and lighting only the centre of the room, with the rest of the room remaining in the shadows.

'Your father is not really one of my friends...' the man seized speaking as Felix spoke and he started to listen, 'I know you...you Money Sling, you manage Alexander Kim the current reigning Sud Republic Sanshou champion, he has survived the Lei Tai countless of times, but has never won.' 'Yea, Yea,' said Money Sling as he chuckled. 'How do you know who I am?' asked Felix. 'I can recognise that Harmonious Fist anywhere...ha! And only a Sobek can apply it with such high proficiency.' 'How do you know...' before Felix could finish his supposed question, Money Sling jumped on it, 'How do I know your father? Your family? Well, business and just plain street history. Nothing more nothing less. Listen here kid, you have a lot of potential, why don't you come fight for me? I will pay you well.'

Felix shook his head as he sighed and said, 'I am done with that life, I just came out of prison I am not going to resume getting into street brawls for a quick buck…I AM GOING TO BE CHAMPION…THE LEI TAI CROWN IS MINE! WARN YOUR FIGHTER.' With those final roaring words, Felix suddenly stood up in a burst, snapping his handcuffs as they slid off his hands like water washing down and the ropes binding his legs snapped. The chair was also a victim as it broke, dissembling itself. 'Impressive', muttered Money Sling who closely observed Felix. 'In prison, they use special handcuffs that either electrocuted me or if that failed needles in the handcuff injected me with some substance that rendered me powerless. I am a Sobek after all,' said Felix. 'Indeed,' replied Money Sling and as he said that another of his henchmen appeared whispering something in his ear. Felix stood there with a mild frown appearing in his face.

'Kid you might want to see this,' said Money Sling and one of his bouncers laid out a device on the ground and seemed to fiddle with his wristwatch. The device vertically projected a beam of light, which then started to show images. It was telehologram, a three-dimensional television. The images on display were part of a news coverage and there stood a female news reporter.

'…reporting live from our studio in the Sud Republic. As it has been announced by the Union of Nations for a week now, they have sent special agents assigned to contain and investigate a report that said that the Sud Republic was the heartland of the Separatists movement. It appears that this report is true right now we have live images of Union Guards raiding the home of the once-famous General, Frederick Sobek, who once was the supreme commander for union troops that brought back peace in the East-South Union. It is believed that Frederick Sobek is one of the key leaders of the Separatists movement and the authorities are already charging him with being responsible for the attacks that happened at the Westick Mall. Authorities have currently updated us that no one was found at the home. It seems the former General Frederick Sobek is on the run with his family...' The tele-hologram was switched off by one of Money Sling's henchmen, as Felix dashed off, he had seen enough. Money Sling stopped his men who tried to stop Felix as he said, 'Leave him, that kid has enough trouble as it is.'

Felix's heart pumped, he was relieved to find out that Charles and Aunt Catherina were not at the house. His certain Uncle Fred kept them safe somewhere, and then he thought about himself surely the authorities will come for him and his father. Felix tried to calm down as he caught a taxi and headed for his house. Once he arrived, to his relief there was no police car parked outside of the house. Storming in he was met with an angry Mrs Wilkins in her nightgown. 'What is this raucous! Young man!' she snarled. Felix just anxiously smiled and hugged her, she pushed him off as he flew off stumbling and regained his footing. 'So now you on drugs!' she said. 'No! Have you not seen the news!' exclaimed Felix. Mrs Wilkins tempered herself down, 'So you found out,' she said. 'Does my father know?' asked Felix. Mrs Wilkins sighed and answered, 'Go speak to your father his in his office,' yawning she ended it with, 'I am too old I need my beauty sleep.' Felix sighed and reluctantly headed for his father's office. He opened the door, the light was on, but Carl Sobek was nowhere in sight, switching off the light he closed the door.

Staying awake the whole evening till the morning in his room, Felix went outside by the pool and there he saw his father suited up and seating at the dining table near the pool. He was talking to a woman. Felix made his way towards them. 'See there is my son like I told you, he has no idea of my brothers doing,' said Carl as he glanced at Felix and then back at the woman. 'Felix take a seat,' he said, and Felix calmly sat down.

The woman was part of the police and was just questioning Carl Sobek on his whereabouts and was questioning where Felix was as well. Luckily Carl covered for him. Once she was done with the questioning she left. Carl turned to his son as he sighed and said, 'They will be watching us for now, she said. Well, I might not be Gaia Corp, but my connections shield us. Your Uncle and the rest are fine in a safe house, no one will find them.' 'So, you also on this? You also part of the Separatists?' Felix asked looking slightly annoyed. Carl smirked and replied,

'You could say so...' 'I do not want any part of this, I just want to be champion.' said Felix. 'As a lineage holder of the Harmonious Fist, you will join us. It is a matter of time,' said Carl. 'Eddy...What about Eddy?' asked Felix. Carl sighed as he said, 'Your uncle has vehemently disagreed with this theory. But I think Eddy is behind the raid. I could be wrong of course however my men are on to him.' 'His family he....' Felix's words drowned in silence as Carl interrupted with, 'Yea, yea, you and your uncle can sometimes be so alike.' 'You really suspect him don't you,' said Felix. Carl just nodded. Felix then got up and said, 'I am done with this, it is too much,' then he quickly walked away. 'Where you going!?' yelled Carl. 'Money Sling!' Felix yelled back. Carl frowning muttered to himself, 'Money Sling. This kid...'

Felix got a few of his stuff that remained in the house and stuffed it all in a rucksack and headed for town, he was short on money. He used what he was left with to get a taxi to town and made his way to Money Sling's bar. Felix was going to take a chance with Money Sling, he did not care that Money Sling represented Alexander Kim. But if he wanted Felix to fight for him then it would be in the Lei Tai.

Being day-time, the bar was closed, and Felix arrived seeing staff cleaning up the place. He asked for Money Sling and he was pointed to a room in the corner. There was Money Sling with a few of his henchmen. The office was small and with Felix stepping in it felt even more cramped up. Money Sling was seated on his table busy browsing through the touch screen of his tablet; the office walls had posters of fighters from yesteryear and above behind his seat was a large painting of himself smoking a cigar.

'Close the door,' he said as Felix stepped in. 'So, what can I do for you today?' he asked as him and two of his henchmen who stood on both of his sides gazed at Felix. 'I want you to be my manager for the Sanshou,' said Felix. 'I am already managing Alexander kid,' said Money Sling. 'So, you can manage the both of us, besides I have a better chance of being champion then Alexander,' said Felix. 'Well, you know you will fight him in the Sanshou right,' said Money Sling, Felix showing no emotion of worry replied, 'I am not bothered, the people that he can defeat will not be in the Sanshou for the Sud Republic or even in the Lei Tai.' 'Great! Let's get to work kid! I am assuming with that bag you will need a place to stay.' Money Sling turned to one of his henchmen as he snapped his fingers, 'Get him in one of the hotels. Tomorrow we begin training.'

The Sud Republic's Sanshou competition took place in the ancient city of Sud, outside the Loham Temple. It was a weekend event, ending the last day of the weekend. The first two days Felix had defeated all his opponents, most of them were knocked out or simply pushed off the raised platform. If you fell out you automatically lost the fight, others were known to jump willingly to forfeit. Or they would simply bow down to their opponents and give up.

As Felix had predicted the final fight was going to be against Alexander Kim.

The man was older than Felix a veteran of Sanshou competitions and the Lei Tai. He was black, tall and brawny; renowned for his tiger style. Sud was originally his city of birth and despite having learned different martial art styles from the Loham Temple, the tiger style was his speciality.

Felix was slightly nervous on the prospect of fighting Alexander now that the time had come, as he stepped on the raised platform. He was the first one there and despite having defeated so many opponents a large, 'BOOOO!' rang across the crowd that had built up around the area.

The event happened in the open, there was no stadium in Sud City. It kept many of the traditions of the past and the raised platform was slightly higher than the standard built modern platforms. Alexander Kim stepped last raising his hands as the crowd went wild, everyone screaming his name. That moment Felix could feel his heartbeat in every part of his body and for a split second he nervously glanced around, he then sighed himself to relaxation as he gazed at his opponent. They both greeted each other using the yin-yang gestures in a martial manner and then to the crowd. After that the fight began; they slowly circled each other, sussing each other out. With a blink of an eye, Felix launched at Alexander with a short kick to his shin. Alexander stepped back, avoiding it and then came Felix's right fist, which he deflected and then seized using the tiger grip (his fingers were bent and piercing) as he grabbed the forearm of Felix's right hand. With his thumb putting pressure on a pressure point, a grimacing Felix suddenly relaxed that area of his body and then sent a surge coming up from his body into Alexander. His whole arm shook in a sudden, sending him stumbling near the edge of the platform. He regained his footing in time smiling at Felix, but as he dashed forward to attack he suddenly fell on his knees. Felix frowned slightly something was wrong, the crowd was pitch quiet each one of them looking in disbelief. Alexander Kim started to cough and struggled to get up, his nose had slow streaks of blood coming out of it. Regardless, seizing the opportunity Felix stepped forward launching a front kick and the Sud City champion went flying off the ground landing near the edge as he rolled off the platform. Felix was now the Sud Republic's champion to compete in the Lei Tai.

Panting slightly in confusion Felix raised his hands, however, the Sud City's faithful still booed him. He did not hold it against them, something was wrong.

After the fight and comforted by the luxury of his hotel suite Felix felt a series of mixed emotions. He switched on the TV and there the news was onto him. A reporter asked one of the spectators what they thought about the fight, 'That boy Felix is good, but clearly our champ was poisoned,' Another angry spectator voiced her opinion, 'That Wobbleton City punk is a fraud! He was lucky Alexander was poisoned! He is a phoney!' Felix switched off the television and pondered. It did seem like Alexander was poisoned; something was fishy and most definitely not smelling good. Getting up, he headed for Money Sling's hotel suite, where he saw a healthy-looking Alexander Kim with Money Sling and his henchmen. Alexander held what looked like a suitcase filled with money and Felix zeroed in on it. He had thrown the fight away, so Felix could win, and he could get paid.

'So, that fight was just a joke!' snarled Felix. 'No! that fight was business! Kid!' exclaimed Money Sling.

'You would have won the fight anyway, even if he did not throw away the fight,' he added sounding calmer. 'True kid, that Harmonious Fist of yours is amazing. Besides I am done with the Sanshou and the Lei Tai. It's a new era and things are not like back in the days. Anyway, this is my retirement money,' said Alexander and then he added, 'Money that stuff really helped with my poison performance thanks... Anyway, I am out, it has been good doing business with you.' He shook Money Sling's hand and left the room.

Felix was still not consoled by those words he needed a real challenge, a real fight. Even if it would end up easy, it had to be of his own accord, no foul play.

'So how much money did you and him make?' asked Felix. 'A lot, it was simple, the odds were against you, so us betting against Alexander's supposed win. We made a lot of money. You made money too, that hundred thousand Dinares you just made is a small fortune,' said Money Sling. Felix had forgotten about the prize money, remembering made him smile a little as he left heading back to his room.

Meanwhile back in Wobbleton City, on a windy evening by a tree in a park lit by street lamps was Uncle Fred and Eddy. Uncle Fred wore a black trench coat and a black hat that slightly concealed his face. Eddy was in his business suit.

'Hi son, how have you been?' Asked Uncle Fred. 'I am fine', replied Eddy coldly. 'Well I wanted us to meet quickly, it has been a short while since we last spoke. Your mother and Charles are safe… look I did not want you to find out the way you did,' said Uncle Fred. 'Oh, I knew…dear father,' said Eddy. 'What?' asked Uncle Fred. 'I am the one that told them…of everything, are you that naïve. You were well hidden after all,' Eddy pulled out a gun attached with a silencer. 'Why? Eddy Why!?' asked Uncle Fred. 'You joined the people that killed my biological parents, plus the way you have ignored me…I mastered the Harmonious fist all these years…it is always about Felix this, Felix that…well fuck that and fuck you!' Eddy held back his tears and with no regret and a sense of relief he pulled the trigger multiple times, with the first bullet hitting Uncle Fred on the forehead and the next on his throat. Within those few seconds of carnage, his body fell backwards hitting the ground with a thud, as his blood streamed out into the grass of the park. Eddy walked over to his body pointing the gun at it, Uncle Fred was already gone, his lifeless body flat on its back while his eyes and mouth were wide open with a facial expression of horror.

Moments later another figure appeared out of the darkness, the person seemed to have been watching the whole show from far. It was a male wearing a hooded black robe, he strolled towards Eddy putting his hand around his shoulders as he said, 'What a sacrifice, welcome to the Brotherhood.'

# CHAPTER FIVE-
# THE LEI TAI

In Main Central, Wobbleton City's maximum prison, a few hours after the event at the park. Silver received a piece of paper slipped into his prison cell by one of the guards, underneath his cell door. He picked it up and read it and once he was done, he took a deep breath and then calmly exhaled. 'Time to leave,' he muttered to himself and in that moment his cell door flew open off its hinges as if someone had used explosives. This was suddenly picked up by the prison cameras and the sirens went off. All prison personnel geared up, first thinking it was a prison riot before they could get a perfect idea as to what was exactly happening. Silver moved within those crucial seconds. Bashing open other cell doors letting prisoners out, this created confusion. The warden and prison guards never knew the full extent of his capabilities, what was thought of as myth became a reality. Silver made his way to the prison main entrance after busting open some doors and crushing skulls with his bare hands. Stealing one of the trucks in the prison parking bay, he busted his way out smashing the entrance boom out of place and running over one of the prison guards who had shot at the truck. He broke into a burst of erratic laughter as he drove off, Silver was free.

Felix received a call from Carl that shuttered him, his father let him know that Uncle Fred had been killed. Everything Carl had told Felix was what he later saw on the news, that Uncle Fred was tracked down and shot by a special counter-terror unit of the Union Guards. Felix had tears trickle down when no one looked. However, setting his mind on the Lei Tai, he intensively meditated emptying himself, his training became less physical as he worked on his mind.

Felix, Money Sling and a few of his henchmen had boarded flights, for the big buzzing cosmopolitan metropolis that was Feiville, where the Lei Tai took place. As per, history thousands of years ago, it was the village were the legendary General Fei was born; Feiville was situated in Eastland, it was the commercial capital of the country. It had the highest population of people and the city was littered with skyscrapers, the tallest being the Fei Tower. It was also where the Union of Nations had its headquarters and on the outskirts of the city, was the famous Dragon's Lair mountains, where ancient Daoist hermits once dwelled.

Given that it was Lei Tai season, the whole world had flocked to Feiville, security was tight, with

Union Troops and Eastland police patrolling the streets with a twenty-four-seven presence. The Lei Tai was to take place in the Red Crow Arena, a mammoth of a stadium with a seating capacity of five hundred thousand.

Felix and the rest were staying at a hotel exclusively for the fighters and their entourage and just like in the Sanshou, the Lei Tai began on the first day of the weekend and ended on the last day of the weekend.

They had arrived on the fourth day of the week, where fighters were interviewed and signed autographs. Felix was not the only new face out of the eight fighters from across the world. It was him and four others.

From the Northern Republics was the tall and large Emike Larson, she had short blonde hair and icy blue eyes synonymous with the cold of her country. Emike was pale and when in combat her skin reddened at a tinge; she was an aggressive fighter known for her tiger style. The Nordic East had Ana Nzinga, she was dark of complexion like milk with a drop of coffee. Her hair was thick, black and tied up to a ponytail, her wide eyes were dark brown tending towards black with eyes that barely had any crease.

Looking very feminine with a petite thin curvy structure of a body, Ana was deceptively fierce and a sight for eyes just like the many women from her region, she was known for her Loham Snake style. Igor Blade was the champion from The Nordic West, he was short, white with a stocky build. He had short brown hair, and greenish like eyes. His tiger style was what brought him to the Lei Tai and The United West had Kel Marr, he was black, bald, and was tall with a thin frame; crane style was his speciality. His victory over the former champion of the United West resulted in the former champion's death.

The veterans comprised of East-South Union's Bill Sterk, a tall muscular white man with a slightly greying full beard, he did not have a style to name. His survival in the past Lei Tai competitions was him losing by falling off the platform like the other returning competitors. The Sud-West Republics had Jim Stones, known for his tiger-crane style. He had an intimidating face and sharp piercing blue eyes; he was a force to be reckoned with. Last was the local Eastland reigning champion, Sun Guan, he was about Felix's height, fairly lighter of complexion with small hazel eyes, that had no crease.

He had a boyish face, was beardless with thick black hair and he was a magnet to his many female fans. A practitioner of Shi San Shi as it was called in the ancient Daoist tongue, meaning thirteen postures. Its origins were from Dragon's Lair and it was said to have come from the Water School; it was the martial arts practised by General Fei and was passed down by Yu Guan (General Red Crow).

The first day of the weekend (first leg of the Lei

Tai) determined who were the next four to progress to the second day of the weekend. Then the outcome on the second day of the weekend determined who the final two fighters will be on the last day of the weekend. It was simple and the battle on the last day was the conclusion to who would be crowned champion.

On that first day, Felix was feeling keen and nervous as he stepped in the Lei Tai platform exhaling and inhaling calmly a few centimetres below his abdomen. The raised platform was cylindrical and a meter and half off the ground with steps leading to the platform. The same structure as the Sanshou platforms, the distinct difference was the cheering crowd inside the stadium, it was at full capacity and the crowd's roar deafened any other sound. This made Felix feel tingling sensations as he waited for his opponent to come up the platform.

His first adversary was Bill Sterk, who jogged up the steps into the platform, lifting his hands and beating his chest as he then turned towards Felix giving him an intimidating stare. The crowd warmed up to Bill, Felix was not booed, but he did not receive any significant cheer.

'Ladies! And gentlemen! We have our two gladiators ready to fight it out!' exclaimed James Jets, as his voice went around the stadium projected by a microphone. He was the event MC, a world-renowned entertainer, James Jets paraded around the stadium, bubbly and full of energy with a face full of make-up. 'Oh, my gawwd doesn't he look handsome...um, yummy, ladies and gentlemen our usual Bill Sterk! Seems like they about to start,' he said as Felix and Bill circled each other. After a few seconds, Felix stood still, and then came the commentary, 'Our newcomer has stopped moving, oooh the suspense!' Bill made his move as he launched a front kick, which Felix dodged moving backwards. The front kick was followed by a series of rapid punches; the first and second deflected and then on the third as Felix deflected it he launched a left vertical straight punch. Aimed at Bill's chest, it made him lose his footing once on impact. He stumbled and fell, he tried to quickly get up and ended up kneeling on one knee with one hand on the ground and the other to his side as he looked at Felix in disbelief. Felix looked back with barely an ounce of emotion and the crowd including James were quiet. Not giving up easily, Bill got up grimacing as he felt the internal pain linger. He grabbed hold of his chest as he took his first step forward, the pain increased. 'Jump off you lose, continue you die,' said Felix. Bill responded with a wry smile and then kept silent. Felix felt a bit hesitant to make the final blow, and then muttering 'fuck it,' he dashed towards Bill. Using his reach and pumped on his last bit of adrenaline, Bill launched a front kick knocking the wind out of Felix who stepped back, grimacing for a split second feeling the pain and he stepped forward again. Then came Bill's roundhouse kick aimed at

Felix's head. Felix raised his arm blocking and deflecting the kick as his front leg and body were at a forty-five-degree angle. Simultaneously his other hand moved and like a cannon (as Felix sunk his body a bit low) hitting Bill on his groin. Bill let out a cry of pain as he fell to the floor grabbing his groin area and leg. The fight was over and as a sign of forfeit Bill crawled towards the steps exiting the platform.

'Ohhh nooo, my sweet Bill oh…it is okay I will nurse you! However, our winner! From…The Sud Republic is none other than Felix Sobek!' said James with added theatrics. The crowd then started to scream, 'Felix! Felix! Felix!'

'What a fight!' exclaimed Money Sling slapping Felix on his shoulder. 'That kick though…my chest I will need some massage,' said Felix who was rubbing his chest. 'Don't look at me, go to the medical bay they will help!' said Money Sling as he frowned. They were back at the hotel and Felix did indeed get a massage at the medical bay. He had made it to the second leg of the Lei Tai, it was just two more fights and then he would be crowned champion. Felix thought of Uncle Fred and then he remembered the promise he had made to his mother to bring him back to the ground.

The remaining fighters were Emike, Felix, Ana and Sun, Felix's next fight was against Ana who had easily crushed her adversary Jim Stones. Emike had torn the arm off, of her adversary on the first leg using her bare hands, a testament of the brute force of her tiger style, her next opponent was none other than the remaining veteran and reigning champion, Sun. His fight on the first leg was short, with a powerful snapping sidekick he had Kel Marr land flat on his back out of the Lei Tai platform.

The first fight of the next day was what every-body considered the de facto main event of the day, Sun Guan against Emike. 'Oooooh our handsome Sun look at him, hmmm would not mind him teaching me that Shi San Shi form of his…Awwh and there our hideo…I mean ferocious she male…manly!' as James entertained the crowd, Emike replied to him by displaying her middle finger and he continued, nonetheless.

Both fighters greeted each other with martial yin-yang gestures bowing their heads slightly and the fight begun. Casting a sneering look at Sun after the greeting, Emike exclaimed, 'Little man I am gonna fuck you up!' Sun immediately replied with a blank facial expression, 'Your brute strength is no match for my internal strength, bring it!' Smirking Emike charged for Sun and the crowd went crazy, she grabbed both of his hands and Sun looked up as she towered over him. Looking relaxed as Emike held his hands firmly by the wrists, he immediately pivoted his wrists up. A sudden internal current came to birth flowing from his feet, surging up and out his body. It went into Emike and as it went in her body she suddenly shook and was projected up in the air. Once it left her body she was out of the Lei Tai platform landing flat on her back. She looked shocked struggling to get up and panting with bewilderment. 'And the winner is SUN!!!!' exclaimed James as the crowd roared.

Up next was Felix and Ana; Felix was enchanted by her looks prior, as he peered at her fighting, focusing as much as he could he knew any form of softening towards the siren Ana would be his defeat. Once they greeted each other the fight begun in that instant, Ana was coiling and springing out like a snake. Her blows aimed at vital areas like the eyes. Moving quickly with the fingers of her hand, held together and the thumbs tucked in, looking like the head of a snake. Managing to grab her as she mistakenly stepped forward and was double weighted, Felix tossed her from his back. She broke the fall rolling up and turned to launch her next attack. Felix had enough, he deflected her attack with his one hand as the other one simultaneously struck her abdomen. Stopping her in a sudden as she knelt grimacing and groaning. Felix grabbed her ponytail pulling her to face him, 'You give up!' he barked. Tears trickled down her eyes as she muttered, 'Yes.' The fight was over, she struggled to walk out the platform and was assisted by medics that came in. The crowd had mixed emotions some cheering, some silent, 'Oooh this fella is cold! The winner is Felix! Would not mind that piece of candy!' commented James with his usual theatrics. Felix forced a smile with an uncomfortable look on his face at James' words.

'Kid, rest well tomorrow is the big one!' said Money Sling and continued, 'Ten million Dinares… sweet Daruma that is a lot of money.' 'Yes, we going fifty-fifty don't you forget,' said Felix. 'Yea, yea kid,' chuckled Money Sling, 'can you believe this kid', he added as he looked at one of his henchmen.

Felix had not spoken to Carl, ever since the San-shou he thought of calling his father and then rejected the idea. His mind was on the next fight and Felix knew of the Shi San Shi style. It shared many similarities to the Harmonious Fist. The difference was the Harmonious Fist favoured an offensive strategy and Shi San Shi the opposite, this distinction was only at the beginning levels of both styles.

A boisterous crowd was at sight the final day of the Lei Tai in the Red Crow Arena, with the local faithful filling most of the stadium, the name Sun Guan was heard the most. However, the Sudese from the Sud-Republic managed to get the name Felix heard. Sun Guan looked supremely confident stepping into the platform the same time as Felix. After all, not only was he the local favourite, the name of the stadium was named after his ancestor of whom he was a direct descendant.

No time was wasted and even James was silenced as everybody watched the two gladiators go at each other. Sun struck Felix with his shoulder after Felix deflected his one punch down and he stepped forward seizing the opportunity. Felix hit the ground feeling as if his body was electrocuted, quickly standing up, he threw a jab as Sun approached, Sun dodged it but did not see Felix's sweeping leg. He tried to quickly to maintain his balance however after the sweep, Felix had immediately struck Sun's abdomen with both his palms. Sun stumbled backwards, they both stared at each other and a smirk appeared on Sun's face, 'The Harmonious Fist...ha! Just remember softness defeats hardness', he sniggered as he lifted both hands settling into a fighting posture. 'Yes, and yang is but a manifestation of yin,' replied Felix with a blank expression on his face as he charged forward. He launched a vertical straight punch feeling his energy surge like an electrical current flowing up and out his fist. Sun deflected it with his left as he internally spiralled, externally turning to the left as his waist moved and his right hand did the same coming down Felix's elbow joint. Sun's left hand held Felix's wrist (he struck with his left hand) and Felix was kneeling a little. He relaxed before they could snap his joints and quickly slipped his left foot behind Sun's right foot tripping him backwards as Felix's launched himself up.

Sun rolled backwards and then stood upright, that is when Felix launched at him with a fly kick. Just missing Sun who dodged it. He then gave Felix a front kick pushing him close to the edge of the platform. The crowd was in suspense and Sun's arrogance got the best of him, as he launched another front kick, which Felix caught. His one foot stepped slightly to the side as he turned his body blending in with the momentum of Sun's kick and leading Sun out of the platform. Sun fell outside the platform and Felix had won. He was the champion; his supporters now dominated with their voices, while Felix was then trying to assess the aftermath walking to the centre of the platform, he lifted both hands joyfully looking at the crowd around him. 'Yes!' he yelled, his childhood dream had finally come true. Tears trickled down his cheeks as he thought of his mother and Uncle Fred.

Celebrations and fireworks marked the end of the event, and the city was ignited to party till the sun came up. Felix was back at the hotel and away from the mayhem, he was looking for Money Sling who he had lost spoken to at the hotel lobby. To his surprise, he received a call from Carl, 'Hi Felix, I am very proud of you son.' Felix felt delighted and appreciated those words, he replied with, 'Thanks.' Carl then told him he had to go, they did not talk about anything else. Felix then thought of Uncle Fred for a few minutes as he headed to Money Sling's room.

Knocking on the door, he realised that it was already slightly open. Stepping inside he was astonished to catch the glimpse of blood on the floor. On the one side were Money Sling's henchmen lying dead and on the other side the lifeless body of Money Sling, face down with the eyes open and his tongue out touching the floor. Felix was swarmed with feelings of confusion and as he immediately decided to call for help. He felt an electrical zapping sensation from behind that propelled him forward into a fall as he shook uncontrollably. Suddenly, his eyes closed, and everything just went black.

Felix woke up panting and breathing heavily as he looked around, it took seconds as he thought what he last saw must have been a nightmare. Then he realised where he was currently, his legs were handcuffed and so were his hands, he could not break them, they were prison standard. He knew with experience should they sense any intent from him to free himself it would trigger the sensors of the handcuff, which would then electrocute him to a momentary paralysis. It was a very unpleasant sensation. Glancing further around, he realised he was inside a moving van used to transport prisoners. He did not know what was going on, then he remembered the dead bodies, and getting electrocuted from behind. His mind felt like exploding as he yelled, 'NOOOOO!'

Back in Wobbleton City, Silver was trying to calm down a fuming Carl Sobek, who paced up and down the pool at the mansion. 'Carl if we try anything now they will lure us out, we need to be calm!' Silver's words did not enter the ears of Carl who grunted back, 'You don't have a son, what do you know!' Silver's eyes sparked up for a split second, and Carl whom he gazed at stopped dead on his track. Carl could not move his body, only his head as he looked back stunned, 'Wha...' his words drowned as he choked. Silver walked towards him and said, 'I looked after that boy in prison...your brother knew and respected me, even your boy knows better than to act like a fool in my presence. We will save Felix but today we wait!' After that, he walked away and Carl in disbelief regained his mobility as he gasped for air. 'You bastard!' he snapped as he rubbed his throat. Silver laughed at Carl and said, 'Fred ironically said you and I would get along...on the serious, it is a revolution Carl and our enemies are outside as well as inside the movement. We need to be careful. I promise we will save Felix, as we know they are framing him as an alleged killer...we also need to clear his name.' Carl who was calm by now, fixing his red necktie said, 'Fine I agree, you just lucky my Harmonious Fist is not half as good as my brothers'.' Silver just smiled and said, 'Ah...the Sobeks...your distinct pride is surely a family trait.'

*"Zhan Zhuang is what the Daoists called it, but in the Sol Islands, the standing meditation was an ancient practice allowing one to connect to the earth and the heavens, bringing the two together in the vessel that was the body. A healing exercise that was used by the warriors of the Sol Islands to harmonise the body, thus improving the body's movements while the mind stood still. Daruma had mastered the meditation, and when he was back from his odyssey, his movements and teachings were given the name, "The Harmonious Fist". It was not meant to be a style, but it became one and the people of the Sol Islands went as far as calling it the father of all martial arts. It was not powerful because of its techniques and forms. Its power was in the essence of obtaining harmony; whole-body movement. The fist when striking out did so with the rest of the body like a unit"-Ancient Tales of Daruma, The Wanderer.*

# PART TWO

# THE DUELLIST AND THE EMPEROR

# CHAPTER SIX-FALLEN CHAMPION

He dodged the first punch as he stepped back and his legs mildly trembled, a symptom of his alcohol consumption. The crowd cheered with some spitting profanities; his opponent was an oversized street fighter towering over him and swinging hard with a combination of stomping kicks. This deadly duel took place in an underground parking lot in the late hours of the night in the metropolis that was Feiville.

More combos of death came his way and despite being in a drunk state, he was still able to dodge the attacks. This frustrated his behemoth of an opponent who then managed to snatch him by the neck, lifting him with incredible might. This fighter who was smaller in comparison was Sun Guan and he struggled to free himself, wrestling with both his hands as he tried to remove his opponent's hand off his neck. Some in the crowd thought the fight was over as Sun was thrown on the hard ground and they followed with whistles and applauds.

Sun quickly rose up and unexpectedly in that time, he started to have flashes from the Lei Tai which had occurred three weeks ago. Remembering how he had underestimated Felix Sobek, the current champion of the Lei Tai.

This moment triggered a rage that neutralised the drunkenness and sobering anger erupted within. Sun exhaled as he gained some self-control and then stared at his opponent, gesturing at him to come close. The giant street fighter fell for the bait as he rushed forth. He swung once and then twice but Sun remained evasive and as the opponent tried a third time before he could complete his movement, Sun threw a straight punch that was sudden and powerful. His opponents face was lit in a state of shock as his eyes widened, feeling the impact of the punch, that was delivered to the body.

The opponent fell to his knees with his head down, he grunted in pain as he struggled to stand up. In that time, Sun wondered if he should finish him off. Friends of the opponent emerged from the crowd, to assist their friend. They helped him up and made their way off with him as he struggled to walk. Sun lifted his hand in the air as a sign of a celebration as some in the crowd cheered in delight and the others booed.

Flashes of light illuminated the area as they

suddenly appeared out of nowhere, followed by the sounds of police sirens. A voice from a megaphone deafened the sound of the crowd, 'THIS IS THE POLICE, WE HAVE YOU SURROUNDED...' as the voice kept talking. The crowd morphed into a state of frenzy as everybody ran in different directions giving birth to an atmosphere of mayhem. Sun remained calm, standing in the same spot as he glanced about.

The police emerged with batons, beating and catching who they could in the crowd and sneaking behind the still intoxicated Sun was an officer who struck him hard on the head. Sun found himself immersed in darkness and when his eyelids opened, he was sitting down on a chair, with his hands handcuffed. A mild headache surfaced just between his eyebrows and as he closed his eyes frowning, the pain got worse. Looking around he was in an office; the door was open and walking in was a man with some paperwork. He had his police badge on his chest, and he wore a shirt with rolled-up sleeves, grey pants and maroon shining shoes. His red tie was loose, and the top button of his shirt was unbuttoned.

The police officer was cleanly shaven with short black hair, he was white, and he had hazel eyes, he looked just a few years older than Sun. But the job had taken some of his youth away, although his eyes still showed some keen enthusiasm for the job. He sighed as he sat opposite Sun and they gazed at each other.

'Detective James…Stockhorn.' said Sun. 'Yeah, so we meet again, another street fight bout…wow…' pausing, Detective James opened his drawer and took out an air freshener as he sprayed it around his office, which reeked of booze. 'Look! Just because you come from a rich family! Do not think for one second you will not end in prison! Losing the Lei Tai tournament does not give you the right to get rowdy…' Detective James sprung forth placing both his hands on the table as his head moved slightly forward, and he glared. 'This is the second time you get in trouble! I do not know what it is about you fallen champions or former Lei Tai champions! Felix Sobek is in prison awaiting trial! And now I have you!'

Sun was not fazed by the yelling coming from the detective, he just needed a pill for his headache, lifting his hands he massaged the area between his eyebrows and closed his eyes sighing. 'Are you fucking listening to me!' Detective James slammed his hands on the table causing some documents to fall off, including his wireless mouse.

Sun who was mute at this time just stared back dazed, tired and not bothered. 'Stockhorn!' bellowed a voice from across the door. Detective James was not startled, but Sun shook a bit and caught the glimpse of a tall dark-skinned bald man by the door. The man was in uniform with his badge and stripes showing his superior ranking. He had very dark brown eyes and a hawkish look.

Detective James looked at his superior blankly masking his contempt. 'Let the kid go! His family lawyer called in, the last thing we want is trouble with the Guan family. Besides that, this kid is a national hero! If this was ancient times you will be hanged...no decapitated! Remove those handcuffs! DAMMIT!' Despite having dark skin, the man's face reddened to a visible tinge. Detective James reluctantly made his way towards Sun as he uncuffed him. 'Kid, you safe to go home, your driver is waiting for you,' said the man. Sun struggled to stand up at first and once he was up, he walked out.

Once he was gone, Detective James' superior slammed the door shut, 'Commander Dylan Wilson...' began Detective James but was shut down as Commander Dylan snapped, 'Shut! Your trap! James!' The commander then opened the door and slammed it again on his way out.

# CHAPTER SEVEN- THE GUAN FAMILY

The Guan family was an ancient clan, whose name was marked in history by its great ancestral patriarch, Yu Guan. Known in antiquity as General Red Crow, he was a close disciple of the semi-mythical Emperor Fei Yue and the emperor's best general.

All the knowledge coming from the Water School of Daoism was passed on to Yu Guan by Emperor Fei Yue. He was the only one to know it and was responsible for its survival and this knowledge remained a close secret of the Guan family.

It was him that gave the Water School's fighting art a name, using the Daoist term, "Shi San Shi," meaning thirteen postures.

Over the thousands of years, the clan survived the times.

They had a long history of Lei Tai champions, and every family member was involved in the military. This only changed within the few hundred years till modern times, with some becoming entrepreneurs, journalists or they followed alternative careers. However, the fighting tradition was kept in the family. Given that they were descendants of Yu Guan, who became a king himself carving up most of the Fei Empire during its decline, the family, therefore, was of a noble line. Many of its family members settled in Eastland.

Although they historically aligned themselves with the military, few became politicians. Phoenix Guan, Sun's father was an example, he was the standard-bearer of the Guan family's Shi San Shi fighting method and its Water School knowledge, he focused on being a Lei Tai champion never losing the title until he retired. He was also the clan head, in control of many of the family's businesses. He used a large portion of the family's wealth to fund Gaia Corp, which was a very rewarding investment as Gaia Corp evolved into the biggest corporation in the world.

Daniel Faris the founder of Gaia Corp had become close friends with Phoenix, who even married Daniel's sister Estelle, Sun's mother. The Guan family became intertwined in the affairs of Gaia Corp. When the marriage of Estelle and Phoenix Guan slowly began to decay, they separated. Sun was thirteen years old at the time and then in an inexplicable bizarre act, Phoenix disappeared into obscurity.

His last words to his son were, 'Never forget the

teachings of the Water School and train hard. Honour yourself and honour our ancestor, Yu Guan.' Sun remembers his father looking sad at the time, however the next day the man had disappeared. The Guan family were shocked not by the divorce but by his disappearance. No one heard from him again and nor could he be found. Kelly Kray his twin sister, born Kelly Guan, continued training Sun. She loathed Estelle, blaming her for her brother's disappearance. Replacing her brother, Kelly became the Guan family head, highly suspicious of Daniel Faris and his Gaia Corp.

# CHAPTER EIGHT-
# THE DEVIL IS IN
# THE DETAIL

Standing one shoulder-width apart, with both his hands up in line with his shoulders, was Felix Sobek. Back in prison uniform and in solitary confinement. He had been held for close to three weeks, awaiting trial. The reason he was isolated into a private cell, was because he was considered too dangerous to be with other people awaiting trial as well.

Calmly breathing in and out just below his navel, meditating standing up, he calmed his mind to silence. It was interrupted as the door of his cell opened and there stood one of the guards.

'Time to go see the judge,' said the guard, as Felix's eyes slowly opened with his hands following in sync as they dropped down. It was his second time seeing the judge within those three weeks, that day the judge was going come to a final verdict.

Felix was handcuffed and transported to the court, in a prison van. Once there, he waited below the courtroom, where there was a cell housing all the accused. Felix calmly waited silently sitting on a wooden bench, he felt no hopelessness just pent up anger. He did not know how to prove his innocence to the murder of Money Sling, his manager during the Lei Tai. They did not have any evidence against him, it was his previous record that made the authorities suspect him.

Another accused approached Felix with his gang, 'Alo...nice prison uniform,' he began as he placed his hand on Felix's shoulder. In an instant, the man found himself in a joint lock, with Felix prepared to break his arm. His friends backed away and Felix shoved the man away causing him to fall. The accused got up quickly, stunned as he walked to his friends. 'I will kill you all before you hear the judge's judgement!' barked Felix.

The day before Felix going to trial, Detective James Stockhorn was reviewing Felix's case. It had too many holes, they did not have evidence pointing out that Felix was behind the murder. There were factual accounts that he was found passed out on the floor amongst the murdered victims-Money Sling and his henchmen. This is what led him to review the case causing a heated debate with Commander Dylan Wilson. What concerned him even more, was Commander Dylan Wilson pushing to

close the case as Felix being the suspected murderer.

James then decided to visit Felix, sitting in the
visitation room of the prison. A handcuffed Felix
appeared with an army of prison guards. A frowning
James stood up from his seat and said, 'Remove the
handcuffs, there is no need for that.' The guards first
looked at each other and then they accepted the request removing the handcuffs. Felix's feet were also
handcuffed, making it hard for him to walk. James'
request lit up Felix's face with a mild surprise, as far
as Felix was concerned the detective hated him.

James asked the guards to leave to their astonishment and they yielded to his demands. Felix and
James sat facing each other, with James opening up
the conversation, 'So...I did not come here to see
your ugly face. I just have one question...why would
you kill Money Sling?' 'Yea...Why would I kill him?'
replied Felix as he did his best to calm his nerves.
'I am going to the prosecutor tomorrow, we have
nothing on you in terms of evidence. This case is not
closed, but you not the murderer,' said James and
Felix stared back blankly not knowing if he should
smile.

Wondering if James was simply pulling his leg. 'I
still think you a spoilt rich kid, who did not learn
from his first conviction,' James stood up and then
barked, 'Guards!' once they were in, he left.

'Felix Sobek! Sobek!' Felix's eyes widened as he

heard his name being yelled, it came from a female police officer who had gone down to collect him. He got up and walked to the front of the cell and the officer opened the cell door, then she led Felix up some stairs to the courtroom.

Felix glanced around, the courtroom was brighter in light than the cell underneath it. At the back was the gallery, with a few seated people. He noticed a familiar figure. It was a black man who wore a black suit and a navy blue tie with small polka white dots. The man was his father, Carl Sobek. In front was the judge and below the judges elevated seat was the prosecutor and for the first time since his arrest, Felix noticed a figure that he safely assumed was his lawyer. He glanced back at his father and they nodded at each other. It was a way of Felix saying thanks. He knew his father had brought the lawyer; it was also the first time since Felix's arrest that his father came to see him. Felix felt a sense of relief, also amongst the crowd in the gallery, he noticed the figure of Detective James Stockhorn.

'Right Mr Sobek how are you feeling today?' asked the judge. Felix sighed and replied, 'Good.' Then the judge continued, 'Mr Sobek today is your lucky day...' pausing and clearing his throat the judge put on his glasses and then he quickly read a piece of paper he held in his hand. He then said, 'The state of Eastland, has no evidence against you and the prosecution has withdrawn the case, you should thank

Detective Stockhorn. Right, you are free to go!' The judge's words evoked a soothing feeling of relief and forced a smile on Felix's face, as he could not resist.

Outside the courtroom towering over Felix's lawyer was Carl Sobek. Interrupting their conversation was the presence of Detective James. 'Thanks, Carl,' said the lawyer as they shook hands and concluded their conversation. As the lawyer walked away, Carl turned to James who looked up.

'Mr Stockhorn,' said Carl. 'Mr Sobek,' replied Detective James. 'Thanks, your investigation has freed my son,' once saying that Carl patted Detective James on his shoulder. 'Well the case is still unresolved, and I am not a fan of your son. If he ever causes trouble in Feiville, know that he will deal with me!' said Detective James as his eyes lit with fury. Carl replied with a cocky grin as he stared back and as Detective James walked away Carl muttered, 'Fool.'

'Money Sling...' murmured Detective James as he read some documents from work, that he had brought with him to his apartment. The detective had become obsessed with the case having even travelled to Wobbleton, in the Sud Republic. The police force there shared the information they had on Money Sling, who was known to mingle with unsavoury characters.

The Wobbleton trip did not reveal anything that Detective James did not expect, it was when he travelled back to Eastland that he saw the devil in the detail. There was camera footage of Felix going into Money Sling's hotel room. But there was something wrong with the footage it seemed edited, something Detective James cannot believe he overlooked. The specialist at the police station confirmed it as well, so Detective James interrogated the head of security from the hotel, who then spilt the beans, 'Look…he said he will kill my family!' anxiously said the head of security at the hotel. 'Your family will be alright…describe how this man looks like,' said Detective James.

Better than the physical description of the man, was the original footage, which the head of security had kept by saving it during the editing process. Detective James took every visual note with his eyes as he looked at the man who had committed the murder. The man was white, bald with a flat snake-like nose and a black goatee. He looked like he was in his thirties with narrow eyes that had no crease and were yellow wolf-like eyes.

The footage showed how he had entered Money Sling's hotel room and how he had left minutes after Felix's arrival. His face was not in any of the police databases and the head of security at the hotel did not know his name. Boiling with excitement and knowing he had solved the crime. Detective James tried in vain to track down the killer and although reluctant at first, he still presented the evidence to Commander Dylan Wilson, who scoffed at the footage.

'You heard me, we are closing this case! We simply going to tell the public that it was Money Sling's own involvement with the underworld that led to his death!' barked the commander. 'That is bullshit!' grunted Detective James, his blood boiling at that point as he gazed up at Commander Dylan Wilson. The commander looked shocked, and he responded with, 'You bastard! I am suspending you!' Left with no words, Detective James removed his badge and threw it against Commander Wilson's wall. He removed his gun dropping it on the floor as he marched for the door. Opening it he turned around looking at the commander and exclaimed, 'I QUIT!' then he slammed the door.

James was done with the police and out of a job, he headed to his uncle who was a famous bounty hunter known as Drasul Stockhorn. His uncle had been James' guardian since James was the age of five. James had lost his parents to a plane crash.

Drasul Stockhorn was also a high calibre martial artist, using the rare and nearly extinct Dragon Style. He had passed down his knowledge of the martial art to his nephew who was also a great practitioner of the style. The Stockhorns were descendants of an ancient clan of dragon handlers who dwelled in the mountains of the Dragon's Lair long before the Daoists. Legends say that they were dragons themselves manifested as humans physically.

Drasul's office was downtown and it consisted of one staff, himself. Despite the nature of his work and unlike his nephew, he always had a joyful spirit, expressed with a permanent smile on his face. He was excited his nephew had finally joined him. Detective James Stockhorn had surprisingly failed the tests to become a Union Guard and instead of taking the tests again, he joined Eastland's police force.

'Anyone can become a bounty hunter, but your experience makes you more than qualified,' said Drasul. Sitting in his spacious open office and calmly smoking his pipe as he caressed his grey hair, he gazed at his nephew with his piercing sky blue eyes. Drasul was clean-shaven and was darker in complexion compared to his nephew. 'One thing I like about this gig is I do not have to worry about bureaucracy,' said James as he gazed around the office and then spotted the desk that his uncle had set up for him, he went there and sat down. 'Yes but, there are no rules in the bounty business my boy! We catch our prey dead or alive, depending on the requests. You have the skills, but you will need to cure yourself of the bureaucracy you experienced in the police force. Because whether you like it or not you were infected,' Drasul chuckled as he took a puff from his pipe and continued, 'On another note, I have a case for you. There is a wanted man known as Mr Biggs, a criminal element from the South. Word in the street is that he is in Feiville. The bastard is hiding and still operating, his currently exploiting young girls using them as sex slaves,' pausing Drasul threw a flash drive James' direction, James caught it and Drasul continued speaking, 'The details are on the flash drive, more importantly, it's your first task. There is big money there.' 'Thanks, uncle!' said James excitedly, as he had already put the flash drive on his laptop and was going through the data Drasul had compiled on Mr Biggs.

A minute into going through the info, James thought of the assassin who had killed Money Sling. It was still an unresolved case and he felt guilty when he heard that the head of security from the hotel and his family were found murdered in their home. James saw this on the news and his gut feeling knew the assassin was behind it, but there was nothing he could do now that he was no longer in the police force. He tried to brush the thoughts away, concentrating his mind on catching Mr Biggs.

'Wassup?' enquired Drasul, looking at the frown that conjured itself on the silent James. 'Nothing...' James replied, maintaining the frown as he gazed at his uncle. 'You know off topic, Mr Biggs is involved with a weird secret society it would seem,' began Drasul, 'there is a lot of weird shit going on in Feiville, in fact, the world. Especially with the Separatists...' James immediately jumped in and exclaimed, 'Crazy bunch!' 'I am sympathetic to their cause...terrorist they call them. But the Lei Tai and the union are slowly by surely changing to filth. It's amazing is it not?' Drasul paused upon that question as he looked at James expecting him to know what he was on about, but James replied with a question, 'What is amazing?' 'Well,' began Drasul, 'Felix Sobek is the nephew of one of the leaders of the Separatist movement. Well former leader, since he died. Rest his soul.'

'Look...if I was still in the force, I would investigate you now...I am just saying, uncle. Regardless of cause or not...There are outlaws,' said James. 'Bounty hunters operate outside the law!' snapped Drasul as he then broke into wild laughter.

Mr Biggs was on the list of the most wanted in the world, ranking as number two, below Silver Serpent who ranked number one. Drasul did not directly go after him, even when he found out the man was living in Feiville. He had not even shared the information with the police. The intel was that Mr Biggs shipped in girls from across the world into Feiville, to work as sex workers for high-end clients. These girls were sex slaves, and some were underage, being as young as fourteen years of age. Drasul had found out the girls were brought in by trucks, he just did not know where in Feiville those trucks dropped the girls as this information would indicate where exactly Mr Biggs was in Feiville.

James was going to find out, he fished for information amongst truck drivers who dwelled in the downtown sleazy bars and brothels where they hung out. Taking the little break, they had from their crazy work shifts. His snooping around led him to gather the information that there was a truck delivering weird cargo, some witnesses claimed to have heard people inside the truck. The truck was coming in during the day, avoiding the heavy control from the police that they will get at night. It delivered its cargo to a warehouse and James suspected the warehouse was where he would find Mr Biggs.

James waited in hiding near the suspected warehouse waiting for the truck to come around. He had noticed that the guards guarding the warehouse were too tense and not your usual security. Something important must have been inside the warehouse.

The truck came and was allowed in after all the necessary checks. Muttering, 'Fuck it!' James headed towards the warehouse; he disposed of the guards outside using his Dragon Style. Not killing them, just rendering them unconscious. Marauding around for a brief minute he climbed a ladder leading to the roof. There he found a door which he entered and found himself inside an attic. There was an opening on the floor allowing him to see what was below in the warehouse. James caught a glimpse of the girls, two guards and Mr Biggs.

Remembering his face from the data that Drasul had given him, Mr Biggs was a short chubby old man.

He had a black beard which was greying at the end; his skin was darker in comparison to James' and he wore a black suit and a black bow tie.

Peering down James could see the girls looked frightened as Mr Biggs touched them against their will, feeling them up. The two guards followed suit with predatory smiles on their faces. 'Did you guys pay the driver?!' snarled Mr Biggs as he turned to the guards who looked at each other in confusion, before one of them said, 'His been paid.' Mr Biggs turned back his attention to the girls and said, 'Take these whores away and bring me the girl I asked to be prepped.' Obeying his orders, the guards barked at the girls to move.

James watched patiently, something told him to wait. Although his heart quaked, he used his will power to calm down. Minutes later, the guards brought a girl who they shoved towards Mr Biggs who grabbed her as he smiled. The girl was barely dressed and tried to maintain a brave face.

'So, you the virgin,' he said licking his lips and then continued, 'I promised a friend of mine, that he would taste you first before the big event with the Brotherhood.' Mr Biggs lit with excitement as he spoke and then James wondered who were the Brotherhood? Were they not the secret society his uncle had mentioned? All these thoughts raced in his mind as he closely watched the events before him.

'Medil!' shouted Mr Biggs, and a person came forth, strolling towards Mr Biggs and stopping once he was beside him. Mr Biggs pushed the girl towards him and he grabbed her saying, 'You are going to enjoy me.' 'Just do not kill the bitch...please. Well, I am going to go taste one of the other girls myself,' said Mr Biggs, sniggering as he walked away. James could not see the stranger's face as he wore a hood. He watched the stranger drag the girl away, meeting no resistance. James immediately stood up and made his way out of the attic and back on the roof. From the top he took a few steps and saw Mr Biggs entering a large container with a girl, the container had been converted into a room and not far was another container where the stranger took the girl he was with. 'Ok, time to make a move,' muttered James.

Inside the container and wearing nothing but white shorts was Mr Biggs; standing behind a girl who lay bent over and naked, with her torso and head laying on the bed. 'I am gonna fu...' Mr Biggs words froze in a sudden as the door to the container busted open and there stood James with his gun pointing it at him. Mr Biggs immediately put his hands in the air, as he stared back. James motioned with his head for the girl to leave and she ran away.

'I am here to collect my bounty...Mr Biggs, you are coming with me,' he said as a grin appeared on his face. 'It's amazing how you caught me,' began

Mr Biggs as he composed himself to a calm demeanour, 'I am well connected with people in high places.' 'I am not surprised, that is why you have been able to operate and hide this long,' said James. 'The Brotherhood...will teach you a lesson!' hissed Mr Biggs. 'The Brotherhood?' asked James. 'You a dead man,' said Mr Biggs as he charged for James who opened fire. Shooting Mr Biggs once between his eyebrows straight in the middle. His head rocked back as he fell flat on his back.

Meanwhile, in the other container room, the stranger was thrusting the girl he was given hard, that she uncontrollably moaned while tears trickled down her eyes. This further aroused him, until he heard the gunshot. He suddenly got off the girl, put on his clothes at an incredible speed; dashing for the door. When he turned to look at the container room where Mr Biggs was and saw the eyes of James peering back at him. James recognised those eyes, yellow and wolf-like, the stranger was the assassin. The man who had murdered Money Sling.

James pointed his gun at the stranger who put his hands up in the air and walked towards James smiling. 'Medil! That is your name, right?' asked James. But the stranger only responded with an arrogant grin on his face. 'Oh, you the silent type...maybe I should shoot your leg,' said James, and when he glanced at Medil's leg it was gone. Looking up, he felt a sudden punch that made him stumble back. He touched his nose as he felt warm blood trickling down. 'That was just a warning…next one is going to kill you,' sneered Medil. James chuckled as he put his gun back into its holster and said, 'So you can fight…I see my gun is going to be futile given your skills.' James raised his hands sizing up Medil who in astonishing speed charged for James, striking him with his hands which he shaped up like the head of a snake. His thumb bent and tucked with all fingers held together. James deflected them and gave Medil a front kick, which made him take a few steps back. 'That's…' James tried to catch his breath and then Medil said what James wanted to say, 'Yes that is the Serpent Style.' Then he launched at James coiling in like a snake and then striking out with great speed with his right hand.

James deflected the attack with his right hand as he spiralled to the right; his right foot had first crossed stepped to the left, in front of his left leg. His left foot then came forward from the back during the spiral. At this time, he was positioned at an angle away from Medil's attack. James' left foot ended behind Medil feet and his left hand came forward above his right. Using his left hand and left foot he swooped Medil up in the air, who landed hard on the ground. As he landed James attempted to stomp him. But as he stomped, Medil using his astonishing speed was no longer on the ground.

'That evasive movement…Dragon Style,' said Medil. James smirked and then lit his face back in seriousness as he glared at Medil. 'You killed Money

Sling,' he said. Medil laughed and then ran towards James, picking up an instantaneous speed and then disappeared in a blur. James glanced around in disbelief as he sighed; Medil was gone.

James was awarded quite significantly for the bounty on Mr Biggs, as it did not matter that the man was dead. The money was enough for him to retire but he was not going to rest, two things were on his mind, the Brotherhood and Medil the Assassin.

# CHAPTER NINE-THE BROTHERHOOD

'The Serpent Style,' began Drasul as he took a puff from his pipe, 'From the Slang Nyoka clan, it's rare you can say extinct. Well, the Loham Snake has replaced it. But the Serpent Style is more powerful or better to say the complete package. I am just wondering where this assassin learned or studied this style,' Drasul scratched his chin and then looked at James. But the former Detective had no answer but a swarm of questions buzzing on his mind. 'He did have the yellow eyes of the Slang Nyoka people,' he said. Drasul nodded and then said after taking another puff from his pipe, 'Silver Serpent is the only known grandmaster in that martial art and no one can believe what he's capable of, his escape from Wobbleton's prison was incredible. I saw some videos online,' pausing with a chuckle he continued with a question, 'You said this assassin had some form of superhuman speed?' 'Yes, the man moved to a blur and disappeared,' answered James.

'Our Dragon Style can manage the Serpent Style, whereas they can issue with incredible power, we… well we can be evasive with our circular motion,' said Drasul, as he grinned. 'Regardless, he was toying with me,' replied James.

The assassin and the Brotherhood had become a central theme of discussion at the Stockhorn bounty office. The bounty on the dead Mr Biggs was quite the fortune that James did his private investigation on the Brotherhood, he knew if he could track down members of this secret society than that would lead him to the assassin. His uncle did not object, Drasul just told him to be prudent on the matter.

Frustration sunk in as the investigation was going no-where, days had gone by and there was not a single lead. James then decided to cool off at a high-end luxury bar one evening on the second day of the weekend. Ordering his beer at the bar, something caught his attention, an old man had come in with a group of young beautiful ladies. James slightly grinned at what he saw as he took a sip of his cold beer. 'Old geyser has a lot of money and all the honey…those gals sold their souls to the devil,' said the barman as he wiped a glass. 'The geyser is having a good time and so are those girls,' said James.

'Trust me, those gals have sold themselves to a demon…I just have a bad gut feeling about it all,' persisted the barman. James just smiled not seeing anything wrong. One of the ladies in the group walked to the bar. She was in high spirits, but James knew by the look in her eyes it was the effects of whatever drugs she was on.

She ordered shots as the barman put on a fake smile and got to work, she then turned to James, 'Hey big guy,' she said. 'Hi,' replied James calmly turning his attention towards her. 'The guy over there is a big shot, he knows everyone his taking us to a party where Feiville's big shots go! People like Daniel Faris are going to be there...even some policemen...' she paused as the barman came back with a tray of the shots she had ordered. Triggering his curiosity James asked her, 'Cops will be at that party?' 'Yes, people like Commander Dylan Wilson,' she said. As he heard that, a frown appeared on James' face. 'What's wrong?' asked the girl. 'Nothing,' he immediately replied and then added, 'enjoy the party.' The girl smiled back in response as she carried the tray of shots back to her group who were sitting at a table.

His heart had begun to pound that he could hear its beat in his ears, slowly drinking his beer he waited for the man and his entourage of young pretty girls to leave. As they did, James hurryingly paid his bill and dashed for the door. Once outside, he saw them get into a limousine and he quickly made his way to his car which was not far away.

James followed the limousine, which headed for

another hotel not far away. He waited in his car, as the old man and his harem of ladies got out of the limousine and headed for the entrance of the hotel. 'How can I get in?' James muttered to himself and then he decided to get out the car. He did not know how to get in, but he strolled hands in his pocket towards the entrance regardless. As he did so, something caught his attention as he turned not far away from where he was and saw two young men in their twenties. They looked like they came from affluent homes and they were harassing a homeless man. The man had long black hair and a full black beard that had been greying at its ends. He was slightly darker than James in skin tone with narrow eyes with creaseless eyelids.

James without knowing got slightly closer and became an audience to the altercation before his eyes. 'Leave me alone, please,' pleaded the homeless man. 'Not a chance, here give us your dog!' grunted one of the young men as he seized the small dog of the homeless man. The young man grabbed the small dog's leg causing the dog to cry out. James turned side to side to notice if he was the only one witnessing this abuse. Before he could march through to stop the unfolding events, the homeless man rushed towards the young man who held his small dog. The young man dropped the small dog, which stood up. As the homeless man got close, the young man threw a punch with his right hand, which the old man parried away with his right hand

and stepped forward to the left with his right foot. Moving around the young man, as his left arm came up and down around the young man's neck, who ended up in a lock bent backwards. All of this happened in seconds as James stared in awe. 'Listen here kid, you do not know who the fuck I am! I will snap your neck!' snarled the homeless man, as the other young man's friend ran for his life, leaving his friend behind. The homeless man then released the young man, who looked horror-stricken and followed his friend by sprinting away.

'That's some real martial skills,' the old man turned to see who had said that and caught a glimpse of James. Instead of responding, the man picked up his small dog and gently caressed the dogs head and then he kissed it. 'You a cop?' asked the old man now that he had his attention turned to James. 'Used to be,' James immediately answered, and then a frown appeared in his face as he asked, 'Why you ask?'

The homeless man grinned and then said, 'I saw you following that old man and his entourage.' 'Is it that obvious?' James turned to look at the hotel entrance and back at the homeless man. 'Whoever or whatever you are, I will entrust you with this information...' pausing with a sigh the homeless man continued, 'They are having their meeting as we speak, the Brotherhood, you can get through using the tunnels there,' the homeless man pointed to an alleyway filled with bins. 'How do you...' James' words were immediately interrupted by the homeless man who exclaimed, 'HURRY!' James turned to look at the alley filled with bins and then when he turned to look at the homeless man, he was gone.

James wondered who the man was, he realised he forgot to ask the man his name. Regardless he had work to do. He headed quickly for the alley and was embraced by the strong horrific smells coming from the bins. In front was just a brick-layered wall and James wondered where this tunnel entrance was. His eyes looked down at the ground and he noticed a manhole that seemed to have been tampered with or opened before. He wrestled to remove the manhole cover and put it aside looking down he saw nothing but pitch-black darkness. Digging his hand in his pocket, he felt a small torch, which he used to light up the sewer. The torch revealed a ladder leading down and putting the torch in his mouth he headed down. Once on the ground, it was not wet like he expected. Lighting up the area with his torch, he noticed that there were no rats just him in silence as he felt his adrenaline pump. The room was completely vacant of anything or anybody; ahead was a door and before opening the door James pulled out his gun. Placing the hand that held the torch on top of the one that held the gun.

The next room was also vacant of anything as he peered around, ready to pull the trigger. 'Not a single rat?' he murmured to himself. The room led to a narrow passage, evoking claustrophobic feelings that James ignored with his will as he walked. The passage got steeper as the path went into an incline and seemed endless. As he walked, the path was back to level ground and then the ceiling got smaller to the point that James began to crawl. Chattering voices and noise could begin to be heard, the more he crawled. Stopping, he glanced down at a puny rectangular hole; he could make out what was being said, however peering down he could not see faces.

'The current police commissioner must go!' barked a voice that sounded familiar to James, it was Commander Dylan Wilson. With a loud beating heart, James widened his ears ready to take in everything he was to hear.

'Indeed, it is a shame the very thing that made him a good police officer during his career, is what will get him killed. I am sure you are happy to replace him…right Commander Wilson,' the voice came from a man who James did not know where he had heard the voice before. A door opened and the person who had opened the door said, 'The girls are getting a tad impatient.' The other men in the room laughed as if it was a private joke between them. 'I am sure Medil is going to be doing a good job, anyway enough of that let's get this orgy going,' said Commander Wilson. 'For the brotherhood!' exclaimed the voice James had heard before but could not recall who it was.

Hearing enough, James quickly crawled away

brewing in thought. They were going to use Medil to assassinate the current police commissioner of Eastland, so he can be replaced by Commander Dylan Wilson. James then wondered about the voice of the person that sounded so familiar. It then dawned on him as he bumped his head and grimaced in pain, rubbing his head and astounded he muttered, 'Daniel Faris.'

It was a sunny day, with bits of clouds marauding the skies of Feiville. A crowd of people had gathered around a man, standing in a podium in front of the renovated Central Police Academy. The man was the police commissioner and he smiled gleefully, excited about the events as he spoke to the crowd. In the corner near the edges of the podium was Commander Dylan Wilson, who put up the masquerade of being happy with the events as well.

Blocks away from the event in an abandoned building, watching from his scope, was Medil. He peered at his target, ready to pull the trigger. Exhaling as his index finger was about to fire the shot, he saw the crowd go into a sudden frenzy. The commissioner glanced frantically around, as he pulled out his gun and so did Commander Wilson. Gunshots had been fired and were the cause of the turmoil. 'The fuck,' muttered Medil as he put his rifle aside and replaced it with binoculars. His eyes moved away from the target and he looked around to see if he could spot who had fired those gunshots. 'They hired some other idiot to do the job and he missed…

idiots!' Angrily putting his binoculars away, Medil hurriedly drew out his handgun and started rubbing away his fingerprints on the equipment that was set up for him. Leaving the rifle and binoculars, he headed to the commotion disappearing in a blur. He was going to finish the job from up close.

Blocks closer to where the mayhem was occurring, was James peering down from his binoculars as he slightly panted for breath. His gunshot had come from another building, which he was focusing on now as he saw police rushed in there since that is the direction where the bullets came from. He had aimed at a wall, so he knew the bullet had hit no one. He planned to flash out the assassin, by causing chaos. He knew if it did not work at least the commissioner will be saved for the time being.

He motioned his binoculars back on the ground, to see what was happening with the commissioner and saw the commissioner barking orders at his men. Commander Dylan Wilson did the same, but James knew that was a farce. By sudden luck, he caught a glimpse of a hooded figure moving the opposite direction from the crowd, making his way towards the commissioner. 'There you are, you little bastard!' he exclaimed, and in a rush of adrenaline, he made his way down to the chaos.

James pushed the frantic people away, apologising as his eyes focused on Medil who got closer to his target. Medil pointed his gun which had a silencer and now that he was within range he pulled the trigger. In that instant, he felt someone tackle him from the side as he crashed down gritting his teeth. The tackler was James, who immediately glanced at the commissioner. The commissioner was not fine but not dead, the bullet had grazed his shoulder which he grabbed as he fell to his knees in pain. James turned his attention back on Medil who punched him, causing James to fall. He quickly got back to his feet, but the assassin was gone using his superspeed.

'JAMES!' yelled Commander Wilson and continued as he raged, 'ARREST THAT MAN, ARREST HIM!' the police officers looked bemused. They knew James had just saved the commissioner's life. 'What are you doing? He did not shoot me,' said the commissioner. Realising there was nothing he could do to James; Wilson was speechless.

The news paraded James as a hero, but he refused to speak to the press, in his mind he wondered how he was going to stop the Brotherhood. His uncle was proud of him but reminded him again to be cautious. James agreed however, he still disagreed with his uncle's sympathy towards the Separatist movement. But far away from the office of the bounty hunters, were two hooded men meeting. It was Medil and another man. 'You have failed the Brotherhood,' said the man. 'Failed...nooo!' Medil started to raise his voice, 'I HAVE A PEST PESTERING ME!' 'What do you mean?' asked the man. 'There is a man, a former cop. His name is James

Stockhorn,' answered Medil. 'The Dragon's nephew,' said the man. 'What do you mean,' enquired a frowning Medil. The man just chuckled and then said, 'Tie up that loose end.' 'Tet that is your name right,' said Medil. The man sighed, 'If you only knew who I really was...anyway, kill James.' Both men then parted ways.

James Stockhorn shuddered in horror, one afternoon as he entered the bounty office. Everything had been turned upside down. He looked around for his uncle and Drasul was not in sight, instead, he heard a murmur, 'James.' Frantically turning his head to see where the voice came from he saw his uncle. Who seemed to have been buried underneath his desk and other mess. James moved the desk and the other objects hiding his uncle. There he caught a glimpse of Drasul, who was covered in blood. His eyes got wet as he helped his uncle to a chair. 'James...' Drasul's words were drowned as James hushed him, so he could save what remained of Drasul's energy. But Drasul insisted on using what was left to speak, 'The assassin, the ser...pent style.' Struggling with his words, James concluded, that Drasul was trying to say that Medil was behind this. 'That piece of shit...do not worry, everything is gonna be okay,' said James caressing his uncle's hair. 'I am calling an ambulance, I am taking you to the hospital,' wiping his tears James immediately reached for his cell phone.

He stayed at his uncle's side at the hospital and

the doctor told him that Drasul should have died, enduring the injuries that he did. But his uncle had fallen into a coma, and the doctor was monitoring Drasul. It still looked very bad and a shattered James decided to sit outside the ward in the reception room, his hands covering his face. He had always been strong mentally and had not shed tears since his childhood, but now he was weeping like a little boy. Having lost his parents, he did not want to lose his uncle, the closest family he had.

'Since when do men…excuse me, since when does a man of your calibre weep like a little boy!' grunted a man who had happened to have just sat next to James. James turned and looked at the man as he wiped his tears. The yellow eyes looked familiar, James never forgot a face he had come across in the police criminal data, or if it was a wanted criminal he had seen on the news. The man next to him was Silver Serpent. 'What…' James was confused, what was the most wanted man in the world doing seating next to him, did the Brotherhood send him to finish the job? Silver immediately shed some light as to why he was present, 'I am here to save you and your uncle boy. Now time is against us, I am surprised you have lasted a day here. Buckle yourself up! You are a dragon are you not? Young people of today do not understand the significance of lineage. Anyway, we will need to get Drasul into a life tank if he is to survive.' 'Why are you helping?' James asked. 'Your uncle is one of us and I hope you will join. We are the Separatists,' a small smile appeared on his face once he was done. 'Now come!' he barked, as he suddenly stood up and grabbed James by the arm causing him to stand up as well.

# CHAPTER TEN- BAD BLOO D

Back in Wobbleton, Felix had finally found some peace and being a champion had brought in a lot of attention. However, he kept his feet on the ground and moved in with his aunt Catherina. Felix did a few interviews with the media, because of his fame his Journal account was crowded with friend requests, he had to decline a lot of them. He had started training his young cousin, Charles Sobek who was seven years old. Felix had used his fortune he had made in the Sanshou and Lei Tai to revamp the kwoon.

The authorities left the whole family alone, despite Uncle Fred involvement in the Separatist Movement. Carl Sobek who himself was in the Separatist movement, was still suspicious. He reminded his son that his paranoia is what kept him off the radar of the authorities.

'We should have started training you when you were two,' said Felix, inspecting his little cousin who was in a horse stance. His feet were about two shoulders width apart; knees bent with his tail bone tucked in, squatting at a ninety-degree angle. Charles was shaking and slowly coming up, but Felix would put his hand on his cousin's shoulders pushing him down, back to the required position. He did that and fixed any other posture errors. 'Hey! Endure the pain!' he barked, Charles looked like he was in agony and four minutes of this hell had already passed with tears crawling out of his eyes. Felix wanted Charles to stay in the horse stance for the required minimum time of five minutes, but with ten seconds left his cousin shot up giving up within those lost seconds. 'Dammit! Charlie!' grunted Felix, sighing and shaking his head, he added, 'And wipe those tears.'

The arduous training took place in the kwoon, with a big painting portrait of Uncle Fred on top of the altar, which was at the centre. Positioned on top, he looked at them with his hawkish gaze and thick eyebrows.

Felix glanced at the painting, holding back his emotions and his tears that were about to wash his eyes. Training his cousin hard and the sudden glance at his uncle's portrait evoked dormant pain. Shrugging it off, he sighed and turned to Charles, 'Charlie you are doing well, next time give me five minutes...you were sooo close,' as he ended speaking, he gestured on the clock with his hand, showing how close Charles was to achieving the goal. Charles wiped the remainder of his tears as he obeyed his older cousin with a nod. 'Come here,' Felix spread his arms and his cousin rushed forth for a hug and Felix held him tight, lifting him as Charles giggled.

'You guys having fun I see,' those words came from someone who had entered the kwoon, this person was a brunette whose hair was short. Her eyes where grey and her figure exceeded the fantasy of the average man on female beauty. This person was aunt Catherina. 'It is hell out here, wanna train?' Felix had put Charles down and his aunt responded to the question with a frown before answering, 'No thank you,' as she crossed her arms. Felix laughed lightly, 'Anyway we done aunty,' he said. 'Great, you guys can have some light snack just to let you know everything is ready for your uncle's funeral,' said Catherina, and for a few seconds, there was silence as each one took in another dose of the reality that Frederick Sobek had passed away. 'Anyway, see you guys in the house,' said Aunt Catherina as she broke the silence and strolled out the kwoon.

Frederick Sobek's body was cremated and the ashes were stored in a crimson urn with Daoist symbols and images of Daruma the founder of the Harmonious Fist. A Daoist priest blessed the urn before casting the ashes into the ocean. It was a small gathering of Carl Sobek, Felix, Aunt Catherina, Charles, Eddy and a few family friends. From afar watching the events was Silver Serpent, secretly invited by Carl.

There were two special guests also invited to the funeral, family from the Sobeks ancestral home, the Sol Islands. The two guests were, Kek Subek and the other was Kazak Subek. Kek was the father and Kazak the son, Kek was the brother of Carl and Frederick's grandfather. Therefore, he was Felix and Eddy's great grand uncle and Kazak was the grand uncle. They looked like they were in their fifties, but they were far older than that.

Kek had a thick long white beard, hazel eyes with creaseless eyelids, with the trademark thick eyebrows of the Sobek's and the one very visible feature he shared with the likes of someone like Frederick Sobek. However, they were not black, but light-skinned in comparison like milk with a hint of black coffee. Both men were bald and looked almost like identical twins except Kazak was completely bald, and very tall. Kek was short and sturdy. They both still carried muscles of athletic young men, it was their faces that showed the evidence that they were old men.

The original family surname was, Subek. Xavier Subek, Felix's great-grandfather and Kek's brother changed the name to Sobek upon arriving in the Sud Republic. The reason for the name change was to distinguish it from "Subek".

Xavier Subek was a rebel in the family and did not get along with his father, who had arranged for him to marry a young girl from another clan. But the stubborn Xavier who was older than Kek resisted. It ended in him fighting his father in a duel, which he lost, and he was banished; changing the family name was his act of defiance. Regardless, his father and Kek still kept contact later in the years, especially when Felix Senior, Frederick and Carl's father was born. He was Kazak's cousin and Felix's grandfather.

Kek and Kazak were different in skin tone and other features, compared to the family in the Sud Republic, due to Xavier Subek marrying a darker woman in the Sud Republic and his son followed suit.

The Sol Islands was the original home of the Harmonious fist and the home of its founder, the legendary semi-mythical figure, Daruma. Originally a warrior, he travelled the world and returned a holy man to the Sol Islands. There he shared his fighting art and philosophy to his wife's brother, his brother law Sung Subek. That is how the family came to inherit the art, fighting system and way of life.

Felix had not spoken to Eddy since they last fought, however, they had greeted each other with nods before the funeral and then kept their distances. Carl kept his poker face despite his suspicions of his nephew. He knew Eddy was behind the exposure of his brother, but what he did not know was he was also the murderer. After the funeral, there was a small gathering at Carl Sobek's house for tea, and the funeral was the first time Felix or Eddy had met their great and grand-uncle.

Kek Subek was quiet, not uttering a single word, it was his son that did all the talking. 'Lovely home you have Carl, lovely home,' said Kazak as he glanced around. Everybody was gathered at the pool dining table, enjoying some green tea which was being served by an old stocky lady, this was Mrs Wilkins. 'Thank you, uncle,' replied Carl. 'I have so many questions to ask you, I do not even know where to begin,' said an excited Felix, beaming at both his great and grand uncle with eyes of admiration. Both Kek and Kazak glanced at each other and laughed. 'Well, I am happy to finally meet the two of you. I am sure there is a lot you can teach me. Or take over where my father left off,' said Eddy. 'Yes, we have been talking about that father and I. Eddy you are very talented, your father always used to say, bless his soul,' said Grand-Uncle Kazak. Eddy smiled nervously and responded with a rapid, 'Thank you.' Then Grand Uncle Kazak continued as he turned to Felix, 'First I would like to congratulate you on becoming the new Lei Tai champion, my father thinks otherwise. For him, the Lei Tai is below a Subek.' He beamed at Felix and then glanced at Great Grand-Uncle Kek who grunted in disapproval. Grand Uncle Kazak laughed at this and then added, 'He is still proud of you, of course, we would like to invite you to stay and train with us at the Sol Islands. Your uncle, my nephew recommended it.' Felix was boiling with excitement internally hearing the invitation but gaining some form of composure he beamed and said, 'thank you.' 'Someone will have to train Charlie though,' said Felix remembering his little cousin's training. 'I got it!' Carl quickly said. Felix nodded at his father who he knew had begun training seriously again in the Harmonious Fist, sparring with the housekeeper Mrs Wilkins.

Quietly listening to all of this and simmering in disapproval was Eddy, a sour look had painted itself on his face, and he broke his silence by making a scoffing sound and then he said, 'Again my late father has disappointed me by recommending Felix to go to the Sol Islands to train, I feel that I am a better candidate...' 'Edward!' interrupted Aunt Catherina, but Eddy ignored her and continued, 'We are martial artists, I think I should challenge him here right now! After all, Sobek or Subek, it was in the Sol Islands that the concept of the Lei Tai was conceived and exported to the world by Daruma... Did YOU EVEN KNOW THAT!' lashing out at Felix as he glared at him with disgust. Great Grand Uncle Kek was now amused as he smiled at the unfolding events. Felix could feel his blood rush as he masqueraded an air of calmness. 'Fine...let's do this,' he said springing up. Aunt Catherina just stared back in disagreement, she, however, knew this was the Sobek way, solving their differences with a duel; fighting was in their veins and with Eddy now part of his mentality.

Both Felix and Eddy walked away from the dining table as everybody peered at them, and it was Eddy who launched the first attack throwing a fury of punches. Missing his target as Felix evaded them, Eddy then threw a roundhouse kick to Felix's face that made him fall as he tried to evade it. Eddy then charged aggressively to end things, but Felix rolled back up to his feet. His cousin threw another savage combination, each punch expressing his hate. Felix deflected them and in a sudden Eddy felt a shocking sensation as he uncontrollably bounced up and down, landing a few meters away from Felix. He had struck Eddy with his palm, striking him on his chest. Eddy struggled to stand up, still feeling the effects and now panting heavily with his eyes wide open he threw a fit growling angrily. 'You have lost,' said Great Grand Uncle Kek. 'Screw all of you! I am leaving!' yelled Eddy as he marched away. Aunt Catherina shook her head, as tears trickled down.

Felix looked unfazed by the events, but inside he felt a feeling of satisfaction, having defeated his cousin who had beaten him up months earlier before the Lei Tai. Great Grand Uncle Kek turned to Carl and said, 'I know what you know, but that boy is still family since he is part of the lineage. He has a tormented soul.' 'Yes Shirgung,' Carl replied nodding. Shirgung meant grandmaster, both Kek and Kazak where grandmasters to each Sobek or Subek relative that was born after them.

The Subeks had left a few days later and Felix was excited that he was going to join them. The Sol Islands was composed of sparsely populated islands, with one large island serving as the mainland, where the capital city was situated. It was known as Sol City; the islands had a population of about a million people. The islands were autonomous and did not belong to any of the other eight world nations. Throughout antiquity the island had always been independent, but when the Union of Nations was formed. The leaders of the islands and the unionist came to a deal. The island kept it militia (since it did not have a professional army, navy or air force) and that no union troops will be allowed in the islands. No Solese ever competed in the Lei Tai, those who did were the ones who had immigrated to the Sud Republic. The islands were situated in the Dragon Ocean, East of the Sud-Republic. In the times of the Sud Empire and prior, the Solese traded with the Southern States. The Solese were historically pirates or fishermen, that were fierce warriors who mostly fought each other or acted as mercenary forces in ancient times. They were the ones who aided the Southern States in ancient times when they fought the Fei Empire.

Somewhere in an undisclosed area in the East-South Union city of Easex, was Silver Serpent and James Stockhorn. They were in a room, accompanied by a doctor and his assistant who monitored Drasul Stockhorn, as he was immersed in a yellowish-brown liquid. Floating naked, inside the life tank; his mouth was covered by a tube, supplying him with oxygen. His eyes were closed as he slept in a deep coma.

'So, you say a man of the Slang Nyoka clan did this?' asked Silver Serpent. 'Yes, he seemed proficient in using the Serpent Style as well. It was not Loham Snake with its wider horse stance...Hell the bastard also had this weird super speed,' replied James. 'I doubt it was this assassin you call Medil that did this...I have fought five hundred duels, not losing a single of those battles, which is the reason for my infamous status. Regardless, there a few men that can be my equals or are even beyond me. They are some old lineage holders of the Harmonious Fist in the Sol Islands and there is this man! Right here in front of me the Dragon!' Done speaking Silver took a few steps forward watching Drasul and then he added, 'Superhuman...or moving like a blur is nothing! I am wondering if your uncle has ever beaten you to a pulp, so you can understand his ability. James chuckled and then asked as his face transformed to seriousness, 'Who then do you think did this?' 'Someone very powerful, an expert in Shi San Shi perhaps,' replied Silver holding his chin. 'A member of the Guan family? I doubt that' responded James. 'Well, you the detective...figure it out. But rule this Medil character out,' those were Silver's last words as he walked away. Looking at his uncle heal, James muttered the words, 'Heal up uncle…I will avenge you.'

The training in the Sol Islands was not a breeze, Felix had flown in and landed in hell. As soon as he had arrived so did his training. The horse stance in the islands for those who thought they had mastered it, was modified to make it more challenging. Heavy rings were added on each arm as they were stretched out forward, hands forming horizontal fists. He also had to hold different other postures and stay like that for hours. 'You must be able to hold your stance, relax into it and have no problem. The horse stance then becomes really meditative, do it till it has become second nature,' Grand Uncle Kazak would repeat, Felix hated those words and felt nothing but pain. An hour was fine, but to hold the positions for beyond four hours seemed mad. Great Grand Uncle Kek, held his horse stance for the whole day with no water and food, only eating the next day. Felix was amazed, and his teachers did not yet reveal their capabilities.

As Felix had expected the islands had a kind of rural feel, the had all the modern luxuries, but most of the old ways were kept. There was no kwoon, and Felix was trained in the open, sometimes they would hike up the mountains or train in the jungle.

The islands were surrounded by an armada of the Union Guard Navy, they mandate they said was to keep the peace and protect the Solese. Nevertheless, the inhabitants were very suspicious as they argued they could fend for themselves.

One evening after a gruelling training session, Felix rested by having a hot cup of tea, enjoying the cooler weather that the evening brought. Grand Uncle Kazak approached him and said, 'Grand nephew, there is something I need to tell you.' 'What?' Felix immediately asked. 'A war is about to begin; do you think we going to let those ships surround our islands like that and do nothing!' Grand Uncle Kazak's voice slowly was raised and then calmly dropped again as he continued, 'The Sol Islands is the heart of the Separatist movement, the Council of Masters does not just govern this small nation, we also govern the movement. I ask you to join us, not as another fighter to our cause. I ask you, Felix...to join us as it is your duty and, in your blood, to serve the cause.' Felix was overwhelmed and intimidated; having won the Lei Tai, his one main aim now was to defend it, but that was not the same. If war was brewing, then would they still be a Lei Tai? By the slip of his tongue, he said, 'Yes,' and then wondered if he would regret it. Grand Uncle Kazak beamed at Felix and said, 'Whatever you are feeling now is fear, the what ifs, well...fuck it. There is a great potential in you my boy...great potential. Dark times are coming, but dark times make brave men.'

# CHAPTER ELEVEN-GHOST OF THE PAST

A woman with silver streaks of hair was chopping away onions as she spoke to her husband who sat meters away reading the news on his tablet. She was light of complexion with creaseless eyelids and gazed at her husband with her green eyes. This woman had a permanent natural fierce facial expression, which gazed at her more tranquil husband.

She was Kelly Kray; mature with no heavy signs of ageing. Still carrying an air full of energy just as she did when she was young. Her martial adventures of the past had left her with a tiny scar on her upper lip.

Her husband Wren Kray was tall and very dark of complexion, like the darkest of chocolates. Carrying more muscles than those who were twice younger than him. He was a former union soldier and had never been taught the Guan Family's Shi San

Shi, he was an expert in the Tiger Style, and he came from the Sud-Republic.

The Krays owned a high-end restaurant in Feiville, which they both ran and on that day in the morning, they were closed.

'So, I punched the life out of him!' exclaimed Kelly Kray, not looking at the onions she chopped. Wren kept cool, calm and quiet. 'It is unacceptable, for him to go out get drunk and get into pathetic street fights,' continued Kelly, 'he is the next leader of the family! I cannot have him fall apart. He reminds me of my brother so much... curse that bastard!'

Kelly Kray was complaining about Sun, who she had recently straightened out by beating him up after she had challenged him to a fight. Having been lenient with her nephew, she felt it was the last straw. 'That is why they call you "Crazy Kelly". I agree with you though,' said Wren Kray as he sniggered. 'Look, the boy has finally listened and his even resumed with training our boys,' he added. Kelly sighed putting her knife down as the chopping stopped. 'Well, speak of the devil,' she said catching a glimpse of Sun, who had just walked in with his two cousins whom he was training in the park.

'Hi,' replied Sun, greeting his uncle and aunt. By his side were his young cousins Su and Wren Junior. The boys were identical twins and thirteen years of age, with Su being five minutes older than Wren Junior. Their Shi San Shi training had begun from the moment they could walk, and they were both very proficient given who was their current teacher. Besides training them, Sun had resumed training for the next Lei Tai, focusing on regaining his title.

Sharing the same features, the twins were darker in skin tone compared to their mother and lighter than their father. They had long curly hair and light hazel eyes.

Sun's parents never officially divorced and were just separated when he was thirteen; they still lived together as some form of family. Nevertheless, it was when Phoenix Guan (Sun's father) disappeared that Kelly his twin sister, marched and stormed into Estelle Guan's home (her sister in law and Sun's mother) and demanded Sun live with her. It was Wren who had come to the rescue, dousing his wife's raging anger. Eventually, they agreed Sun was to live with his aunt and uncle, and he would occasionally visit his mother, who he did not share a bond with, he was closer to his uncle, aunt and father.

Estelle Guan was not a martial artist, she was instead a well-known socialite from the United-West where her family was originally from. Kelly believed that Estelle only married her brother because of his wealth, and despite Phoenix and Estelle having a child together, Kelly still mistrusted her sister in law. She did not like the whole Faris family.

'How did the training go?' asked Wren, standing

up from where he sat. 'Great!' replied the twins as they walked away, leaving Sun alone with their parents. 'Mister!' barked Kelly and Sun turned his attention to her. 'So...' begin Kelly pausing as she put the knife aside which she was still holding and strolled towards Sun, 'Your uncle, Daniel Faris wants to see you.' 'About?' Sun frowned in response as he glanced at Wren and back at Kelly. 'Don't know,' she answered turning away. 'He actually told me, and I told her,' said Wren with a grin on his face. 'Ok is it today?' asked Sun. 'Yes, his at their main office here in Feiville...anyway, I am happy you are cleaning yourself up, remember no more street fighting while drunk. I will let you rot in jail,' said Kelly. Sun simply sighed and then grinned as he looked at his uncle who grinned back.

Noon had just set in and Sun had a quick shower before heading to Gaia Corp's main office in Feiville. He wondered what would be the reason for his uncle wanting to see him? Sun remembered the number of times his uncle had proposed for him to work in the company. Despite the tension between his father's side of the family and his mother's family, Sun got along with his uncle. Politely saying no to many of Daniel Faris' offers.

Gaia Corp's main office, like most of its offices around the world, was at the forefront of technology. Its campus was enormous, and Sun was received at the main entrance by a man whose limbs were mostly replaced by machines. Sun frowned upon meeting him, understanding the frown he introduced himself by saying, 'I am a cyborg.' Sun simply nodded in amazement, he followed the cyborg who took him on a small trip to one of the board rooms of the office, where inside awaited Daniel Faris.

'Thank you, you can get to your duty,' Daniel told the cyborg once he left. 'Sun!' he exclaimed excitedly as he stood up, turning his attention to his nephew. Sun simply had a small smile on his face as he returned the gaze. Daniel Faris was a very tall man, dressed in a black suit with a canary silk tie, which had black polka dots. He was olive-skinned, with brown eyes and a shark-like sharp nose. Approaching Sun, he shook his hand, towering over him.

'Hi uncle,' began Sun, 'So what's up?' he asked. 'I am having a...' interrupted by the opening of the door they both glanced and caught the glimpse of a woman. She had a mixture of concern and a kind of wry smile as a facial expression. She had long dark brown hair, straight with curls at its end resting calmly pass her shoulders and stopping mid of her back. She had light hazel eyes and despite her age, her beauty had been preserved. She had an olive skin to accompany her delightful features; this woman was Sun's mother and Daniel Faris' sister, Estelle Faris.

'Sun!' she exclaimed rushing towards him as she

hugged him, and he hugged her back. She attempted to kiss her son on the cheek, but he pulled away, 'That's enough mother,' he said, sounding a little annoyed. 'Come on! I have not seen you since that Lei Tai competition...You really do not care about me! Who paid for your lawyer or bail money! Not your sweet aunt Kelly...me...you, ingrate,' her voice was filled with sadness as tears began to pour down her reddened face. 'Guys...guys...there is no time for this,' said Daniel, as he had salvaged a tissue which he gave his sister, taking a deep breath, he then continued, 'Like I was saying, wanted to see you, to invite you over at a party, I am having at one of my mansions here in Feiville, it sort of like a work function. Look I know you do not want to join the family business, even though I am sure Phoenix, your father who was my closest friend, would have wished or been happy you joined. Just come through it will be fun...look at your mother...she is hurting at least do it for her.'

'Fine!' Sun said reluctantly as he looked at his mother fighting off the bit of guilt he began to feel. 'Great! I will text you the details, during the day,' said Daniel lighting up with a smile. Sun nodded his head and turned heading for the door, ignoring his mother whose red puffy eyes he could feel were looking at him.

He had mixed feelings about the whole thing as he headed out of the campus, at least he will meet new people and even beautiful girls. He smirked at the thought shaking his head; when he was outside the campus something caught his attention. Gazing at the source he saw a homeless bearded man dressed in a worn-out trench coat staring at him. But the moment Sun gazed at him he turned away, walking away with his companion, a small white dog. Sun frowned and then he headed home.

The party at the mansion was filled with executives and managers from across the world, all who worked for Gaia Corp. Arriving there, Sun wished his name was not on the list as the doorman searched for his name on the tablet. His name was there, and he was allowed in. Everybody was well-dressed bow ties, ties, white shirts and the whole works from the men, with the ladies dazzling in different stunning dresses. Nevertheless, Sun Guan simply wore a black leather jacket and he was tie-less, with the top two buttons of his white shirt unbuttoned.

Staring at the alcohol that was being served, he could remember the warning his aunt had given him, "You better not get drunk…or else…especially if you cause chaos!" Smirking Sun then chuckled as he helped himself. His hand swooped in as one of the servants was walking by, 'What is it?' he asked, smelling the drink. 'Martini!' the servant quickly replied, as she walked away. 'Just one…' Sun murmured to himself, as he took a sip and strolled about looking at the people.

He could feel some stares as people recognised

who he was, the former Lei Tai champion. Some ladies approached him, with one pulling out her cell phone for a picture. Sun did not decline, as he pulled his best smile. When the ladies left another one approached him, as she waited for her turn catching Sun by surprise. This lady seemed to be around his age, she had alluring emerald green eyes and she was a brunette. She wore a short canary dress and drowning in her beauty Sun stayed mute as he stared at her frozen. 'I am Arrieta Long,' she said drawing out her hand for a handshake. Sun snatched it quickly, his hand relaxed, but Arrieta Long was caught off guard by the speed. Sun then gently kissed her hand as he said, 'Nice to meet you, I am Sun Guan.'

Arrieta seemed smitten and nervous as she tried to mask her timidity with a smile. Sun was confident she was going to be his. 'Hi! I am Eddy Sobek,' said another voice and Sun saw that it came from a man with piercing blue eyes and short blonde hair. He was formally dressed and now at Arrieta Long's side staring and smiling at Sun while marking his territory. Eddy drew out his hand, but Sun instead responded with the yin yang gesture in a martial manner. The right hand in a fist, with the left-hand open on top with its fingers pointed out and the thumb tucked in. Eddy seeing this immediately replied the gesture. 'A Sobek, first one I met defeated me at the Lei Tai,' said Sun. Eddy laughed smiling and replied, 'Yes my cousin Felix, that was quite a fight you guys had.' 'Hope his well, is he the best in your family?' asked Sun. 'Not by a long shot, his good...but not good enough,' said Eddy as he winked, 'Anyway was nice to meet you. Oh yes, and she is my woman, I see you met,' he added. 'Beautiful woman,' replied Sun. They left him as they strolled away. Sun chuckled to himself as he took another sip from his drink.

Inside his office staring at the mirror as he fixed his tie was Daniel Faris, he turned to a young lady who had just fixed herself and said, 'See you outside.' She in response walked towards him, kissing him on the cheek, before she left shutting the door behind her. Daniel took a deep breath and gleefully lit up a pipe and took a puff. 'That girl nearly broke me,' he muttered and then followed with slight laughter.

'Saw the whole thing, she made me hard...did not want to interrupt,' said someone. Shaken and a tinge red on the face was Daniel, who was about to sit and enjoy his pipe. He moved his head wildly, looking around and by the window behind the curtain he saw the person who had spoken. It was a man and he made himself more visible as he moved away from the curtain and took a few steps forward. He had long black hair and a full black beard, which was getting grey at its ends. The man wore a worn-out trench coat and glared at the shocked Daniel Faris, who gazed at him in disbelief. '...Pho... Phoenix.' stuttered Daniel. 'Yes,' hissed the man, 'I am back old friend like a ghost from the past,' he added as he looked around. 'How has your plotting been a failure these days...hey, the police commissioner is still alive...yes you piece of shit! I was not responsible. I simply hinted to a young man where a secret abandoned tunnel was...hmmm the Dragon's nephew. I see you invited my son to your filth of a party.' The man walked back and forth in a stroll as he spoke, and Daniel Faris mustering the bit of courage he had, quickly looked down at his table where he stood, remembering there was a loaded gun there. He rushed for it and pointed it at Phoenix, struggling to keep his hand steady as it shook. Phoenix sniggered in response and then with a sudden blank expression on his face, Daniel began to grab his throat as he struggled to breathe. Something was choking him, he dropped his gun and held his throat with both hands and then before he was about to pass out. He felt himself getting pushed into the chair as he sat. The choking had stopped, and he was gasping for air.

'I am far stronger than I was before, very strong... strong enough to put up a resistance against your master,' said Phoenix as he took a few steps towards Daniel. Regaining some breath and still panting with a reddened face, Daniel responded, 'No you cannot! You always thought you had it figured out. I am the one who negotiated for your life to be spared. So, he fucked your wife, my sister...' silenced again, he felt himself choking with Phoenix this time gesturing the action with his hand. Daniel was lifted off the chair and was floating slightly above it and Phoenix said, 'You made it look like she cheated on me! But that is not what happened, is it? Now tell me how he is stronger…' his voice fell to a sudden silence as the doorknob moved. Once the door flung open, Daniel fell on his chair as Phoenix and his invisible grip to Daniel's throat both disappeared. Struggling to breathe and slightly coughing with a bit of sweat, he stared at the frowning face of Sun.

'You okay uncle?' asked Sun. 'I am absolutely… okay,' lied Daniel, as he slowly got up masking his trauma with a smile. 'Look thanks a lot for the invite, but I am going to bounce,' said Sun. His uncle simply nodded as his thoughts raced and then Sun closed the door.

# CHAPTER TWELVE-ENEMIES AND ENEMIES WITHIN

Drasul Stockhorn had spent a week inside the life tank, and once he was taken out of the tank, he spent a day still in a deep slumber. When he was awake, he thanked Silver and James but did not mention who had attacked him. Silver did not ask the question, but James did and got no answer. The only thing he got was that it was not the assassin and now that his health was back, the Dragon began to train hard.

One day, James had left and Drasul was training, practising the Dragon Style's famous circle walking. His left hand was out in front, with his index finger in line with his nose. His left palm was facing forward at an angle. His right hand was tucked slightly below the navel and the right palm was facing down. He would plant his foot with the bottom of the toe area touching first and then followed by the heel. Rooting himself, he would spiral back the other away; hands changing when he walked the circle from the other direction. Looking graceful and swift. Silver who was watching clapped once Drasul was done walking the circle. 'Amazing,' he said. 'Always the fundamentals, it's all in the basics,' replied Drasul. 'Indeed,' agreed Silver, 'What happened though, if it was not the assassin who harmed you, who was it?' he asked. It was the first time Silver had asked the question and with his arms crossed, he frowned wondering how his old friend could have been defeated.

'People think it is a rumour or myth that you can breathe, a dragon's breath of fire or even turn into one. But we both know, that is no myth!' continued Silver. 'He struck me before I could display my clan's true power,' said Drasul, his eyes gazing away as his mind recollected the events, 'this man called himself Tet,' he added this time looking at Silver with a frown on his face. 'Tet, how did he look like?' asked Silver. Drasul sighed, and then said, 'He was an old man that was bald, pale and very thin... scrawny kind. His eyes were greyish, and he was definitely very powerful. His fighting style seemed like Shi San Shi...' 'You could recall the style when he was whoopin' your ass,' remarked Silver, and Drasul chuckled before continuing, 'Yes, in fact, the bastard bragged about not being at full power yet, and that he will soon be. He said he was the leader of the Brotherhood. You heard of them, right?' 'Yes, James has mentioned them a few times,' answered Silver. 'Well we not just fighting Gaia Corp and the Union, the Brotherhood is the one that is behind everything,' said Drasul, and Silver nodded before responding, 'So why have you not told James all of this?' 'That kid is a hound, he would have done something stupid and try to seek out this Tet and he would have definitely got killed. That Tet thought I was dead when he left, but where I failed in my martial skills, my dragon heart saved me,' answered Drasul. 'Yes, and the life tank, we might hate Gaia Corp, but Daniel Faris…son of a bitch has got a hell of a machine,' said Silver.

Silver took the Stockhorns, to a Separatist safe house, in a small town in the outskirts of Feiville. Although the Stockhorns were not on the wanted list, they kept a low profile. Silver was originally visiting his old friend and member of the Separatist movement. When he got word of what happened to Drasul, he thought the Union Guards had discovered that Drasul was a Separatist member. He was glad to find out that this was not the case. Nevertheless, with the Brotherhood, the Stockhorns believed that they were going to be hunted down and Silver also believed that this was likely.

They, therefore, decided to head to the ancient city of Sud, in the Sud Republic. A black minivan was parked outside the safe house. The engine was running, and Silver had opened the door for the

Stockhorns to get in, and at that moment. Silver sharply turned around and so did Drasul, meanwhile James did not know what just happened and was still getting in the van. But right behind him stood a bullet, which had stopped and was floating in mid-air. 'What is going…' James words froze as he turned and was shocked to see the bullet. He then looked ahead. Cloaked by his black hood stood Medil, standing from quite a distance, pointing a handgun equipped with a silencer.

Silver snatched the bullet that floated behind James and threw it away angrily. Fuming, as his eyes focused on Medil. 'Who stopped that bullet?' asked James still amazed. 'He did,' answered Drasul pointing at Silver who barked, 'Guys go now!' The Stockhorns then hurriedly got inside the minivan, slamming the door shut and then the minivan's wheels span as they sped away.

Using his super-speed Medil got closer, about a meter away from Silver, appearing in a sudden blur. 'So, you must be the famous Silver Serpent,' begin Medil hissing in tone and looking at Silver in disgust, 'You betrayed your people when they fought each other, so you could travel the world and fight fellow martial artists, in pathetic brawls or duels!' Silver chuckled and stopped with a smirk, looking at Medil up and down. 'I heard rumours that the clan had stopped its war amongst itself and kept to the shadows, being hired to carry the tradition of assassinations. See kid, I am not an assassin to be exact, I am a martial artist,' said Silver. 'You were our most powerful warrior, yet you did nothing to lead us, as we tore each other apart!' yelled Medil, and then he looked at his gun which he still had, 'this will be useless against you!' he grunted putting the gun away. 'So, what now, you guys are the hired hand of the Brotherhood?' asked Silver. 'Their one of our clients yes, are current Grand Priestess would love it, if I brought your head on a platter. It is fine if I missed killing my target. You will do!'

Once his words were said, Medil charged for Silver disappearing in a blur and reappearing closer to Silver, but he stopped in a sudden. Looking down he saw Silver's fist striking his stomach. He groaned in pain, as Silver stepped a few steps back and the hurt Medil then fell to his knees holding his abdominal area.

'Your speed or trick whatever that thing is is no match for what I can do. There is a war brewing, and do you think your enemy will spare the Slang Nyoka when he is done with the Separatists?' Silver knelt a bit down looking furiously at Medil, who was still in too much pain to let out a few words. 'You will take me to where the clan currently is, I have a proposal your Grand Priestess will not refuse,' said Silver.

Silver Serpent had left the Slang Nyoka when the clan fought each other, due to a leadership dispute. Many died, and Silver who was to be their next leader did not want to get involved. He did not like being an assassin despite all five hundred of his duels ending with his adversaries' death. Silver did not see himself as an assassin. Something the Slang Nyoka clan were renowned for, as in ancient times they were used in wars to end them. By killing the opponents of their clients, infamous for their stealth and craftiness.

Carl Sobek had taken Silver Serpent's place, in meeting a faction of the Separatist movement, who disagreed with the way things were being handled in the movement. They wanted more actions to be taken, they were the ones also responsible for the terror attack in a mall in Wobbleton, Sud Republic. An attack, which did not shed a good light on the Separatist group. It was not known to the group that they will be meeting with Carl Sobek instead.

The leader of this faction was led by the young twenty-five-year-old Rochelle Sud, a member of the illustrious Sud family, who once ruled the Southern lands in ancient times when it was known as the Sud Empire. Fierce, proud and like most of her family members, she was proficient in the martial arts of the Loham Temple. As well as the family's Sud Fist, which was a different version of Shi San Shi. It came from the Fire School of Daoism, which was passed down by Emperor Dos Sud a family ancestor.

Rochelle Sud caught the eyes of most men, but behind all of that was a fierce nature. Her soft-looking black skin and lovely hazel eyes were but deception and the man who had somehow won her heart was her lieutenant Jeffrey Mins, a bald tall young man about her age. He was white, with a visible scar across his nose and what was notable about his physical features, was his muscular physique.

The couple and a few of their followers waited in an abandoned storage facility, expecting Silver Serpent who they had never met. They also did not know Carl Sobek either, so when he arrived alone they did not question his identity. He did not introduce himself either and was not happy to have come in Silver's place. In his moodiness, he sneered at Rochelle, 'So young lady and crew, let's wrap this up. You lot, are ruining what we are fighting for,' snorting with laughter as he looked around, 'really, what are you guys thinking?' he added. But Rochelle was not going to tolerate his rudeness as they glared back at him, 'You right let's wrap this up,' she said snapping her fingers and then Jeffrey who stood beside her nodded at a man who appeared behind Carl. 'This was the plan Silver, now the main leaders where ever they are...will listen to us,' said Jeffrey, and Carl frowned realising that they were not aware that he was not Silver. He had also not paid attention to the man behind him and as he spoke, 'Wait I am...' a shocking electric sensation zapped him to silence as he was shocked into a coma.

'Stop!' barked Rochelle and the man immediately stopped, she then turned to Jeffrey, 'all is going as we have planned, let's send them a message and they will understand we mean business.' Jeffrey smiled as he kissed her gently on the lips, lifting her as if she weighed nothing and then gently putting her down. 'Let's fix this mess!' he barked, as a bunch of people that were there, lifted Carl's unconscious body placing him on a chair.

It had been months and a few weeks, since his arrival in the Sol Islands. Felix was beginning to get the hang of things, but his body still ached from the arduous training. One morning he trained in the glare of the sun. Standing in a horse stance at the beach with the view of the sea in front of him, Felix had his right hand's index finger upright. The thumb was bent, and the other fingers bent as well. He breathed out from below his navel, as he pushed his right hand out forward. He made a sound with his mouth, that sounded like a deflating tyre. After a series of repetitions with the right hand, he changed to his left. The exercise was one finger gong, a hard chi kung he had learned from Grand Uncle Kazak, it was something Grand Uncle Kazak had learned from a Loham monk years ago.

Once Felix was done, he stretched and then started to throw random combinations of kicks and punches. Also trying throws, takedowns and simulating joint locks. A few minutes into his shadow-boxing session, he heard someone shouting his name. Felix stopped the shadow boxing and turned to catch the glimpse of a tall, bald muscular man, with narrow creaseless eyelids. It was Boris Subek, Grand Uncle Kazak's son and Felix's uncle.

Felix took a jog towards Boris, who stood to wait with his hands on his waist. 'Felix!' he said in his usual and normal scowling deep voice, always with a serious gaze. Felix was not intimidated and had got used to his uncle speaking like that. It reminded him of Uncle Fred who had sounded similar but that was far milder. 'We need you at the Council of Masters!' he continued. Felix had a small frown on his face, but he did not ask any question and followed his uncle who marched away at a rapid pace.

The Council of Masters was the leadership core of the Separatist movement, consisting mostly of Subek or Sobek family members. Amongst the members was a Sud family member who before the formation of the Separatist movement, had travelled to the Sol Islands. Establishing the Separatist movement at the islands with Great Grand Uncle Kek and Grand Uncle Kazak. The Council of Masters was traditionally the governing power of the Sol Islands, with Grand Uncle Kazak as the Chairman Master. He had replaced Great Grand Uncle Kek, who was also there seated.

Felix had never been inside the chamber of the Council of Masters when he arrived, it was the one thing he had not seen. The chamber was housed in an ancient temple, built in the honour of Felix Subek the First. He was the one who had unified the different clans in the Sol Islands and was the founder of the Council of Masters. Outside the chamber's doors stood a bunch of men and women, including a tall guard who guarded the doors to the chamber. In front of the doors, and like most around the islands was a tall statue of Daruma. The men and women were dressed in military uniforms. Everybody saluted Boris and Felix using the martial yin yang sign as they walked through them. The guard opened the door for Felix and Boris as they strolled in. Inside the chamber were benches where the masters sat, that surrounded a large painting in the centre of the chamber's floor. It was two fishes of different colours that were facing different directions. This painting symbolised the yin yang symbol, and on the ceiling, was a painting of Felix Subek the First, leading his men into a naval battle.

Felix and Boris were in the centre, under the watchful eyes of the masters in the chamber. 'Thank you, Boris,' said Grand Uncle Kazak, Boris nodded as he went up the steps to his seat. Felix was now left alone looking up at all the seated masters. The doors flung open again and strolling inside were the men and women who stood outside. They were the Sol Island's militia. Consisting of commanding officers who were mostly fishermen and one of the Sol Island's finest martial artists.

'Thank you!' began Kazak, as the door closed, 'Ok so let's begin, Felix welcome to the chamber. Today we will begin the operation we have been planning for years, operation Thunder Fist! We will attack the Union Armada surrounding our islands, destroy them. All of you officers have already received the orders and are prepared for this day,' Grand Uncle Kazak's voice was audible in the chamber as no microphone was needed for a voice to be heard. This ancient gathering area had excellent acoustics.

The plan was that they were to launch a surprise attack on the union navy, the first person that would lead the attack was going to be Great-Grand Uncle Kek and Grand Uncle Kazak. There were also talks of deploying the Nautifist, it was a gigantic submarine and the only ship the Sol Islands had. Nevertheless, it was a force to be reckoned with, the issue was that they lacked any warplanes, luckily the Union navy lacked any aircraft carriers.

Listening in, Felix first wondered if the reason he was called in was to participate in this battle that was about to take place. He also wondered what is it that his great and grand uncle were going to do to launch this attack. The Nautifist surely could not take on all the Union ships?

'Felix! The reason we have brought you here,' said Grand Uncle Kazak, as he gestured at one of the militiamen who came forth and placed a tele-hologram on the floor. A three-dimensional image appeared, showing a tied-up Carl Sobek looking unconscious. The image then disappeared, and the militiaman took the tele-hologram. 'As you can see that is your father, he has been kidnapped by our own,' said

Grand Uncle Kazak. Felix had a frown appear on his face and another seated master of the council spoke, 'My niece and her followers have kidnapped your father, they think that he is Silver Serpent, the reason is they want to bend the movement to their will...she is foolish!'

The man who had spoken was Ren Sud, the older brother of Cole Sud. About twenty years ago, Cole held protest marches in the East-South Union against Gaia Corp's involvement with the government. He was shot dead and his death led to a revolution that later led to the formation of the Separatist group. Ren Sud who had friends in the Sol Islands had secretly formed the group with the help and blessing of Great Grand Uncle Kek and Grand Uncle Kazak who were his close friends. He was a tall bearded black man, with thick intimidating eyebrows, he was very wealthy, given his family's history and a great martial artist who had never competed in the Lei Tai.

'Felix, your task is to save your father, you will be taken to Sud City, where James and Drasul Stockhorn will assist you with this task,' said Grand Uncle Kazak. Felix looked even more puzzled, James Stockhorn the detective, things were getting weirder. 'Great! This short meeting is done! Let's crush these sons of bitches!' grunted Great Grand Uncle Kek, as he shot out of his seat. 'Come follow me!' one of the militiamen hurriedly said, as he shoved Felix forward out the chamber.

Great Grand Uncle Kek and Grand Uncle Kazak headed for the beach. Where they could see the Union ships off the coast, it was Great Grand Uncle Kek that began as he first glanced at his son who glanced back. Standing in a horse stance with his hands positioned as if he was giving a hug, he closed his eyes breathing deeply and when they shot open, suddenly currents of electricity flowed around his body getting stronger as he focused, and at that moment, he yelled, 'HA!' A sphere of electricity that surrounded his body emerged and shot out towards the Union ships in the sea.

This left Great Grand Uncle Kek breathing heavily and sweat crawled down his forehead. He and Grand Uncle Kazak watched the ships get demolished, some exploded as the sphere of electrical current that was emitted from Great Grand Uncle Kek, split into multiple smaller spheres causing carnage. Glancing at his son, Great Grand Uncle Kek said as he got out of his horse stance, 'Your turn my son.' Grand Uncle Kazak took a few steps forward and stretched his right hand out, he closed his eyes for a moment and when they flung open, a current of electricity shot out his hand straight into the sea as Grand Uncle Kazak's whole body started to shake. The electric current was like a thunderbolt moving and ravaging the union ships.

Felix could see everything from the top of a mountain, as he and the militia peered for a moment. He was flabbergasted by what he had just seen, the only martial artist he knew that had abilities beyond imagination, was Silver Serpent. But this was something new, after a minute of watching they hurried away. Felix was taken to a cave, where there was an elevator leading down to another cave that exited into the sea. There he took a glimpse of the immense Nautifist floating in the cave's seawater, the Sol Islands' ultimate weapon.

They rushed inside and moments later, the submarine sunk into the waters, once they were out of the cave. The militia captain inside barked out commands to his subjects, buttons were pressed, and missiles were fired from underwater. The missiles ejecting out of the water heading for Union ships. Monitoring the situation, the militia captain could gauge that the Union armada had been crushed with a few harmless ships left. Felix looked around in wonder as this was beyond him, it came to his mind that a great war had begun.

'Okay kid you going to be accompanied in one of our sea pods where you will be dropped in the beaches of Sud City,' said the militia submarine captain. Felix was still a bit stunned as he was then rushed to one of the pods with a group of four other men. Before he knew it, he was inside the pod and they were shot out of the submarine floating underwater in the large sphere that was the pod, within hours they floated up, off the coast of Sud City. Once they hit the beaches and came out the pod, Felix caught a glimpse of two people, recognising James

Stockhorn and not knowing who the other person was; it was getting dark and the sun had begun to slumber away.

'We leaving you here, we have a battle we need to re-join, good luck on your mission! Soldier!' barked one of the militiamen as they rushed back into the pod and rolled quickly back into the sea and then they were out of sight.

James Stockhorn and the other man who happened to be Drasul jogged towards Felix, who waited for them. 'Detective,' begin Felix trying hard not to sneer. 'Felix this is my uncle Drasul, uncle this is Felix,' said James pointing at Drasul who stretched his hand out to shake Felix's hand. Felix shook it and said, 'Hi Drasul.' 'Okay boys,' said Drasul as put his hands on his hips, 'this is what we are going to do. Your father is being confused for Silver Serpent by those brats, do not know if you know. The Council of Masters had taken the liberty of not telling them that they have the wrong person. Ironically, the war those brats want has just started in the Sol Islands. Anyway, we are going to head to the storage facility where they are and speak to them.' 'Speak to them?' frowned Felix. 'If they resist, we fight them,' said James. Felix sighed at that answer and he gazed at James and Drasul. 'Look Felix they are still one of our own,' said Drasul. 'Anyway, we need to head there now!' exclaimed James as he ran off and the other two followed.

Meanwhile, an hour later in the abandoned storage facility, Rochelle was asking around for Jeffrey Mins as it seemed he had gone missing. A now resuscitated Carl, was now cuffed to a chair and grinning till he broke into laughter. 'What's hilarious!?' Rochelle snarled lighting up her eyes, as she motioned towards him. 'Well your lover leaves you, you look worried,' said Carl as he grinned. 'You not worth my time,' said Rochelle as she turned away and sighed. 'Your uncle must be disappointed!' yelled Carl. Rochelle then turned back to him, 'He clearly has forgotten what we are fighting for! The Council of Masters and the Subeks are against the Lei Tai they do not want it to even happen and should it happen there should be blood. They want to reset the Union as the current one is corrupt and heading to a one-world order. I kind of agree with all of that! But we also fighting for the murder of my father!' Rochelle's eyes got watery and she wiped the tears before they could trickle down. Carl scoffed unaffected by Rochelle's words, 'Quit going on! You emotional wreck!' he said. She lifted her hand ready to strike him and then stopped, as she heard a scuffle. Turning around she saw three men who had entered the storage facility and were getting yelled at by her men to put their hands up or they would shoot. 'I assume that is your rescue party,' Rochelle said turning to Carl who peered out noticing Felix.

Felix, James and Drasul had their hands in the air as they strolled forward, looking calm. 'It's okay guys!' exclaimed Rochelle as her men withdrew their weapons but glared at Felix, James and Drasul. 'You may drop your hands,' she said to them and they immediately did so. 'You guys have the wrong guy,' said Felix and a confused Rochelle turned to Carl who was grinning and had not revealed his true identity even after he had come back to consciousness. 'What do you mean!?' she angrily asked. 'That's my father, Carl Sobek,' said Felix. Shocked and taken by surprised she stared back at Felix realising who he was and so did some of her men. 'He is the champion of the Lei Tai!' barked one them.

'I know Silver Serpent! I mean have you not searched him online?' Felix frowned at Rochelle wondering how she could be so stupid. 'There is no way you or your men could hold him down if he were here,' he added making Drasul and James chuckle. 'They right, here is the real Silver Serpent,' said one of Rochelle's men, as he walked towards her with his cell phone, showing her a picture of him. Rochelle gritted her teeth as she murmured, 'Dammit.' 'Your uncle will forgive you, foolish girl, now let me go,' said Carl glaring at her.

'Ah a family gathering!' said a voice and everybody turn around to stare at a man with piercing blue eyes. Next to this man was Jeffrey Mins, towering over him and grinning. 'Jeff...' Rochelle tried to speak but froze as she frowned at her lover. Felix knew that face, it was Eddy and gazed at his cousin frowning as well.

'I knew you would end up part of the Separatists, a scumbag! Just like my dear father,' said Eddy as he looked at Felix in disgust. Felix's could feel his heart racing and then he remembered his father believing it was Eddy that had revealed Uncle Fred's involvement with the Separatists.

'What is going on?' asked Rochelle as she walked towards Jeffrey. Once she was close, he slapped her hard watching her fall to the side, his physical strength was immense, and he glared at her saying, 'Shut up! Bitch!' Holding and shaking she got up looking at him blankly. 'Ok, so we have you maggots surrounded, it's over now. Union troops are outside, there is no way you guys can escape,' said Eddy gleefully, and then he cast a sneering look at Felix. 'You are truly our family's abomination!' begin Felix in a rage, 'because of you my uncle died! You the Scum!' Felix looked ready to pounce on Eddy, but Jeffrey stepped in front of Eddy and Felix looked up at Jeffrey.

'Everybody make a run for it I will handle this! Felix! Help your father! James get them out of here now!' Uncle Drasul impatient, took charge of the situation and James immediately obeyed him as he grabbed Felix by the hand but Felix resisted, 'Hey! We came to save your father,' he said and Felix looking at him then yielded. Rochelle followed them rushing forth to free Carl as she uncuffed him. Her men just peered around confused looking at Eddy and Jeffrey. 'Jeffrey is an agent of the brotherhood, not your lover!' yelled Eddy as he grinned at Rochelle. 'This really is not your day young girl,' said Carl as he massaged his wrists and shook his feet.

'What now?' asked Felix. 'The dragon will save us,' James calmly said. Drasul had got into a small horse stance with his eyes closed and his right hand over his left hand, holding them just under his navel. 'EVERYBODY RUN!' he roared as his eyes shot open. His voice sounded strange, deeper and loud. Like mice escaping a fire, Rochelle's men were set into a frenzy as the whole lot of them made their way out. 'They will get caught,' sniggered Jeffrey and Eddy chuckled in response. They turned back their attention towards Drasul, wondering what he was doing and before they knew it, they saw currents of electricity underneath Drasul's feet. The current shot up and covered Drasul's whole body and his eyes' pupils went red shining and beaming a red light. Eddy and Jeffrey were suddenly taken aback by this, as Eddy said, 'let's get out of here, we stronger outside,' once he said that they both run away.

'WHAT ARE YOU GUYS STILL DOING HERE!?' yelled Drasul. Shaken by the words, Rochelle turned to the rest and said, 'there is a door leading to an underground tunnel, serves as an escape route in case shit hit the fan.' 'Take us there now. My uncle is buying us time!' said James. Rochelle took them to a secret door, which led to the tunnel as they escaped.

Once he felt the presence was gone, Drasul grinned and in a bang of immense bright exploding light, the whole storage facility exploded, and a bright white beam of light shot straight up into the skies.

The explosion overwhelmed Jeffrey and Eddy, including the Union troops outside, as they were pushed meters away backwards by the force of the explosion. Felix and the rest thought the tunnel would cave in as they escaped feeling it tremble, but the tunnel managed to hold its own.

# CHAPTER THIRTEEN- RESURRECTION

Back in the Sol Islands, a strange homeless-looking man had demanded an audience with the Council of Masters, saying it was urgent. The independence declaration of the islands rocked the news and social media. It had caught the world in complete surprise, and the Council of Masters was busy plotting its next military move, he was refused an audience. Instead, the militiamen and women tried to arrest him where they found him on a beach with a fishing boat it seemed he had stolen. The man was Phoenix Guan and he retaliated defeating the militiamen and women with ease.

The doors to the Council of Masters flung open and the guard guarding the entrance fell inside, as the doors opened, sliding on the floor. Stepping inside was Phoenix Guan, 'What is this nonsense!' grunted Boris Subek. 'I have something urgent to tell the council!' said Phoenix not backing down.

'Let him speak,' said Great Grand Uncle Kek. 'Before he does that, we need to know who he is?' asked Grand Uncle Kazak as he frowned at Phoenix. 'I am Phoenix Guan, of the Guan family, a direct descendant of Yu Guan also known in antiquity as General Red Crow,' said Phoenix with pride as he looked around the chamber. 'Impossible!' scoffed Ren Sud, 'the man you say you are, disappeared years ago, the patriarch of the Guan family,' he added. 'Disappeared...but not dead,' responded Phoenix, 'You have announced to the world your independence from the Union, but I have socialised with Separatists members. This council is the main leadership head of the movement,' taking a pause he continued, 'I am sure you have all heard of the Brotherhood, this force is not just what is running things in the Union with the help of Gaia Corp. The man behind the Brotherhood is an ancient evil our forefathers fought!' shooting his gaze at Ren Sud. 'What do you mean?' asked Ren whose shield of scepticism was cracked. 'Years ago, when I became friends with Daniel Faris, he introduced me to a man called Dr Tet Watson, I am sure you guys have heard about this man?' The master's looked at each other more confused than before. But Phoenix continued, 'This Dr Tet, or Tet as he began to call himself was an archaeologist whose career had come to ruins many years ago, I was surprised to...' Boris Subek on the ends of his last bit of patience interrupted, 'What is the point to your story!' 'Boris! Let him finish,' said Grand Uncle Kazak glaring at his impatient son. 'I was surprised because this Tet character was said to have gone missing, I do not know if you all remember the Sword of Carnage?' 'Of course, it's family folktale amongst my family members,' said Ren Sud. 'Same with mine,' said Phoenix and continued, 'The Sword of Carnage was claimed to have been discovered by Dr Tet Watson…his peers, however, did not believe him. They ridiculed him, but this is not what led this man to obscurity. As you all know the sword as told by myth, was the short sword Emperor Fei Yue, had found in his village after his return from the Dragon's Lair. The sword that raiders who had raped and pillaged his village had left behind.' 'I remember such a tale years ago, yes of some crazy archaeologist making these claims…so it was this Tet character?' asked Great Grand Uncle Kek. 'Yes, and it was no myth, my ancestor Yu Guan saw the downfall of Fei Yue, but Fei Yue knew he was going to fall he sensed it with his fear. This set him on a quest to find out how he could be immortal, but not on the goal to just live long but to be truly indestructible,' pausing Phoenix gazed around at the masters.

Then he resumed, 'Fei Yue one day after frustration on pondering how to be indestructible, held the Sword of Carnage, and in holding it managed to transfer a part of his consciousness into it. This was his greatest secret, hiding it and not mentioning the events to my ancestor, his trusted disciple. In doing so, he had achieved some form of indestructible immortality not the long immortality of Daoist sages of antiquity but one that was perverse.' 'So, you are saying that his soul or consciousness lives in the sword?' asked Grand Uncle Kazak, intrigued by the tale. 'Yes, but there is more, Dr Tet Watson is a man that lived about ninety years ago, he was not a martial artist, how could he have lived this long? You see, the ridicule he received from his peers broke him down and his reputation as an academic was tarnished. Holding what he knew was the Sword of Carnage one evening and planning to stab himself with it. His weakness evoked what was left of Fei Yue in the sword and he entered Dr Tet Watson, killing the man that was inside and possessing his body. Then Fei Yue or Dr Tet Watson disappeared into obscurity and over the years plotting his return, he created the Brotherhood an organisation that was behind the formation of the Union of Nations and has become its main driving force. He's not as powerful as he was in the body of Dr Tet, but he still a force to be reckoned with.'

'This is ridiculous! You must think we are fools!' snarled Boris as he crossed his arms. Phoenix ignored him and continued, 'Our family secret or possession is that we have maps leading to Fei Yue's burial place, where his remains are. I gave this information to Daniel Faris after I confronted Dr Tet due him fucking my wife...' Ren interrupted him this time, 'So that is what this is all about!' Phoenix sighed not shaken by their disbeliefs and resumed what he was saying, 'Tet threatened to kill my family and Daniel Faris told me if I revealed where the remains were, my family will be spared. And I did, then disappeared into my own obscurity. To conclude, Gaia Corp's life tank, its new innovation will be used to recreate his body cell by cell using those remains. He will then possess that body and return to his full power. You all have doubts, but as I tell you all this, it could be happening now!'

Boris scoffed at what he had just heard, and Grand Uncle Kazak remained silent. 'If what you say is true, then our enemy has been the Emperor the whole time. The same demon our ancestors fought to bring peace to the world,' said Great Grand Uncle Kek.

Phoenix Guan had his say and agreed to be taken as a prisoner, but he told them that the only way to kill Tet was to find out where the Sword of Carnage was and destroy it. He said the sword was his only weakness, and anchor to the living world. If it was destroyed, Fei Yue would be dead instantly. The Council of Masters then broke into a heated discussion of what had just occurred, after Phoenix was taken to custody by the guard guarding the doors to the chamber. The guard regained consciousness after having been knocked out by Phoenix, who did not resist as the guard took him to his cell.

Back in Feiville in an underground secret laboratory were Daniel Faris and a team of medical doctors monitoring a man that was floating in the life tank. 'His ready I see,' said a voice, and Daniel Faris turned to see an old white man who wore spectacles. 'Tet,' he said and turned back to gaze at the man in the life tank. 'Soon you will call me by my original same,' said Tet as he walked next to Daniel, 'And soon I will be back in my original body,' he added.

The man inside the life tank was tall, darker than Daniel in complexion with narrow mono eyelids. He had the body of an athlete with long white hair stopping at his shoulders. 'It's actually ready, you can give it a try if you want,' said Daniel. Dr Tet closed his eyes for a moment and then suddenly fell unconscious to the floor. The man in the life tank then shot his eyes open, they were light blue and the glass enclosing the tank started to crack, and then it exploded into pieces causing the others to take cover.

Daniel and the medical doctors slowly got up and they caught a glimpse of the man floating naked in the air, with surges of electric current flowing around his body. He floated above them and then slowly vertically descended until his feet touched the ground. He then faced Daniel and the rest who gazed in awe.

'Emperor Fei Yue,' muttered Daniel as he kneeled and so did the medical staff. Fei Yue looked at his feet and hands, himself surprised that he was back.

'Daniel as promised, I will make you a king and you others will have your pieces to the pie. Provided you swear your allegiance to me,' he said as they all did not dare look up but the ground.

Hours after his return, Fei Yue visited the eight permanent elders of the Union of Nations at the Fei Tower, a skyscraper that was the headquarters of the Union and the tallest in the city of Feiville. Barging in he took them by surprise as they discussed the Sol Islands matter.

'Subjects! The emperor is back!' he arrogantly exclaimed. 'Who are YOU!? And how dare interrupt such an important meeting!' one of the elders shot out of his seat furious and fuming. Fei simply laughed, as a smirked appeared on his face and he then pointed his finger at the elder who was a man. The elder looked around anxiously, as he started to float up feeling unbalanced. Fei moved his finger to one side and the elder went flying straight for the wall, hitting it hard and then he fell unconscious. With an evil grin, he scanned the room looking to see if he was to receive further dissent. All the other seven permanent elders looked horrified at what just happened.

'I am Emperor Fei Yue and I have returned back from the ashes of time!' the tone of his voice expressed excitement, mingled with some anger as he spoke to the permanent elders who listened attentively to each word. Fei Yue described how the Brotherhood had taken over and that each Union general was under his thumb and members of his

Brotherhood organisation, and that all he wanted from the elders was their allegiance and loyalty.

Later on, Emperor Fei Yue had an audience, the media was on him like ants foraging on leftover food. The Sol Islands' breaking news was over-shadowed by this event. Online, in the social media sphere, people called it a farce, others commented that it was the end of the world. Watching the news, the Council of Masters in the Sol Islands, had an emergency meeting and they had sent a militia-man to collect Phoenix. However, the militiaman returned pale and shocked as Phoenix had escaped by smashing his prison cell wall, leaving a big hole. The alarm went out and a search party searched for him, but the man had vanished from the Sol Islands.

'Fei Yue is back...that explains a lot, his whole goal like during his time in ancient history was world domination. The irony is that the war our an-cestors fought those thousands of years ago, is now our fight,' said Ren Sud in the chamber of Council of Masters and then went silent, into deep thought. Everybody was silent for a moment reflecting and then Boris broke the silence, 'It would have not made a difference, but if Phoenix were here, I would apologize for my arrogance...there is hope though, we have to find the Sword of Carnage and destroy it.' 'If what Phoenix said about the sword is true, yes there is hope,' remarked Great Grandfather Kek. 'Emperor Fei Yue is back, and he warned us about that. The story about the sword must also be true then,' said Grand Uncle Kazak. 'Have we heard news about Carl Sobek and his son?' inquired Ren. 'Yes, the mission was accomplished, they managed to free Carl Sobek. However, this information comes from the Dragon,' said Boris and he further explained that Drasul had used his dragon power to allow Felix and the rest to escape. When they asked him where Drasul was, he explained that Drasul was not with them. That he had changed his mind meeting them at the safe house in Sud City, because of the current events that have recently occurred. It was then agreed that Boris would make contact with James and the rest. Advising them that Drasul was still alive and that they would be picked up off the coast of Sud City, to be taken to the Sol Islands.

When James received communications from Boris, he was filled with joy knowing that his uncle did not die, in the explosion. He informed Felix and the rest on what was happening, and they all went straight to the coast, where they were to meet up with some militiamen and women, so they could be taken to the Sol Islands. Rochelle had fallen into some form of depression and kept quiet, holding back her tears. The betrayal from Jeffrey Mins had cut her deep and Felix could pick it up, but he focused on his own stress and anger. Eddy had betrayed the family and he did not tell his father yet, but Felix felt that they needed to have evacuated Aunt Catherina and Charles. The paranoia that Eddy was going to harm them, tormented his thoughts and then he remembered Mrs Wilkins. He still struggled to understand what Eddy was doing with the Union troops, but James explained to Felix that Eddy was most likely part of the Brotherhood. James explained the Brotherhood to the rest and how he came across them in Feiville, telling them it was when he was re-investigating Felix's case, also recounting his encounter with Medil.

It was early morning when they arrived on the beaches of the main island of the Sol Islands, the sun was up in splendour, but the good weather did not reflect the mood of Felix and the rest. They were met by the whole Council of Masters and a furious Ren Sud rushed towards Rochelle, slapping her across the face. That she flew backwards, falling on the water. Felix protested by yelling and received a look of disgust from Ren Sud who walked away. Carl Sobek hid his grin and laughter as everybody gazed at Rochelle, she slowly got up finally letting out the tears she held back. Felix felt like comforting her but did know how to begin. He finally walked towards her as she got out the water and muttered, 'Everything will be okay.' 'It's my fault,' said Rochelle sniffing. 'We all mess up,' he said patting her on the back.

Sun wondered if there was going to be another Lei Tai with the return of Emperor Fei Yue. The story on the media was that Dr Tet Watson who had disappeared ninety years ago had indeed discovered the Sword of Carnage. Fei's soul or consciousness was inside the sword and it had possessed his body killing him off, and for years the emperor was inside Dr Tet's body until eventually his remains which were discovered by Gaia Corp under the direction of Daniel Faris was found. Then it was rebuilt using the life tank. The body allowed Fei Yue to be complete again.

Sun was in awe with all of this, his ancestor Yu Guan had challenged Emperor Fei Yue thousands of years ago, and he wondered if the emperor will exact revenge upon his descendants, his family. Historically Fei Yue was only viewed as a tyrant amongst the old families, but to the rest, he was regarded as a powerful leader. The images on the news, showed the rampant riots that occurred across cities, with Union troops called in to calm the situation.

'This is unbelievable,' said Aunt Kelly watching the events, 'Phoenix where are you,' she added. The Guan family held a meeting about the unfolding events, concluding that they stay on guard.

Fei Yue had the whole world under his feet; he announced that there was going to be a coronation. Where he will be crowned emperor of the world and it was to be held within a month.

# CHAPTER FOURTEEN-
# THE GRAND
# PRIESTESS

Medil had taken Silver to the Slang Nyoka clan, where they hid in a mountain filled with caves that housed thousands of them. The mountain was in a forest on the outskirts of the Dragon's Lair and was not far from the ruins of the original village of the Slang Nyoka clan. They were a clan that always lived in secrecy, assassins used throughout history to eliminate whoever the enemies of their clients were. The Union even during its formation, did not try to stop them. The clan was the world's dark secret, lurking the shadows none of the clan's assassins could be caught. With the formation of the Union, most of their clients were criminals.

Silver had left his clan when the civil war had broken out amongst them, his parent's death was the cause of the war as they were assassinated by his uncle, who made a move also on Silver's life. Despite being stronger, Silver escaped into exile leaving power in the hands of his father's brother, who ironically was also assassinated. It was then that he set on a voyage challenging martial artist around the world to deadly duels. When he had amassed five hundred kills did he then allow himself to be caught by the authorities, ending up in Main Central, Wobbleton, the Sud-Republic's most dangerous prison. However, during those duels, he had encountered the Separatists, he joined the movement just before going into prison. But all this time during his self-exile, the Slang Nyoka clan had fallen into chaos, he was keen to find out how the Grand Priestess had brought order into the clan.

Despite taking him back to the clan, Medil did not hide his loathing emotions towards Silver who was amused by them. They were met by an audience of guards and the Grand Priestess, inside one of the caves which were connected with the other caves around the mountain.

Silver recognised the Grand Priestess but could not believe it as he gazed in disbelief. The Grand Priestess was a very thin and short old woman, she was bald with the yellow eyes that everyone who came from the clan had. She walked with a wooden bamboo staff, whose end stopped at her shoulders and were gripped by her bony fingers. Her fierce stare overshadowed her thin physique, as they displayed her internal strength.

'So...are you going to remain silent!' said the Grand Priestess in a serious tone and then a grin appeared on her face. Medil frowned in confusion it was not what he had expected, he knew the Grand Priestess unlike the other members of the clan, did not spit on the ground on hearing the name of Silver Serpent. But she did not object when they cursed his name. He had always assumed this behaviour was her display of loathing towards Silver Serpent and how he was hated in the clan by most. Silver kept quiet his eyes widened with amazement and as he took a few steps forward and the guards drew out their guns and pointed them at Silver. This action rubbed the heavy frown off Medil's face as he smirked gleefully. 'Put your weapons down!' barked the Grand Priestess and her bodyguards immediately obeyed the order, 'Make way!' she added as they gave her way, to walk towards Silver who just watched hypnotised by surprise. She walked up to him and they hugged, shocking everybody else around them.

'Helga...' muttered Silver as they withdrew from each other. Medil had not told Silver that Helga was the Grand Priestess, she was the youngest of all of Silver's siblings to have not only survived the civil war but to have brought peace during those troubling times. Medil's hate towards Silver stemmed from the fact that his parents died in the war. Something he let Silver know when they journeyed to the Slang Nyoka clan. But he could see from the

Grand Priestess's eyes, that she still loved her eldest brother. This did not change his feelings of hate towards Silver, but he was fiercely loyal to Helga who trained and brought him up as an orphan when she gained power.

'So much has happened since your exile... brother,' said Helga. Medil could see for a moment, a vulnerable Silver and his instinct and pulse from years of training told him to pounce on Silver. But he kept calming down, ignoring the urge. 'Well...' begin Silver but was immediately interrupted by Helga who said, 'You both have travelled far, rest first! We will speak tomorrow,' she turned to her bodyguards and added, 'Make rooms for these two! And should anyone make any move on my brother, I will kill them in person with my bare hands!'

Medil did not sleep at night he instead indulged himself into doing push-ups in his room, night time in the clan meant lights out. Unless for those who were training or were on some form of guard duty. Living with the clan meant, there were strict rules to obeyed or one will be punished. Death was more common than banishment to those that were disobedient, and life in the clan was all about discipline and obeying orders. Occasionally they indulged in some form of celebrations where banquets were held. It was the only time the members of the clan took it easy and for those who went on assassination missions like Medil for days or years, it meant more freedom to do as one pleases. Although he occasionally indulged on worldly pleasures, the discipline from the clan was drilled to the bones since birth.

Hearing a knock on his door, Medil immediately got up ready and cautious, he immediately unlocked and opened his door. In front of him was a girl who he immediately recognised and aggressively dragged her inside his room, closing his door and locking it.

The girl had short hair, with eyes that were wider in comparison to most in the Slang Nyoka clan. She was lighter in skin tone with full lips, one of the clans most beautiful females. She gazed seductively at Medil, who gazed back slightly annoyed and said, 'You really want to get into trouble…Adel Hiss…' Medil paused mesmerised by her figure as his eyes motioned up and down.

Adel launched at him wrapping her hands around his neck as they kissed and then Medil turned her around aggressively shoving her away. Adel fell on his bed as he strolled towards her and then turned her face down, 'Hard and rough just like you like it right,' muttered Medil.

She had grown up with Medil and the two would occasionally have an affair, with her investing more of her heart in the interactions. She was in love with Medil who only occasionally would give glimpses of his affection. Regardless, she stayed loyal to him and unlike many in the clan she was more of a thief than an assassin. Preferring to steal highly valuable items but when it came to be killer, she was as deadly as any of them.

The Grand Priestess was jovial of the return of her eldest brother and a banquet was to be held to celebrate his return. This ambience of her content emotions shielded or blinded her from the loathing glances Silver received from most of the clan. Medil not hiding this as he repeatedly told Silver, 'If I could, I will kill you!' Silver would snigger and be carefree at these remarks, this carefree attitude further annoyed Medil. Before the banquet Silver wanted to speak to his sister, as to why he had come back, and a meeting was held in her throne room. Seating on both her sides were her advisers, it was a large room in one of the caves with the walls carved with images of serpents all up to the ceiling. It was lit by burning torches hanging from the walls.

Helga listened patiently to Silver as he spoke about the Separatists and the events that had just occurred. He and Medil on their journey to the Slang Nyoka Clan kept up to date with the return of Fei Yue. Medil had even bragged to Silver about having met Tet, and Silver pleaded to his sister that the clan join the Separatists movement to restore balance in the world.

'Emperor Fei Yue is back, such figures of the past cannot be good for this world or even more importantly, his Brotherhood is your client but, in the end, he will kill you all the moment he fears you!' Silver argued with the advisers, who sneered back at him scoffing at all he had said. Medil was also in the meeting standing up beside Silver. He hated the feeling, but he agreed with Silver having met Fei when he was Tet, it was possible Fei Yue in his twisted state could turn on the Slang Nyoka. The Grand Priestess stepped in as the debate started to heat up and she said, 'We will continue after the banquet, brother I am taking everything you are saying into consideration, but I will only make a decision after the banquet. We live very rigid lives with strict rules. Let's allow ourselves to relax by having a banquet,' those were her last words as she got up and left. Once the Grand Priestess left her advisers whispered sinisterly amongst themselves, Silver glanced at them and then smirked as he strolled away. Medil stayed peering at them and wondering what they were plotting, until one of them spotting that Medil who was still there, approached him.

'We need to get rid of Silver! We are ready to kill him in the banquet,' began the adviser as he hissed at the mention of the name Silver and continued, 'our Grand Priestess will not understand but it needs to be done. Our assassin will poison him, and when the Grand Priestess seeks justice our hands will be clean, but the culprit will die alone.' 'Sinister plan, you will frame your own assassin,' said Medil. The adviser smirked before saying, 'We need to cover our tracks, it's no secret you hate Silver as well, he is the cause of the war!' grunted the adviser and Medil nodded in agreement. Silver had to go, it was unfortunate the Grand Priestess did not understand, thought Medil.

The banquet took place within the following days in a large hall inside one of the caves, the celebration hall had the capacity of housing all the Nyoka. Traditional music was played at the banquet, using ancient musical instruments and the cellars that were barely touched, supplied the wine that was being served in goblets as the Slang Nyoka partied.

Helga sat on the head of her table, clapping and moving her head to the music being played, with her taster next to her observing and tasting the wine being poured into the Grand Priestess' goblet. Silver was also in a jovial mood sitting close to his sister. Medil was next to Silver, not seduced by the ambience surrounding him, he buried himself into eating the meat from a freshly hunted boar, that had been roasted and occasionally sipped on his wine.

The Grand Priestess stood up and in a sudden, the whole room went silent. 'Let me make a toast,' she began as she gazed at her brother and a smile appeared on her face, 'my brother Silver...' Her words were paused by an arrow that flew straight into her throat and a stream of blood began to leak out. The Grand Priestess had a look of shock and fear as she gazed at Silver. It was as if she was asking for his help, with her one hand reaching out for him. Then a barrage of more arrows struck her, piercing her body. Her bodyguards were too slow to act with some of them just standing idly by. Medil and Silver both shot out their seats. Silver run to his sister's collapsed body and Medil run the direction he believed the arrows came from.

Cries from the erupted and with it came chaos, everybody ducked down in fear of more arrows. Silver watched as Helga slowly closed her eyes and he could feel her heart had seized to beat. Feeling the rage, he got up, and the assailant shooting the arrows appeared shooting one straight at Silver who stared back at him. The arrow snapped and broke as it made contact with his chest, bouncing off into fragments and he glared at the assailant whose head split into different parts, a bullet had struck him, and it came from the gun that Medil pointed at him.

The supposed bodyguards of the now-dead Grand Priestess, all pulled out their guns pointing it at Silver who gazed at all of them, with a razor-sharp look of focus on his face. 'Your weapons are futile!' he barked as they all began to choke dropping their guns and they held their throats as they felt the invisible strangulation, gasping for air and shaking uncontrollably as they fell to their last breaths. At that moment, Silver and Medil's eyes met and Medil could feel Silver scanning him for any signs of betrayal. It felt as if Silver was trying to read his thoughts and after a few seconds, Medil using his super-speed vanished in a blur appearing next to Silver where the body of the Grand Priestess lay, kneeling Medil held her as tears trickled down his cheeks, doing his best to hold back, he broke into a sob as he briefly glanced at Silver who did not judge him, in his moment of weakness. Silver eyes were not wet, but he cried inside sharing his pain with Medil.

The mayhem in the hall, saw people rushing out and exiting into the cave corridors leading to other caves. Once the chaos settled, Medil took control of things and with a band of other clan members, brought some order. To his surprise Silver told him that the judgement for the murder of his sister would come later, they first had to mourn her. Nevertheless, there was a shutdown in the caves, with the curfews tightened and no one was to leave.

As was tradition, Helga Serpent was buried in the catacombs reserved for the Grand Priests and Priestesses of the past. After the burial came the judgement, the advisers ironically advised that Silver the rightful heir should become the Grand Priest, to avoid another war. Silver unsurprisingly declined and gave the power to Medil who was taken by surprise and after the crowning ceremony, Medil confessed to Silver about the original plot to have him poisoned. Silver was calm as Medil divulged everything, 'I am aware of that,' he told

Medil, 'you did not make it a secret that you wanted me dead, but the question that you and I have is who plotted for my sister to be killed. They wanted us both dead.' 'I know who wanted you and her dead... the same people that claimed they just wanted you dead,' said Medil.

A meeting was held in council chambers after the crowning ceremony and Silver and Medil's brief chat. Silver simply greeted the advisers and before they knew it, they were all gasping for air, holding their throats as they choked to death, this amused Medil and Silver as they both grinned.

After the macabre event, new advisers and body-guards were immediately appointed by Medil. Then he pledged allegiance to the Separatist group to Silver's delight on the behalf of the clan. However, Medil was to still masquerade the clan as supposed allies of Fei Yue. The day after, the two had a secret meeting, as Silver contacted the Council of Masters in the Sol Islands on an encrypted line. Kazak spoke about the appearance of Phoenix Guan and what he told them about the Sword of Carnage, catching Medil and Silver by surprise.

'So, what is the plan in finding this sword?' inquired Medil. 'He clearly has the sword and has it hidden, you are working for him you could find where it is,' answered Kazak on the other end of the line, then Silver joined the conversation. He said, 'Our troubles have increased exponentially we need to act fast, I am leaving the caves, I will coordinate with our members amongst the eight nations.'

After the meeting, Silver left the caves but what Medil and Silver did not know, was that hidden in the dark shadows, where they held their secret meeting, was the presence of Adel Hiss, who heard everything. With her personal agenda, she left the caves as well, in pursuit of the Sword of Carnage.

# CHAPTER FIFTEEN- CORONATION SHOWDOWN

Shaving his beard off, as he carefully peered in the mirror was Phoenix Guan, gently moving the blade as the shaving cream was removed with the beard. Once he was done, he rinsed his face with some lukewarm water and then he dried his face with a towel, taking another look at his face this time with more admiration as he grinned.

After having left the Sol Islands, Phoenix Guan had made his way to an inn in the outskirts of Feiville. During a planned encounter with a drug dealer, Phoenix took the opportunity to beat the drug dealer to sleep and steal his suitcase full of cash. He then used the money to rent a room in the inn and purchased new clothes.

Sitting down on his bed he grabbed the remote

and switched on the television, with his heart already pumping to the news that he suspected, Fei Yue was being talked about. Phoenix listened carefully as the breaking news was on Emperor Fei Yue's coronation as the Emperor of the world. He also gave the Separatists, the ultimatum to yield or be destroyed this same message was also given to the Council of Masters in the Sol Islands. The part of the announcement that gripped Phoenix's attention, was when Fei mentioned the Guan family amongst the list of prominent families, to be invited to attend the events as proof of their allegiance.

Slowing down his racing heart and breathing deeply Phoenix had a flashback of Daniel Farris telling him about the Sword of Carnage, and how Fei had divulged the secret to him arrogantly. That the sword was the root to him still being alive, should it be destroyed, Fei will die as the sword was his vulnerability to his immortality.

Emperor Fei held a meeting at the Fei Tower, with all the Union Guard Generals who were secretly members of the Brotherhood, and fiercely loyal to Fei. It was certain to them, that the Separatists were not going to yield to their demands and Separatist suspects were rounded and arrested. The other major subject was the invasion of the Sol Islands, it was clear after Jeffrey Mins relayed the information that the Separatist leaders were in the Sol Islands' Council of Masters. After the meeting, Fei had another visitor, Medil who pulled a brave face as he gazed at Fei.

'Medil Serr!' exclaimed Fei, with a grin on his face and Medil replied with a nod and a more blank facial expression. 'You finally see me in my true body… you clearly did not know who I was then…but Tet,' Fei sniggered once he spoke his words. 'So, you wanted to see me, what is it?' asked Medil getting straight to the point.

'How is the clan and the Grand Priestess?' replied Fei with a question. 'She was assassinated…' Medil's words were interrupted by Fei, 'So you killed her…crafty bunch your clan.' Medil kept quiet not bothering to correct Fei's assumption. 'So, you are now the Grand Priest I suppose?' continued Fei and Medil immediately responded, 'Yes I am and on the behalf of my clan I pledge our allegiance to you, Emperor Fei,.' Fei feeling flattered slightly laughed and put his hand on Medil's shoulder and then said, 'Loyalty is very important for me Medil, double cross me, and I will kill you, and every slithering member of your serpent, snake praying, bunch of people.' Fei's eyes lit up not with a glare but some form of intimidated expression but Medil seemed unfazed.

The streets of Feiville was lit with people as if another Lei Tai was about to take place, the only difference is people had more a facial expression of curiosity than that of excitement. It was the day of the coronation of Fei as emperor of the world and the official stamp of his tyranny. It took place midday, with the glare of the sun as it reigned supreme with the lack of clouds and a soft wind to blow off the heat. A parade was on display and the crowning was taking place at the square outside of the Fei Tower, where a podium was set up with a majestic throne, with steps looking down at the podium and this is where the crowned Fei sat. Further away from the podium were seated dignitaries with the Guan family in front. Sun sat next to Aunt Kelly baffled by the events and wondering what this meant to the world. Amongst them was Dylan Wilson who was now appointed police commissioner, by Fei after the previous police commissioner and his whole family committed suicide suspiciously, their deaths were reported as a suicide by the media.

The journalist took pictures with their cameras' peering flashes, some pulled their phones streaming the event live online, as Fei slowly descended from his throne ready to make a speech. The area was filled with heavily armed Union Guards and police, monitoring and scanning for a supposed attack by the Separatists.

Once he reached the podium with a grin on his face Emperor Fei spoke, 'I have been waiting for this moment in my life for thousands of years, it is unbelievable to most of you I know. I am living proof of what happens when one pushes the limits of the ancient knowledge of the Daoists...Fear me not my children, my enemies have thought they could write history and put my name in the shadows, yet it is I who tried to unify the world and bring peace.

One of the teachers of the Water School told me something before I foolishly slay them due to the horrors I had witnessed once I got back from my village...' pausing for a second he continued, 'he said... and I will never forget this, "This is our end, and your beginning, although you will succeed in many battles that await you. Today is one war you have lost." I had been my worst enemy and as my power and influence grew, so did my fear. I knew my end was coming, so using the knowledge I had, I took precautions. Upon returning to my village and witnessing the carnage, there was a short sword, which I had picked up if you are familiar with history or as the myth goes this short sword is known as the Sword of Carnage. So, I kept this sword as a reminder of the chaos around me and how my goal of world peace was important. But more importantly the fear, that I felt of losing it all drove me to find out how I could be immortal. So, sensing my end I transferred part of me into the sword, part of my consciousness stayed in the sword, using the Daoist knowledge I had I was able to pull this magnificent feat,' Fei continued talking, twisting the truth that when the sword was discovered by Dr Tet Watson, it was Dr Tet Watson who himself sacrificed his body as a vessel for Fei's consciousness or soul knowing that he will die in the process. During this time Sun and Aunt Kelly cast each other shocked looks at what they were hearing. 'His immortal, a sort of demi-god,' muttered Aunt Kelly, to Wren her husband who sat on her other side not cloaking his concern.

One of the Union Guards not far from the podium removed his military beret and threw it on the ground and then aimed with his rifle as he started to shoot at Fei. This caused immediate mayhem, with screams and all the dignitaries took cover, while the crowds that were close and far scrambled for safety.

Some of the Guans who crouched down looked up and to everybody's surprise, none of the bullets had hit Fei. The bullets lost momentum and bounced off to the sides. Other Union Guards jumped on the Union guard firing the shots. It was Phoenix Guan, he was tackled to the ground, surprisingly not resisting as his weapon was snatched away from him; flat on the ground he glared at Fei. Kelly peered not believing her eyes and stood up ignoring the turmoil around her. She held her breath for about ten seconds frozen in time before she started to breathe again, and her mouth and eyes slightly opened in awe. She could not believe she had just caught a glimpse of her brother. The other flabbergasted party was Sun as he whispered, 'Dad,' covering his forehead with a heavy frown.

Fei was not fazed, it was his coronation and his day, his response to Phoenix's glare who lay pinned flat on his stomach by the other guards was a grin. 'Hold him up!' barked Fei and the Union Guards still holding Phoenix lifted him to his feet and he did not show again any signs of resistance. Fei strolled a few steps away from the podium towards Phoenix's direction and then said as he stopped, 'Phoenix Guan...' but his words were shot down by Phoenix who interjected with a snarl, 'You are the world's greatest evil! Those shots were just to see how powerful you really are! But I will make you pay for everything!' At that moment of his last words, closing his eyes the guards who held him suddenly bounced off him rolling on the ground in different directions. The guards then pointed their guns, but before they could pull the trigger, they suddenly found themselves struggling to breathe as an invisible hand choked them. 'Your ancestor was close... you are not even close enough,' said Fei and then he pointed his hands at Phoenix. He briefly closed his eyes and then shot them open, firing a lightning spark that zapped Phoenix off his feet, sending him flying out the square, into the road filled with people running about for safety. A combination of Union Guards and police officers rushed for him amongst the moving crowd, but Phoenix was gone.

The events did not affect the proceedings that were to occur later, like the coronation ball. Fei had used the opportunity to display his ability. Something only a few old martial art masters knew was capable, images of him shooting lightning sparks went viral online and the fact that this thousands of year-old figure had resurrected himself, made people see him like a god and the rest simply feared him. The security forces were able to douse the flames of turmoil and bring peace, with that a tighter security. Commissioner Dylan used the opportunity to settle any remaining scores by arresting people on trumped-up charges, that they were Separatists who aided Phoenix Guan.

Phoenix Guan was another subject, the news kept talking about him and to Sun's anger, his father was portrayed as a mad man and a bad father who wanted to live by his ancestor's legacy by attempting to kill Emperor Fei. As for Kelly Kray, once the dust settled, she did the unspeakable and denounced her brother much to Sun's horror agreeing with the media's narrative and pledging on the behalf of the Guans, their allegiance to Emperor Fei as she was interviewed before the coronation ball, where the Guans were also invited to attend.

The ball occurred at night, as it rained taking place in one of the halls of the Fei Tower and Kelly who was about to meet with Emperor Fei to personally display her loyalty, had noticed the sourness in Sun's face who occasionally shot her glaring glances. 'I did what I did, to protect our family...you show me some respect!' she said as she launched a slap towards Sun's cheek, but her wrist was grabbed before the slap could reach his face. Sun held her hand tight fuming with anger, 'When I was small, I respected you...if I yielded to your demands, it is because of that respect. But today you disgust me,' he said and then shoved her hand away. Wren blankly watched not wanting to get involved as Sun hurried away leaving the hall. 'He has a point,' said

Wren. 'He does not know…So for now. I need to pro-tect the family from that monster…' Kelly's words froze into silence as Emperor Fei appeared walking towards them, her heart raced but she knew what to say.

After the ball, Daniel Faris who was one of the guests at the ball was summoned by Emperor Fei. 'Your friend has returned,' began Emperor Fei as his eyes scanned Daniel suspiciously, 'you pleaded for his life, but I wanted that vermin dead just like his ancestor. I guess his angry that I had my way with his wife,' finishing his words with a snigger. 'I…' Daniel tried to respond but he could not, a sud-den choking sensation blocked the necessary air to speak and just before he could pass out, the sen-sation disappeared as he panted for air holding his throat. 'Eddy!' barked Emperor Fei and Eddy Sobek walked in glancing at an uncomfortable Daniel, he then gazed at Emperor Fei. 'Look here Daniel, see this boy…he will be your successor of that com-pany you love so much…now get out of my sight!' said Emperor Fei and without muttering a word Daniel left.

# CHAPTER SIXTEEN- HORRIFIC ACT

With his mind in disarray, Sun surprisingly made his way to his mother's mansion that evening after leaving the ball. She had not attended and was overwhelmed by her son's visit, she hugged him tightly as her eyes crawled with tears.

Sitting down on the dining table, she prepared some green tea which they both drank, Sun liking the bitter taste as he served himself again, once his cup was empty. As he took a sip of his refill, Sun noticed that his mother had new tears streaming down her face and she quickly wiped them off. 'What is wrong now?' he asked. 'That Tet man who is now Fei raped me...' pausing as she sobbed and tried to control herself, 'Your father thought me and that Tet guy had an affair, but the story is he forced himself on me.'

Estelle revealed to Sun, what had happened in the

past, Dr Tet Watson who Fei possessed was infatu-
ated by Estelle when she visited Phoenix and Daniel
at one of the Gaia Corp offices. One day she waited
in Daniel's office as he was running late, and Dr Tet
entered the office locked the door and had his way
with her. Phoenix had discovered them together as
he was wanting to meet with Daniel and was heading to his office, that is when he saw Tet coming out
Daniel's office together with Estelle. She told her
son how Phoenix did not believe a word she said.
Daniel had revealed to her that Dr Tet was powerful beyond measure and she believed him because
Phoenix who had confronted him was beaten to the
ground when he fought Dr Tet. She never knew that
he was Fei or anything about the sword, all she knew
was that Daniel her brother told her that to protect
Sun, it was better she complies with Dr Tet who
would visit her and have his way until he eventually
got bored of her and seized paying her those visits
she dreaded. She explained to Sun that is why his
aunt hated her so much and that she had thought of
suicide many times. Gazing at his mom with an expression of remorse he could see she was a broken
woman.

'You can stop crying woman,' said a voice and Sun
and Estelle both quickly got out of their chairs with
Sun lifting his cup ready to throw it at the intruder,
who he could not see. Then he appeared before
them hiding behind the curtains of the window; the
intruder was Phoenix Guan. 'Phoenix!' cried Estelle

star-struck, he joined them on the table looking calm. 'Dry your tears, Estelle. I figured out everything, after a year of anger and isolation. Gaia Corp was a booming company, but you're forever ambitious brother wanted more, so he sold his soul to the devil and that devil wanted you in return. The day you were to meet your brother, I was supposed to meet him too. When I confronted Tet for touching you consensual or not, he beat me. Your brother revealed who Dr Tet Watson really was...' pausing Phoenix grabbed the hand of Estelle, 'I have always loved you and I am sorry for not believing you when you told me the truth, about you and Tet, and I ridiculed you. My sister hating you was my doing...I am sorry.' Phoenix stood up and he kissed his wife on the forehead before turning to his son, 'Ha! You have grown up, Lei Tai champion like his father, I know you may think I have never been there, but I have watched you grow from a distant.' 'Were you the homeless man I saw outside when I was leaving the Gaia Corp campus?' asked Sun. 'Yes, it was me, like I said I have seen you grow from a distant,' answered Phoenix. 'So...' before Sun could carry on, Phoenix interrupted him, 'Son I want you to join me time is of the essence, and Estelle I promise you I will make Fei pay, I know how to kill him.' Phoenix told them about the Sword of Carnage if destroyed it destruction will lead to Fei's death as was revealed to him by Daniel Faris. 'The sword is like his anchor for him to stay alive,' he said. 'Then why has uncle not destroyed it?' enquired Sun. 'We need to find it, as arrogant as Fei is, he is not going to make it that easy for us,' replied Phoenix.

Sun accepted in joining his father who told him he was in contact with some Separatists and that they needed to prepare. What surprised Sun though, was that his father did not mention anything about Aunt Kelly denouncing him live on television. They left Estelle, disappearing into the night, leaving her with a sense of hope.

Back in the Sol Islands Felix felt very uneasy about Aunt Catherina and Charles still being in the Sud Republic. He kept having the paranoid thought that Eddy will harm them, the feeling kept bubbling inside that eventually he told Carl, who also felt the same.

'I have struggled to get hold of my contacts and even Mrs Wilkins! I feel your pain. Eddy is sick in his head,' said Carl as he glared out into the sea, wishing his nephew was before him so he could strangle him. 'The Baron is no more,' he added as he sighed hoping his frustration would diminish.

Carl had his fears to add to what Felix felt, he knew the Union Guards had probably raided his mansion and it was not far from the truth. As they were to later hear on the news, Mrs Wilkins defended the Sobek resident and was eventually killed, to Felix and Carl's delight she had died taking away the lives of a couple of the Union Guards during the raid. Carl and Felix were also on the wanted list as Separatist leaders and operators. Felix remembered when his Uncle Fred asked him to join the movement, but he was too caught up on proving his worth, by winning the Lei Tai. He wondered if he had joined the movement instead and not worried about the Lei Tai, would Uncle Fred still be alive? Felix then brushed those thoughts away. What he realised about the movement though, was that its leaders in the Council of Masters were actually against the Lei Tai and not worried if it turned into a sport. The Lei Tai a concept originally from the Sol Islands and it was imported to the rest of the world by Daruma as an ancient way to solve conflict and avoid blood being shed on the battlefield. It was not for gladiator-like entertainment, and to people like Grand Great Uncle Kek, it was nonsense to say it commemorated the past. They also saw the Union of Nations as a tyrannical organisation, that had enslaved and divided the world into eight nations. This was different from the message you got online from Separatist propaganda, which Felix came to realise was done and run by Rochelle Sud and her followers.

Aunt Catherina and Charles lived in fear, she wondered what was going on and had not heard from anyone. She was relieved when Eddy visited her, he had come with a tall friend of his who she did not know was Jeffrey Mins.

'Have you heard from Carl?' Aunt Catherina anxiously asked Eddy who quenched his thirst with a glass of water. They were in the kitchen while Jeffrey and Charles wherein the living room. 'Those criminals are done for,' sneered Eddy. 'How can you say that?' Aunt Catherina frowned in disapproval. Eddy gave her a cold look and an evil grin appeared on his face as he strolled towards her. 'You not even my real mom,' he said brushing her hair with his hands. 'I have always loved you like you were my own I...' Eddy silenced her as he put his finger on her lips and Aunt Catherina hit them away. 'How dare you!?' she snapped, and Eddy suddenly slapped her, shocking her as she stared at him horrified. He slowly got closer to her, 'What are you willing to do to save Charles?' he asked her, and Aunt Catherina realising she had raised a monster did not understand what was happening. Eddy got closer and then launched himself at her grabbing her. She completely felt overpowered, feeling slight jolts of electricity at that moment as he turned her around with his chin brushing her head. Holding her against the wall as her face faced the wall, he ripped the back of the dress she wore as she yelled, 'EDDY NOOO!' laughing sinisterly he rubbed against her, thrusting and then ripping her underwear, tears appeared on her face. 'Fight me and I kill Charles, now make your buttocks jiggle,' he muttered. Once he was inside her, he violently started to thrust, breathing heavily as he enjoyed himself.

Charles had tried to rush to his mom's aid from the living room when he heard her yell, but after two steps into his sprinting dash, he was knocked out by a single blow from Jeffrey who he watched the television with. Eddy climaxed after ten minutes of hard thrusting as his one hand held Aunt Catherina breast and the other her bare posterior's cheek, watching it bounce with each pounding thrust. 'I am the one who killed your miserable husband...now you going to offer me that body of yours when I visit,' said Eddy, as he got off her and Aunt Catherina, kneeled to the floor. She was silent, still going through the trauma she had just experienced.

A new armada of ships had surrounded the Sol Islands, with Fei not making it a secret that he was in one of the ships. The Union navy had its aircraft carriers with planes flying out within sight as a sign of intimidation. Commercial flights at the Sol Islands' international airport was stopped, and a decision was made at the Council of Masters after days of heated debate.

They all agreed they would make a stand and not yield to Fei, fighting to their last breaths but the disagreement came with Boris, who was appointed to command five hundred militiamen including Felix, James, Rochelle, Carl and Drasul. His father Grand Uncle Kazak had appointed him, and the rest of the masters were to remain and fight, Boris finally yielded.

They were to all escape in the Nautifist and although it could cause damage to the new armada surrounding the islands. A Union victory was inevitable and Great Grand Uncle Kek and Grand Uncle Kazak could sense Fei's enormous power.

After a quick meeting that was stopped, just as the Sol Islands surprised the Union forces with their anti-aircraft missiles, Boris headed with Felix and the rest to the Nautifist where the five hundred men awaited them. Everybody kept quiet, but the mood was sombre, they knew some of their loved ones left in the islands would die. The Nautifist was the Separatists lost hope and will serve as the movements main centre of command, it stealthily moved undetected under the depths of the sea, as Union Naval ships closed in.

Back in the Sol Islands, Union planes had finally started to destroy the islands' airspace defence, supported by the Union Naval power. Ren Sud, Great Grand Uncle Kek and Grand Uncle Kazak, headed to one of the beaches where Union Marines had landed, and ran head-on, like a swarm of ants popping out of a crack, in a wall. A few hundred militiamen stood hundreds of meters behind waiting for the four masters to display their power.

Ren Sud stepped formed and with a simple stretch of his hands, a lighting spark burst out of his palm shocking hundreds of marines till there were dead all dropping where they stood. He was exhausted after that and stepped back, with Great Grand Uncle Kek and Grand Uncle Kazak stepping forward. Ren Sud looked out into the ocean as he wiped the sweat off his forehead and his eyes widened in amazement. The Subeks gazed at each other in disbelief once they caught a glimpse of what Ren was seeing, it was Fei who was floating in the air with currents rapidly surging around his body, with sparks shooting out of his feet, hitting the ocean. His hair stood up and he was quickly coming their way, looking fiercer as he got closer. 'He emits his energy to the point where he can fly like that...impressive,' said Great Grand Uncle Kek. 'Death to a worthy opponent,' he added wryly, with a grin on his face as he turned to Ren and Grand Uncle Kazak. The Union Marines on that beach stopped at the shore as Fei dressed in his military uniform softly landed to a splash on the shore and marched towards Great Grand Uncle Kek, Grand Uncle Kazak and Ren Sud. He stopped a few meters away from them as he gauged at them with his eyes scanning. 'It is funny thousands of years ago I fought your very ancestors, you two are clearly Subeks and you...' Fei paused staring at the glare of disgust coming from Ren who then said, 'I am the descendant of the great Rey Sud, Ren Sud!' Fei sneered at Ren and before the two Subeks could blink, like thunder striking, the Emperor passed them and struck Ren with his fist, piercing the body right through. In seconds he had defeated and killed one of the world's most powerful martial artists. He removed his bloodied hand and Ren who was dying, just choked and fell to the ground his body shaking slightly. Fei stomped and crushed his head, mashing the skull to put Ren out of his misery, before he turned to the Subeks, 'If I was in the body of that Tet I would have been equal or no match for both of you or him,' he said spitting on what was now the corpse of Ren. 'Son let's give him all we got!' barked Great Grand Uncle Kek as he and Grand Uncle Kazak charged for Fei, who zapped them before they got close as he drew both his hands, shooting bolts of electrical sparks. The Subeks were electrocuted as they yelled in pain and both fell within half a minute. Their bodies were fried beyond recognition.

The militiamen who stood by watching the downfall of their masters, then made their move despite all of them knowing their fate. Although some of them pissed in fear as they rushed for Emperor Fei knowing he could issue enough energy to wipe them all. Nevertheless, bravery was in every part of their bones, embedded in their genetic make-up. They were vaporised within seconds much to the shock and awe of Union Troops who watched in disbelief.

Within hours the Union forces controlled the islands with a few remaining militiamen who were pleaded by the few masters of the council that remained, to seize to fight. They knew they had played their part as the Nautifist moved underneath the Dragon Ocean.

Rochelle looked in wonder as she glanced around the submarine, surprised at its unusual size, it was a nuclear-powered monster and probably the world's biggest naval vessel, it was self-sustaining to its inhabitants. It also housed other vessels and was armed with state-of-the-art weapons and was undetectable from radar with stealth technology.

Boris spoke through the intercoms and to the few militiamen who stood before him, 'We are the movements last hope and we will not fail them. We are going to head for the coast of Feiville and as planned we will avenge our brothers and sisters. Most of all restore balance to this world! If history repeats itself, then Emperor Fei's time is coming soon!'

Later on, Boris met with Felix and the rest in the Nautifist's unusually big conning tower, a few things where discussed, and Carl managed to communicate with Silver Serpent, who was busy mobilising what was left of the movement around the world. He and Felix pleaded for Silver to go and fetch Aunt Catherina and Charles, Silver agreed with no resistance. He was to collect them and take them to Eastland.

Silver had taken a few days to arrive in Wobbleton, sneaking into Aunt Catherina's house he came across Jeffrey who he choked from a distance by staring at him till he died. He had found Jeffrey and Charles in the living room. Charles was sobbing, while the television played at the maximum volume. Charles had never met Silver, but his presence began to dry his tears and the young boy's intuition led him to trust Silver, who tapped him on the head and muttered with a smile, 'Wait for me, my boy.' Silver headed to Aunt Catherina's room, whereas he got closer, he heard the groaning sounds of a man, confused and frowning he opened the door and found Eddy on top of Aunt Catherina, who was naked and silent with tears coming down, as she looked into the distance with her chin resting on the pillow. Meanwhile, her backside stuck out bare, sandwiched on top by Eddy.

Silver's presence quickly made Eddy Jump off and rush for his clothing he looked drunk as he stumbled and jumped onto the curtains covering the window, which he smashed with his jump. Wearing nothing but shorts and barefoot he ran away. Silver quickly covered Aunt Catherina, she was speechless and distraught. 'I am here on the behalf of Carl Sobek, I am here to save you and Charles,' said Silver. 'Who...are you?' asked Aunt Catherina as she struggled to speak. 'I am Silver an old friend of Frederick, wash and pack, I will assist Charles,' replied Silver as he left the bedroom.

He assisted Charles in packing the little he could, and when he went back for Aunt Catherina, he saw her this time lying in the bed bleeding, she had grabbed one of the broken glasses from the broken window and stabbed herself.

Crying in pain she looked at Silver and said, 'That bastard...raped me, I brought him up... me and Frederick...he confessed,' pausing as she breathed heavily, 'he told me...it was him that killed Frederick...' Aunt Catherina began to murmur gibberish as she cried moving her head side to side, regathering some of her senses, she muttered to Silver, 'take my life...please, take away this pain, tell Charles I love him...' before she could continue Silver gently placed his hand on her chest closer to the left and a sudden surge of electric current flowing from his lower abdomen went straight to her heart and she suddenly gasped for air as her eyes and mouths widened and then she was dead. Her eyes were now closed, and a smile appeared on her face. 'You are now at peace Catherina,' said Silver.

Silver left the house with Charles who had a bag pack on his back, holding Silver by the hand. 'Your mom killed herself kid...but she told me to tell you she loves you, the pain she carried, a woman does not deserve,' said Silver as he walked away from the house with Charles. 'I can relate sort of, I am also hurting my youngest and only sibling that was alive was murdered,' he added but Charles kept quiet with a blank facial expression.

# CHAPTER SEVENTEEN- THE SWORD OF CARNAGE

A week had passed, and Eddy who was in a state of insanity killed Arrieta Long after making love to her. He had choked her to death with his bare hands and the murder was kept quiet as the mess was cleaned up by a Union Guard General who had visited him, to pass the message that Fei was summoning him.

Eddy had moved to Feiville, living there in an apartment, when he came back from Wobbleton. He had lied to Fei about the events that had occurred in Wobbleton, telling the Emperor he had decided to kill his foster mother and little brother out of hate for the Separatist movement. Eddy said that when he killed Aunt Catherina, Silver had shown up and killed Jeffrey, and he had to run away as he was not on the same level as Silver. Now that he was summoned, he wondered what the Emperor wanted from him.

During the meeting, he realised that the Emperor had summoned him for other reasons. 'Edward...my boy,' began Fei as his eyes pierced through Eddy, 'I have an important task for you, there is an item that will be transported and brought to me. It is a power-ful relic, and if you are successful in protecting it during its transit. I might share some of that power with you.' 'What...' Fei interjected as he said, 'Do not by any means open or try to find out what the item is...I will reveal it to you, depending on how well you carry this task...' pausing Fei continued, 'You and I, are very similar...I see your thirst for power and your ambition.'

Eddy was excited after the meeting, and as he walked the corridors of the Fei tower he bumped into Daniel, who it seemed was going to see Fei. 'Eddy...How are you?' asked Daniel. 'I am all good boss,' replied Eddy candidly, which annoyed Dan-iel who tapped Eddy on the shoulder as he turned away, forcing him to look back at Daniel. 'I would not be too happy if I were you, you think you can replace me,' said Daniel, as he slightly glared at Eddy who stared back at Daniel defiant and unafraid. 'I will be in charge of the security of an item that is being transported here in Feiville...I have already replaced you!' he said as he strolled away. Daniel's heart began to race, he knew what the item was, it had to be the Sword of Carnage he thought.

Sun and his father headed to a bar downtown in Feiville, where they secretly were going to meet with someone. Phoenix did not say who it was and told Sun that he will see who the person was once they arrive at the bar. The individual was a man who hid beneath a hood and was patiently enjoying his whisky, it was Daniel Faris as he revealed himself and then hid back in his hood. Someone else was coming to the bar, Phoenix revealed to Sun. And this person he said was from the Separatist movement. As Phoenix had been in contact with a few of their members.

This Separatist member was none other than Boris Subek, who joined the table where they sat. 'So, let's get to business time is ticking,' he aggressively said, without greeting anyone as he sat. 'Wow,' Daniel Faris gazed at him astonished by his rudeness. 'You heard the man Danny, what is it you want to desperately tell us?' asked Phoenix himself looking impatient. 'The sword,' began Daniel, 'I know you do not trust me, but I have come here to this filthy place, that is probably filled with Separatist loyalists…Anyway, Fei has entrusted Eddy with the security of an important item that is being transported here to Fei.' 'And…' Phoenix paused as he realised, he was raising his voice and brought it back down still sounding angry, 'So you think that is the sword?' 'What else could it be, he was careful not to tell Eddy what the item is, and after my snooping around with some Union Guards, the item will be heavily guarded, and they will be travelling from the outskirts up north of the city,' said Daniel, and all he got was a look of suspicion from Phoenix. 'Uncle...you not bull shitting us, right?' enquired Sun, who expressed signs of trust. 'Look I believe the son of a bitch, I will have my men on it, just give the exact location they will be travelling from,' said Boris as he stood up ready to leave the bar. Daniel gave the rest of the details he had, and the exact location he had retrieved from one of the Union Guards. Then Boris immediately left, once he got what he came for and as Phoenix and Sun were about to leave Daniel said, 'I also want to rid the world of Fei, believe me when I say that.'

Not too far from their table, was another hooded figure who had increased her hearing to a supernatural level, that she heard everything as if it had been directly whispered into her ear. It was Adel Hiss who had been obsessing on how to find the Sword of Carnage and now she knew how.

In a small beach somewhere in Feiville, was Felix and Carl waiting for Silver to arrive with Charles. Once Felix saw them, Charles who was holding Silver's hand let go and rushed towards Felix, who lifted him with a bright smile on his face. Carl grinned at the two and was even happy to see Silver, who had told them of the ordeal Aunt Catherina experienced, and how she wanted to kill herself. After the reunion, they all watched the ocean with its waves crashing as the wind blew.

Boris had selected Felix, James, Rochelle and Drasul, including ten militiamen, to retrieve the item which was believed to be the Sword of Carnage. The group launched their attack on a heavily guarded convoy travelling towards Feiville in the North. Drasul helped with the weakening of the enemy's heavy guard, displaying his ability with awe, he killed the majority of them. One figure popped out though not scared and ready to defend the item, it was Eddy. He had caught a glimpse of a raging and charging Felix who tackled him to the ground and started hitting him, with murderous fists. Each punch carrying with it a murderous intent to kill, with every single blow. Eddy managed somehow to push him off and they both stood up, going at it again, while everybody watched. Eddy threw a front kick and Felix snatched the leg and tripped Eddy. He rushed for Felix as he quickly got up and was stopped by a sudden punch which sent shocking sensations across his body as if he had been tasered. Whimpering, Eddy struggled to get up as Felix spat at him, glaring in disgust. Rochelle drew out her gun pointing it at Eddy, but James lowered her hand as he muttered, 'This is Felix's kill.' Felix strolled towards Eddy and gazed down at his cousin. Then he said as he held back his tears and replaced his feelings with erupting rage, 'You a sick fuck! And you need to die,' Before Felix could stomp Eddy to death, a helicopter appeared out of nowhere.

It was a Union helicopter and it began firing its machine guns, which ripped the grass with dust rising as the bullets pierced the soil and everybody took cover. From a distance Drasul spotted another convoy coming, yelling at James and the rest he said, 'GUYS! I WILL TAKE CARE OF THIS, LEAVE THEY HAVE REINFORCEMENTS!' James heard his uncle clearly and he was not happy as he muttered to himself, 'Dammit why must you always play the hero.'

Accepting fate, James shouted for the rest to go inside their vehicles and as they moved, Drasul began to glow. James somehow knew this time his uncle will sacrifice himself and as they drove off. Drasul's body exploded into pieces, in a beam of electric light that spread out causing the helicopter to crash, the Dragon vanished into a large electromagnetic pulse.

Eddy sniggered, as he finally got up and watched Felix and the rest escape. James wiped a small tear as he looked back, it was war and his uncle's sacrifice allowed them to escape. The electromagnetic shockwave from the explosion, fried the electronic systems of the incoming Union reinforcements causing them to stop. The Separatist were using old vehicles that were not affected by the electronic magnetic pulse.

Retreating from the battle Felix felt like a failure, the supposed Sword of Carnage was right there for them to grasp. When they got back to the Nautifist, Boris did not seem phased by their retreat, instead of with some excitement he spoke of a second plan. 'The Nautifist is a supreme weapon, we will launch various missiles on the outskirts of Feiville causing them to rush to those areas, and then we will launch an all-out assault on the Fei Tower,' he said. 'Fei will vaporise all of us by himself,' objected James. Boris chuckled, causing everybody to frown except Carl and Silver who grinned in silence. 'Is there something we do not know?' asked Felix himself feeling more confused. 'The Slang Nyoka have the sword as we speak, one of their agents stole it and replaced the original with a wooden sword,' said Boris. 'That means we have won!' exclaimed James, as his eyes lit with joy. 'Indeed, Medil will destroy the sword tonight and we will launch our attack tomorrow. We only find out about this, minutes before you guys came back,' said Silver.

The agent from the Slang Nyoka who had stolen the Sword of Carnage was none other than Adel Hiss, baffling the Separatists as to how it was done. Included by this surprise was Medil himself, he had never sent Adel, who revealed to him that she had eavesdropped on him and Silver, hearing about the sword. Medil took the sword to a volcano in the Dragon's Lair, where he threw the sword in a lake of lava, watching it melt. At that moment, a furious Fei found out that the item had been stolen and replaced with a wooden sword. After summoning Eddy, he physically had him off the ground, as he strangled him to his death with his one hand. Back at the volcano, as the sword was completely immersed and gone in the lava, Fei suddenly let go off Eddy who hit the ground gasping for air. He felt a weird and lethargic sensation creep in, as he kneeled on the ground struggling to come up. He knew then that the sword had been destroyed, but what confused him was why was he still alive? The lethargic sensations then vanished, and he quickly stood up looking at his hands. Something was different, his power was not the same and he could feel it was as if the destruction of the sword had taken his power back to the level he had when he was in Tet's body.

Eddy finally managed to stand up as well as he struggled, once he was up, he glanced at Fei and then tried to run but was stopped as he felt an invisible hand choke his throat. 'I may have lost some strength but the people who are equal to me at this level, are all dead,' said Fei and with his lost words, Eddy's lifeless body fell as he was now dead.

Boris and Carl where to stay in the Nautifist and Felix, Rochelle and James and two hundred and fifty of the militiamen, were to launch the attack on the Fei Tower. They were to be joined by other Separatists, led by Silver from around the world that had managed to hide from Fei's grasp.

Sun and Phoenix met with other Guan family

members and to Sun's surprise, Aunt Kelly was there, she explained to him that it was all a farce what she had done, and it was to protect the family. It was all part of the plan, which Phoenix understood. Sun felt a bit foolish and told Aunt Kelly to forgive him for being so blind. It was also communicated that the Guans were going to assist with the attack. Nevertheless, everybody waited for the announcement of Fei's demise, but it did not come. Boris in communications with the rest told them it does not matter the attack had to go on, he was convinced Fei must have been weakened by the destruction of the Sword of Carnage. 'If all else fails we will retreat and I will use the nuclear warheads we have on the Nautifist,' he said sending a cataclysmic ripple as this was something no one had thought about. 'Millions will die!' barked Carl as this was discussed in the conning tower of the Nautifist before the attack. 'It is the last resort and an option I also wish not to consider,' said Boris.

The attack began as was planned, with a couple of missiles landing on the outskirts of the city of Feiville. Prompting Union forces from across the world to gather and set up the immediate surface to air defences. The Feiville police and the few Union Guards around the Fei Tower were caught off guard as the Separatist moved in like a swarm of bees, overwhelming them after a few minutes of gunfire. With snipers firing from unknown locations.

Felix and the rest rushed into the Fei Tower with

Rochelle taking the lead, the elevators were immediately made not operational and the only way up was through the stairs, where they started to meet some resistance. Rochelle, James and a handful of militiamen got stuck fighting in the corridors, while Felix decided to continue to the top floor of the skyscraper where Fei was supposed to be. Shaking his leg as the fatigue from climbing the stairs kicked in, Felix rushed inside the room where he saw Fei waiting for him and the corpse of Eddy.

'Felix Sobek,' began Fei, sneering in tone, 'the Separatist have definitely got me, you guys managed to steal and destroy the Sword of Carnage…the irony is I hated that thing. It is what killed my mother after all.' Felix kept quiet pulling a brave face as he shook inside, Fei was very powerful, and he ignored the voice in his head that told him he was stupid, to have abandoned the others so he could try to challenge Fei by himself. Regardless, he was there now, and he glanced at Eddy's corpse satisfied to see the cousin he once loved, was dead.

'Pull that brave face all you want, but I know deep down inside you are scared,' said Fei and continued, 'before we start this fight, I do not know if you are familiar on how you and I are connected. This whole war is not just an ancient affair, it is also one big family affair.' Felix who kept silent begin to frown and wonder what Fei was getting at. 'My mother was married off to a man from the Sol Islands. He had conquered all the clans in the islands and my mother was a faraway foreigner, to add to his list of concubines. His abusive behaviour caused her to escape from the Sol Islands when she was pregnant with me...' pausing Fei chuckled and then continued, 'She never returned to her original village and instead was accepted in one close to the Dragon's Lair. Do you know who conquered all the clans unifying them in the Sol Islands?' Felix could not believe what he was hearing, and the question asked meant that Fei was a relative. 'That is a tale that is not even recorded in the history books, your direct patrilineal forefather! Felix Subek the First! Was my father and that makes me your great, great, great, great, grand uncle!' Fei's voice rose in tone with hints of anger. 'That bastard sailed the seas searching for my mother, given that the Subeks were fierce pirates who raided coastal towns. Once he had found which village my mother was in, he and his band of filth raided, raped and pillaged the place. The Sword of Carnage came from the Sol Islands. My father had received his revenge by killing my mother.' 'Well all of that is in the past now!' grunted Felix. 'The past,' muttered Fei as he looked down and then glared at Felix who began to choke, and his body felt paralysed.

Busting into the room, appeared Sun and Phoenix. Sun wasted no time as he fired a few shots at Fei who stumbled back, and Felix was free as he breathed heavily. 'You done! You scum!' snarled Phoenix. Fei defiantly got up, looking at his bullet wounds as blood trickled down. 'Boris' prediction was right, destroying the sword has weakened him instead,' said Felix as he finally regained most of his breath. 'Well he dies today,' muttered Sun. Phoenix drew out his hand opening his palm as currents of electricity shot out, zapping Fei who yelled in pain for a couple of seconds and then fell to his death. Phoenix began to sweat and pant as the attack had drained him.

The eight elders of the Union of Nations were liberated, as Fei had them in some form of house arrest and the generals of the Union of Guards were all executed by a firing squad. The elders announced the death of Fei and the restoration of peace around the world. A new system of world governance was being discussed, with what remained of the Separatist movement's leadership. Phoenix had got back with Estelle and Daniel Faris was found dead, he had shot himself, and with his death, Gaia Corp was split into different corporate companies.

Five years had passed, and a twenty-eight-year-old Felix contemplated the craziness of that year, the world was now a different place. The Lei Tai as per his Great Grand Uncle Kek's desire was no longer, it was replaced ironically with combat sports and the world still had some turmoil. However, the greatest of them all was finally gone.

*"After three months of trekking the mountainous region that was the dragon's lair, Daruma had finally come across some Daoist sages of the Fire School. Their movements were slow and then they had fast patterns, finishing off in stillness. Daruma observed this for months and then continued on his trek until he came across the Daoist Sages of the water school. This school, focused on harmonising the body with slow movements, seeking stillness in motion. Here, he introduced them to the Zhan Zhuang technique, the standing meditation of which they gave the name Zhan Zhuang"-Ancient Tales of Daruma, The Wanderer.*

# PART THREE

# SOBEK LEGACY

# CHAPTER EIGHTEEN- A WANDERING BRAWLER

The smoke that fumed out of his cigar started to hurt his eyes and he began to have tears trickle down. He got rid of his cigar as he sat by the bar and wiped his tears. The permanent hawkish facial expression he carried, glanced around with an austere gaze at the rest of the bar's patrons. It was a high-end fancy bar and this man stood out like a sore thumb compared to the rest, who were somehow formally dressed or dazzling in their outfits. He instead wore a faded out black leather jacket, with a red shirt and his hair was black, wild and curly. Accompanied by a thick black beard, covering the bottom of his face. His eyebrows were thick and intimidating, just like the atmosphere of intensity he brought with him. He had a dark complexion with very dark brown eyes. This man was Charles Sobek, but most people who knew him called him Chuck.

Chuck downed the rest of the whiskey he was drinking and felt a bit drowsy as he turned his attention fixed to a voice. The drowsiness was the effect of the booze, but even that could not drown his senses, as he stared at the person whose voice grabbed his attention. This person had appeared on the stage of the bar singing, catching many of the people by surprise with the beauty of her voice and her fascinating physical features. She was a brunette with very light hazel eyes and full lips and had no back-up singer, it was just her voice and the glittering white dress she had on. Chuck had come to see her as she was the one element that softened and calmed the flames that brew inside of him.

When her eyes connected with his, he felt a warmth and he stood up, the inside voice of his mind mocked the feelings or sensations Chuck felt. But he drowned this inside voice, he needed the positivity that evening. Nevertheless, like a sixth sense something caught his attention, a man wearing a fine suit surrounded by bouncers all stared at Chuck. The man in the fine suit and red tie was blonde with greenish eyes. Beardless and well-groomed, he had a tall imposing height. Yet he was not as muscular or stocky like Chuck. This man was Otto Von, a man from a wealthy family and he owned the high-end bar. He and Chuck did not know each other; however, seeds of hate were planted in both men and that evening they had grown and blossomed into lively flowers.

They strolled towards Chuck and Otto began, 'Hi, I assume you know me, I am Otto,' he stretched out his hand for a handshake and Chuck first looked at the hand blankly for a second, before shaking the hand. 'Would you like one more drink?' Otto asked, masking his dislike for Chuck by masquerading it with benevolence. But Chuck could see through him and immediately replied with, 'No thanks, I am on my way.' 'Before you leave my men and I would like a chat with you...in my office,' said Otto. By this time the bouncers had surrounded Chuck who kept his eyes on Otto but was aware of his surroundings. 'I am not going anywhere,' said Chuck as his blood began to boil, he could feel the heat in his ears. 'Well, let me get to the point,' began Otto as his eyes lit up and his head slightly moved forward, 'Helga has complained about you...' Frowning Chuck tried to interrupt but was hushed by Otto, who raised his finger and continued, 'I do not care, since you not going to have one more drink. I want you to leave my establishment and never come back.' His last words were heard, but Chuck cast a look at Helga, the woman singing. She stared back and could notice what was going on but continued singing this time with more focus on her performance.

Chuck sighed and looked at the ground before casting a glaring look at Otto, 'You introduced yourself, but you clearly don't know who I am,' he said. 'Who gives a shit!' grunted Otto taking a step closer. A split second later, he was holding his throat as he stumbled back making choking noises. Chuck had struck his throat and the bouncers froze before they could react. 'I am the devil and you better give a shit!' snarled Chuck. With those last words before the bouncers could seize him, he was on the offensive. Thirty seconds in and he was done with them, as they groaned struggling to get up. The rest of the patrons stared in shock and silence. Helga had suddenly made her way off the stage and rushed for Otto.

'Are you alright?' she asked, frowning anxiously as she held Otto. Gathering some strength as he gently cleared his throat, he glanced back at her and then pulled on a brave face. He glared at Chuck who was strolling towards one of the exits. Full of rage, Otto sprinted for Chuck as he bellowed, 'COME BACK HERE! I AM NOT DONE WITH YOU!' Once he was close, he lunged with a hook from behind. A grinning Chuck went low dodging the blow and like a coiling snake, he immediately turned around punching Otto in the abdomen. Otto slightly hopped up as he stumbled backwards. His eyes were wide open in disbelief as the pain built up and he gasped for air, causing him to kneel on his knees.

'A little more dosage on that punch and I would have ruptured your spleen, perforated your small intestines...listen, rich boy...I am not one to be fucked with,' those were Chuck's last words as he turned back and strolled towards the exit, finally leaving the bar.

Charles "Chuck" Sobek was a member of the Sobek family, a martial arts family whose original family name was Subek. Members of the family who resided in the Sol Islands the family's original home still used the "Subek" name. The family's martial art was called, "The Harmonious Fist," an ancient martial arts system, thought to be the first martial art. Put together and founded by Daruma who also came from the Sol Islands. The legend is that after his odyssey around the world, Daruma had compiled all the knowledge he had gathered and with the Sol Islands' traditional standing meditation he created the Harmonious Fist. His brother in law was a Subek, and Daruma passed the knowledge down to his brother in law. This was how the Subeks or Sobeks came to inherit the Harmonious Fist. Felix Sobek, Chuck's older cousin had trained Chuck in the ways of the Harmonious Fist. But once Chuck was eighteen years of age, the two had a major fall out resulting in Chuck leaving his cousin and setting his path in life. This was seven years ago, Chuck was now twenty-five years of age and he had become a hound for the underworld. If he did not have a job to do, he would wander the streets picking fights or engage in duels, fighting was in his blood.

# CHAPTER NINETEEN- DAILY PERILS

Deep in his sleep and the depths of his mind, Chuck saw images of his seven-year-old self. There in his dream, he caught a glimpse of a woman. She was a brunette with short hair and greyish eyes, she beamed at the young Chuck, calling him, 'Charles,' and the young Chuck responded with, 'Mom.' Another person appeared, a black man with thick eyebrows, looking stern yet with a hidden smile that made the young Chuck beam at him.

The man was Chuck's father Frederick Sobek and his mother was Catherina Sobek. Another figure appeared, a young man with short blonde hair and piercing blue eyes, he smiled at the young Chuck and the young Chuck did not smile back. The presence of this figure instead brought crippling fear into the young Chuck. Feeling a deep sense of distress, the young Chuck started to run. He heard a gunshot and the yells of a woman getting raped, he hated that he was running, he hated himself. Chuck kept screaming at the young Chuck to turn around, but he did not and then in a sudden, Chuck's eyes popped open as he woke up from his dream. Sighing, he muttered, 'I was weak,' and with a wry smile he sprung out of his bed.

It was morning time and the sun had not risen yet, Chuck immediately began stretching, unwinding himself for about forty minutes before getting into a horse stance. With his thighs positioned ninety degrees to the ground, he crouched down and remained standing till the first sound of the morning birds. A bit of sweat was evidence to the gruelling exercise of standing in a horse stance, feeling empty and calm. He moved on to doing push-ups and various other exercises before having a quick shower.

The people he was hired to work for, had set him up with a room in one of the hotels they owned, in the bustling city of Feiville. Being a proud vagabond, the luxury did not amaze Chuck, although he did not refuse the hospitality when it was offered. At least he now had a decent place to take women or prostitutes to, to spend the evening with. After his quick cold shower, he made his way to the hotel lobby where he was to meet with a man dressed in a suit who waited seated in a table. The man quickly got up when he caught a glimpse of Chuck, the two shook hands before Chuck took a seat.

This man had the same skin tone as Chuck, with slightly wide eyes and few creases in his eyelids. His eyes were yellow like a wolf and he had a short goatee for a beard.

The man enjoyed a small cup of green hot liquid that was matcha and still hot, there was a second cup of black sugarless coffee. This cup was for Chuck and he immediately helped himself to it as the man gazed at him with a slight frown. 'What?' asked Chuck. 'How do you know if I did not poison you?' remarked the man. 'I am reckless and foolish I guess...like the caffeine that is now circulating through my veins,' answered Chuck nonchalantly as he took another sip of his cup, shrugging his shoulders as he gazed at the man. 'You definitely are...we have heard of your troubles with a prominent member of the Von family,' sneered the man, causing Chuck's eyes to flare up. Nevertheless, controlling the surge of adrenaline that pumped in his blood, he calmly said, 'I am a free agent...' pausing as the man interrupted him, Chuck hushed him as he raised his hand and continued, 'I am about to squeeze you like a zit...now like I was saying, I am not an assassin, although I may get rid of your organisation's headaches. I simply get shit done, most of the time using my martial skills. I am not from the Slang Nyoka, I am not a professional assassin,' with those last words Chuck took his last sip of coffee and stood up ready to leave. However, the man had one more question, 'So what are you then?' Chuck who had his back turned ready to leave, turned around immediately and said, 'I am a martial artist, a wandering vagabond and a warrior for hire.' After his response Chuck left, making his way to the exit door of the hotel.

Hours later, away from the prominent areas of Feiville and further downtown, inside an empty bar, below in its cellar, were two men taking on one man. The cellar was large enough to house a crowd that cheered them on, it was lit by burning lamps attached to the walls. The fight had just begun, and the two men were twice the size of what seemed to be a prey to them. Their supposed prey was the other man and he was not puny in stature in his own right. He took the liberty of simply dodging their blows. Moving around in the confined space that the crowd had freed up for the brawl to take place. The two men had suddenly become frustrated with their opponent. Seconds had already passed, and he ridiculed them with his evasiveness, gently tapping them as a reminder he could deliver blows at will.

The crowd were entertained but many were also disappointed, the bout had the two men as favourites and the majority in the crowd had placed their bets on them winning. Struggling to get a finger on the supposed underdog who was Chuck, one of the men launched themselves at his legs, catching him by surprise as they tackled him to the ground.

Chuck then ferociously begun to swing at the man's face who tucked it down as the fists landed at the back of his head. The other men then rushed in, Chuck who was aware of this, used his pelvic area to shove the man who was on the top forward and using other manoeuvres swapped their positions. He was now on top and his tackler at the bottom. Chuck quickly stood up and took a step backwards muttering, 'Playtime is over'. Both men at this time looked tired and desperate as they stared at Chuck panting. A large part of the crowd was now booing at them and they glanced at each other gritting their teeth and then grunted as they rushed for Chuck again. This time his evasive footwork accompanied a counter-assault of savage proportion as he finished them both with straight vertical punches to their foreheads. It brought them to an abrupt stop, putting them on the ground with their hands and feet first sticking in the air before falling like the rest of their bodies. The act had brought a sudden silence amongst the crowd as they gazed in disbelief and Chuck looked around smirking gleefully.

After the fight, Chuck collected his winnings in a brown paper bag filled with cash, 'Not bad, next time I will take on three men,' he said when the money was given to him and the response was a sneer from the man who gave him the money. Chuck then marched away and once he was out of the bar, a gang of men waited for him outside, with one of them pointing a pistol at Chuck.

'We not losing our cash so easily, you scum! We are going to take our betting money back and including the extra,' said one of the men amongst the gang as the other chuckled to his words. He seemed to have been their leader. By this time Chuck was trying to control his heartbeat and was deciding whether to fight, hand the money or run in the hope that the man pointing the pistol would miss. Besides that, it would not surprise him if they still killed him, even after he had given them the money. Nevertheless, in that moment of thought a parked white van's door had flung open and the man who Chuck had spoken to from the hotel, sprung out with a gun and a silencer attached to it. The man indiscriminately started to fire away, the first person to hit the ground was the man pointing the gun at Chuck. His shots were so accurate with each bullet being fired ended in or through the skulls of the gang's members. He had only fired four shots and with four dead the rest scurried away in different directions like quick crawling ants.

'Impressive, I think it's time I asked you your name,' said Chuck. The man had made a scoffing sound and replied, 'You never asked before besides, unlike you...I like to be nameless,' After saying that he turned to two other men that had stepped out of the white van and said, 'Call clean up.' 'Well thank you anyway, Mr Nameless,' said Chuck. 'It's a pleasure, just do not count on it, next time. Also, I would advise you to get a gun, given your daily perils. Anyway, cutting to the chase I am here because the boss, Gringer Solace has summoned you. We do not have time to waste let's go.'

# CHAPTER TWENTY- A NEPHEW'S REVENGE

Seven years in the past, in a remote mountainous area far from the city of Wobbleton, was a bald black man whose skin tone was like black coffee with a few drops of milk. He had a thick black beard and eyebrows, a common physical trait found in his family. This man was Felix Sobek, who stood half-naked on top of a boulder. Exposing his lean and muscular features to nature, as the sun fried him darker with its scorching heat. Sweat dripped down both side of his arms, coming down from the shoulders and passing his tattoos.

The tattoos were trigrams, the one on the right had two solid lines with one broken one in the middle. On the left hand, it was the opposite, it had one solid line in the middle. The trigram on the right symbolised fire and the one of the left symbolised water. The tattoos were ancient Daoist tri-grams that referred to balancing the two elements within oneself, these symbols were found in most martial arts of the world. But it was especially central to the Sobek or Subek clan's Harmonious Fist.

Felix stood a shoulder-width apart, with his hands up as if he was embracing the air or holding a large ball. His hands were in line with his shoulders and his eyes were open and looking down at a forty-five-degree angle.

Not far from Felix, was an eighteen-year-old Charles Sobek, not known as "Chuck" then and he was drilling through forms. Forms in martial arts were a standardised version of shadow boxing systematically throwing punches and kicks. With hidden applications of grappling and wrestling.

A cool random breeze appeared, not disturbing Felix, however, what caught his attention was the sudden appearance of a figure. The timing was perfect because Felix was done with his meditation, but Charles had stopped his training and was now staring at the figure that had appeared.

The figure was a man dressed in Union Guard brown fatigues. Wearing a red beret with a yellow star in its centre. This was an indication that he was part of the Union Guards' elite special forces unit. One of the few still functioning things in what was a defunct Union of Nations. The man was sprinting fast as if his life depended on it. Nearly stumbling to a fall in his endeavour. Felix and Charles just stared at this point. With frowns on their faces.

The man took a few minutes to get close to Felix as he gasped for air. Charles had simply strolled towards the man, whose attention was fixed on Felix who remained standing up on the boulder.

'Commander,' began the union guard with a salute, 'I have very horrible news, your father...he was found dead! Assassination style!' Felix remained unfazed and calm by the news as for Charles his eyes widened and with boiling questions he asked as his voice rose in tone, 'What you mean his dead!?' The union guard turned to look at Charles finally noticing him. 'We do not know much, it could be anything from an international syndicate group, to simple upstart hoodlums, in Wobbleton.'

Felix jumped off the boulder, landing as his knees bent and he gently straightened himself up and then began to speak, 'I told my father to live a peaceful existence in our original home...the Solese Islands. But he refused, he had to be "the Baron".' After those words, Felix had a wry smile and then chuckled. 'The fuck! What!? Is that supposed to be another one of your sick Daoist impressions! My uncle! Your father was killed, and you sit here calm as if...' Charles words drowned as he tried to control his fury, which pumped in his veins. Felix gazed at him with a slight frown and a look of indifference. 'Leave us and thank you for the information, I will make arrangements for the funeral at once,' he said. The union guard was also shocked by the lack of emotion from Felix, Charles glared at him as he searched for any sign of emotion in Felix's blank eyes.

Felix and Charles had headed back to Wobbleton, where the funeral was held for Carl Sobek, Felix's father and Charles' uncle. Carl Sobek's body was cremated and some of his ashes cast to the sea, what remained of it was buried in an urn, next to Virginia Sobek, Felix's mother. Amongst the people who came to the funeral was Boris Subek, a member of the original branch of the family from the Solese Islands, he was Felix and Charles' uncle.

Silver Serpent had also come to the funeral, he was a close friend of Charles' Father, Frederick Sobek who was Carl Sobek's older brother. Silver was pardoned by the Union of Nations after the war. Before the war and his membership to the Separatist Movement. Silver of the Slang Nyoka clan had infamously killed five hundred men through deadly duels.

'So, who in the underworld wanted your father killed?' asked Silver with no reserve. 'We still do not know,' answered Felix.

After the funeral, there was a gathering at Carl Sobek's mansion. The mansion was damaged during the return and reign of Emperor Fei and during the war after the fall of the emperor. Felix had managed to put it back together during the years of peace.

'So how will you handle matters?' asked Boris Subek, raising his thick eyebrows with a mild frown on his face. Felix sighed a little before responding to everyone's surprise, 'Nothing.' Charles cast him a glance of disgust, which he ignored and continued, 'As we all know, The Baron as he was known to his foes and associates has passed. Yes, he was my father and although I make look or appear to be unaffected by his passing. Trust me when I say, I am. However, I need to stop this vicious cycle in our family, Subek or Sobek. My father was killed based on the unwritten rules of the underworld of crime, a life that he did not want to retire from after the war. I rather let justice take its course, then to take matters in my own hands. Over the years studying my family's history and its martial art and way, The Harmonious Fist. I have come to conclude that my family has never reached the high levels that one should achieve or do his or her best to achieve, that is complete harmony with oneself. The founder Daruma had achieved this level and he was poisoned by his student, the man who coined and gave the name to our family art, Sung Subek. Since that day, powerful martial artists we have had over the generations but none amongst us even me reached harmony. What has happened to my father was just a matter of time. I accept this truth, there is no need to avenge him...' seething in a pot full of fury, Charles scowled at his cousin, no longer able to hear Felix's words as they drowned away and then he exploded,

'CUT THE CRAP!'

Charles shot up from his seat, his breathing slightly heavy, 'I will find the killers and I will kill them!' he grunted, as his eyes shot open and moved around staring at all the guests before returning to Felix. 'You and I are done!' after his last words, Charles left in a fury.

It took months before Charles tracked down the man who had ordered the killing of his uncle. Charles wasted no time in making his move upon his discovery, wielding nothing but his bare hands he beat the man to death, including the man's henchmen. His revenge fell upon the culprits like a message from hell during a cold Wobbleton evening. It was then that he was discovered by Gringer Solace who happened to be the boss of the man who had killed Carl Sobek. Gringer Solace it appeared was not aware of the killing of Carl, and he was surprised to hear that one of his captains in Wobbleton, was killed by one man who happened to be an eighteen-year-old. It was then that Charles who was then to be known as Chuck began to offer his services as a mercenary for the underworld.

# CHAPTER TWENTY-ONE- MAKING AMENDS

Charles had fallen to a slight slumber after riding in the white van for twenty minutes, in that drowsy and half-asleep state he had a mild contemplation of his life and then a random flashback of Felix lecturing him.

There was one thing that his cousin once said to him that stuck and Chuck could recall each of Felix's words, "*The lone wolf does not seek refuge, he is a refuge. He does not seek out the community. He is a community. Now melancholy might settle, and weakness may creep in. So, he seeks advice from the other lone wolves. Regardless, whatever may be the trouble, the lone wolf knows better than to blame the external first. Instead in true Daoist nature examines himself first!*".

'We here,' the man tapped Charles on his shoulder's as his eyes shot open before he slightly yawned and rubbed his eyes. The air was fresh and cool, soothing his nostrils as he breathed and glimpsed around him. Gringer Solace lived in a villa in the hills not too far from the city of Feiville, surrounded by vineyards. The villa was heavily guarded with men in suits marauding around heavily armed.

'Are you still not going to tell me your name?' Chuck had turned to the man who he had the meeting with earlier in the hotel, and who had shot the men that wanted his winnings from the fight he had won. Smirking, Chuck waited for a reply and the man smirked back and said, 'Mr S'. 'Wow, S for shots...I will call you Mr Shots...better yet...just Shots,' Charles immediately responded, but was ignored by Mr S who just smirked gleefully and began to stroll away. Chuck cleared his throat and followed Mr S as a mild glare invaded his face, it was time to meet Gringer Solace.

Mr S who was joined by a group of armed men led Chuck to Gringer Solace's large open office. The door was open with two guards inside, guarding their boss Gringer who was busy going through empty hand forms. Half-naked with black martial loose-fitting trousers, Gringer Solace was a man in good physique as the rest watched him throw kicks with his bare feet and punches that displaced the air like small gusts of wind. He was tall with reddish hair and clear blue eyes, with an unshaven chin. Chuck knew that the "boss" was also a martial artist, something that made Chuck mutually respect Gringer and in turn also made Gringer respect Chuck.

It took him a few seconds to be done and so deeply did he appear to be concentrated, that it felt as if he had just woken up, as he glanced at Chuck and Mr S. Gringer snapped his fingers and one of the guards approached him with a small towel, which he took and gently wiped his sweat off before strolling towards Chuck and Mr S. He glanced at Mr S as they nodded at each other and then he turned his attention to Chuck, and with a mild smirk they shook hands, 'Chuck! How you?' he asked while maintaining his tight grip with a penetrating gaze. Chuck did not budge nor feel intimidated, he maintained his handshake without responding to the crushing gripping force of Gringer. Yielding in some way, yet not retreating neither. 'I am good,' Chuck replied.

After the handshake, Gringer turned to one of his men slightly nodding, the man returned the nod and immediately left the room, only to return a few seconds later. This time with two other people, Charles immediately recognised them. It was Helga and Otto Von, Charles felt his heart sink intuitively knowing he had to make amends for his raucous actions at Otto's bar the day before. However, what made his heart drop even further was the presence of Helga, her beauty stole his gaze for a few seconds longer and when their eyes met, Charles could feel the pump of his heartbeat in his throat. She only acknowledged him with a glance, and then looked down at the ground as she tilted her head.

'Great! Let's wrap this up!' began Gringer as he looked both at Otto and Charles. Then his eyes rested on Charles, 'You fucked up this time Chuck, the Von family are one of my business partners whose loyalty and allegiance I greatly appreciate and cannot simply let go down the drain...' pausing Gringer sighed and continued, 'I have managed to douse the flames you created kid, as you know I once served under your cousin Felix Sobek when we hunted what remained of the Brotherhood...ah the good old days, it has been decided Chuck, instead of your head being served, you will make amends instead. How? Simple, your freedom of being a free agent is over, you will be working for me only. You will be reporting to Mr S, now do not think I am stupid we know what you capable of...' as his words drowned to a pause, Gringer gazed at Otto who had a permanent smirk on his face the whole time. Otto then took over, aggressively grabbing hold of Helga who made a slight moaning noise as a form of resistance yet looked helpless. He pulled her in front of him and then had his arm around her neck as he breathed on her from behind. Otto then begun molesting her, his hands sliding up, till he squeezed one of her breasts. Looking at Charles he said, 'I know how much you love this whore, so I will gladly slit her throat on Gringer's behalf next time you fuck up,' and with those words, he shoved Helga away as she fell forward. Looking distraught she dared not to shed a tear, as she held on to whatever was left of her courage.

Charles responded with a blank stare at Otto who stared back smirking. 'He has understood, you may go now,' said Gringer as he glanced at Charles, whose eyes remained on Otto as if they were the only two in the room. Gringer could sense the volcano was seconds from erupting, even though he had finally had what he always wanted Charles under his thumb, he knew his new pet had a nasty bite.

Otto and Helga left as they were led away by one of Gringer's men and once they were gone, Mr S began to speak, 'Do not get fooled by the damsel in distress, to save her family's debt-ridden, high-end bar, she failed miserably to seduce Otto, who resolved her problems and enslaved her in the process. Her charms, her beauty that is her weapon, if you do not cure yourself of her poison you will end up one of her victims. Otto is already one, where you seek to conquer her heart, he seeks to possess her. You both seek!' Those words sounded like something Felix would say and for a moment Charles thought of his cousin and then he responded as he looked at Gringer, 'Great, now I am reporting to this Daoist philosopher.' Gringer simply chuckled and then cleared his throat, 'I have a task for you, the first step in you making your amends for your wrongs I want you to head to a small town in the Sud-West Republics, I need you to get rid of a little problem for me. Mr S will brief you on the rest,' he said and as he left, he added, 'I have meetings to attend to, Chuck, don't mess up.'

# CHAPTER TWENTY-TWO- THE LAARI BASTARD

In the small town of Mbanza Laari, a village found in the Sud-West Republics. Was the Laari family, of which the small town or village was named after. Back in the old days, the Laari family's original patriarch was a king of the Laari Kingdom that stretched out in most of the Sud-West Republics before being conquered by the Sud Empire. The Laaris were an ancient family that had become a prominent patrician like family in modern times.

Although residing in Mbanza Laari, the main branch of the family was still very wealthy and living a very quiet life in the village. Nzonzi Laari the current patriarch and de-facto chief of the village oversaw a large vineyard, which produced the family's signature iconic red wines. In the vineyard, there was also a large inn, with the small town's biggest restaurant, "Madia".

Nzonzi Laari was the father of two boys, who were a year apart in age, their names were Dioko and Nimi. Dioko was the eldest and besides having two boys, Nzonzi and his wife Maria had adopted a second boy by the name of Lukeni. Lukeni was the son of Nzonzi's younger sister Nzinga who had died giving birth to him. No one knew who Lukeni's father was and Nzinga shamefully kept quiet only giving brief descriptions of the man. Although she did reveal to her older brother that she had been raped.

His sister, in her stubbornness and longing for adventure, had left the family when she was twenty years old. Taking nothing but some clothes, her beauty and wit, as she ventured off to Eastland ending in that country's biggest city and bustling metropolis, Feiville. There like most young girls seeking a fast life, ended up as a prostitute. Once she had discovered she was pregnant, to protect her baby, she made contact with her older brother who had dishonoured her. However reluctant he was to assist his sister, Nzonzi used his contacts to help his sister escape.

She lived far from Mbanza Laari, close to the middle of nowhere until the day came for her to give birth. A nurse was there that day to assist her, hired by Nzonzi. However, Nzinga did not make it and died. The baby, Lukeni was born and different from most Laari family members, his skin was lighter meaning his father must have been of white or lighter skin. As his mother's skin was like the darkest of chocolates. His eyes were light blue when he was a baby within a year of turning one year old, they were hazel with a touch of green. His eyelids hads some crease although wide, an indication of how his father might have looked like. Nzonzi never directly showed any affection to Lukeni, a man with anger like the memory of an elephant, Nzonzi had transferred the anger he felt for his sister towards her son. However, in a twist of his emotions, he felt it necessary as the patriarch of the family to do at least the minimum for the wellbeing of Lukeni.

One of the traditions of the family was that the men had to learn the family's martial art known as "Ngolo," which in the Laari language meant, 'strength or power'. It was not an obligation for the women to learn and Nzonzi like every patriarch before him was an expert. The martial art was founded by Kipura Laari, the founder of the Laari clan. His inspiration came from observing the animals in the area such as the zebra, and its kicks. One of the features of this art was deceptive movements of moving side to side and seizing the opportunity to uproot your opponent. By taking them done and finishing them off. The purpose of the martial art was not just for self-defence, but most important of all was to connect with the ancestors through the body and to train one's spirit. In modern times, like most if not all martial arts this translated to connecting the body and the mind as one.

Lukeni, however, was not fortunate despite being a member of the family, to be taught this art, science and philosophy. When his cousins were six and seven and were being taught for the first time by their father, Nzonzi lashed out at the then four-year-old Lukeni, shaking him beyond belief, that he did not dare ever try to make himself visible during Nzonzi's tutoring of the martial art, the words still rang loud in Lukeni's mind over the years, 'What are you doing here! What are you doing here! You are bastard! I feed you! clothe you! What more do you want! They know you out there as the Laari Bastard...You are born of filth and disgrace!' Each word cut the young four-year-old Lukeni to the core. His eyes remained wide open, it was his aunt Maria that had come in frowning in disbelief. She did not bother uttering a word to her husband but simply cast him a look of disapproval and then turned to Lukeni grabbing him by the hand and dragged him away. Tears only trickled out later as she caressed his forehead. It was only one of the few times his aunt showed tenderness to him. Her calm brought down the heat, condensing the steam and letting the tears pour down like the rain. She never showed signs of hate towards Lukeni, but he will learn over the years that his aunt did not share the same love she had for her sons towards him. It was only her female motherly tenderness that he got, the same one any other child in the village would receive from Maria.

Nevertheless, Lukeni kept a kindness to him, the ordeal and the pain never shattered his innocence, which was an air of candidness he had about him. He was simply kind and appeared naïve to those who felt sorry for him and stupid to those who loathed him.

# CHAPTER TWENTY-THREE-MEETING THE TIGER

When he was seven years of age Lukeni was summoned by uncle Nzonzi, and he wondered fearfully what punishment will befall him. It was outside the restaurant of the vineyard and on that day, he caught a glimpse of two men, one was black and bald with a thick black beard and the other had narrow eyes with a bit crease in his eyelids. He was lighter of complexion and bald too. The lighter skin of complexion man had a sturdy presence and was slightly shorter than the black man and very muscular in stature with big forearms that were exposed by his rolled-up sleeves. With them was a fourteen-year young man with bushy black hair and a pubescent growing beard that had gone through its fiftieth shave.

'Here he is,' said Nzonzi looking at his nephew in disgust once Lukeni appeared. The muscular man not surprised by the treatment glared at Nzonzi and then covered his face with a smile as he glanced at Lukeni who timidly stared at everyone. 'How are you? Young man?' asked the muscular man. Lukeni simply responded with a nod and a facial expression that made a bad attempt at a smile.

'The Brotherhood has been officially eradicated,' began the black man as he glanced at Lukeni, 'however, it would be safe to protect this boy for longer, no one else besides Wong Claw over here and I Felix Sobek know of this child's whereabouts. Our unit is now disbanded but one of the guys I am angry to say has been converted to the remnants of the Brotherhood's ideology.' Nzonzi sighed once the black man who was Felix ended his words, and Nzonzi then spoke, 'Felix with all respect to you and your family and everything you have done for this world. I do not give a fuck! I am simply focusing on this abomination that my sister brought into this world!' His voice rose in tone as he spoke boiling the lighter of complexion man who was Wong Claw. 'You piece...' Wong Claw's words were frozen by a calming gesture from Felix. And then Nzonzi added, 'The real father is you! You raped my sister you scum! And you,' pausing his eyes narrowing them down on Felix, 'are a liar, lying to me about who the father really is and this whole story about the brother...' the words seized as an infuriated Wong Claw shot his eyes wide open and attempted grabbing Nzonzi, who went into a focus mode putting one leg back ready for the assault that was coming his way. Felix was holding Wong back and struggling. 'Let me go! Commander! This piece of shit will experience my Tiger Claw!' yelled Wong in a berserker-like fashion. 'Come at me boy! And I will make you pay for everything,' Nzonzi calmly said with a mild sneer and grin painting itself on his face. 'WONG! Nzinga would not have wished for this,' said Felix and those words soothed Wong immediately making him go on his knees. As he calmly panted away and wiped his eyes immediately. 'Look at you pathetic, like this boy and weak!' snarled Nzonzi.

Felix glanced at Nzonzi and then set his eyes on Wong, 'It's okay old friend you have been holding a lot of pain over these years, but always remember the love you and Nzinga shared.' Wong was silent and sniffed once in response as he knelt with his head done. He then looked up at the bedazzled Lukeni and a smile appeared on his face. And then in a surge of courage he quickly got up and stared at Nzonzi, 'I am taking the kid, he will be under my protection. I sense the abuse you have put him through, and no child deserves this.' 'You will not take him!' exclaimed Nzonzi, 'his...his...his...' the words struggled to come out and Felix jumped in, 'His what? Come now, we did not come to fight clearly this child has been a burden. We have not realised how much a burden the whole ordeal has been for you that we have not formally thanked you. I have fifty thousand Dinares...' Nzonzi interrupted and said, 'I do not need your money.' 'The kid comes with me, I will train him and raise him to be a man,' said Wong. 'Come now, Nzonzi be reasonable,' pleaded Felix. Nzonzi looked at the bushy-haired fourteen-year-old who watched the whole spectacle crossed armed and calm. The young man looked back straight not phased and not smiling either. 'Who is that?' asked Nzonzi, pointing at the young man. 'I am Charles Sobek, his cousin,' the young man immediately answered, uncrossing his arms and staring at Nzonzi with more intensity. Nzonzi grinned at this reaction and then he said as he turned to Wong, 'Take the kid and get out of my sight.'

That day the seven-year-old Lukeni was taken to live with Wong Claw, who had set up shop in the small town of Mbanza Laari as a silk producer an ancient family tradition of his. However, originally his career of which he retired when he adopted Lukeni, was being part of an elite team of Union Guards that were put together during the great world war that started after the fall of Emperor Fei.

The Union of Nations weakened during the war trying to keep the eight nations together with the help of the Separatists. However, after the end, it came out a weaker institution then what it was before. But the elite team of Union Guards led by Felix Sobek was a tight-knit unit that had the main mission of seeking out remnants of the Brotherhood and destroying them. Part of the weakness of the Union of the Nations after the war was the infestation of Brotherhood members that needed to be removed. The elite unit removed them primarily by death without trial.

Wong Claw was a practitioner of the "Tiger Claw style", a style that was an offshoot of the Tiger Style with an emphasis on its joint locks. An external martial art in its very beginning and the deception of brute force being a basis behind the movement of the style. But in fact, its mastery like all complete martial art styles was internal. And Wong Claw's movements were further influenced by Felix's "Harmonious Fist". Using the Harmonious Fist's standing meditation as a foundation in his Tiger Claw style.

Lukeni was very timid at first and Wong Claw was gentle with him for the first few months as they lived together and Lukeni then started to become more open and within three months the martial training began.

Lukeni was nervous his first training session, Wong who had been patient for far too long slapped him across the face. He fell on the ground immediately crying and Wong sighed before he began to speak strolling back and forth, 'This my boy is about life and death...There is a lot I wish to tell you and I cannot, not yet. For now, I need to train you because there will come a time when you will need to protect yourself. And do you want the world to keep pushing you around without you putting up a fight and getting back up? Honour the blood that is coursing through your veins.' Those last words had a sniffing Lukeni look up, with rage and tears in his face. Wong paused with a slight intrigue waiting for what was going to happen next. Lukeni charged for him and got slapped back into the ground when he was within range. Slowly getting back this time with the tears drying up and the rage had completely taken over. In that sudden moment, Lukeni heard a voice inside of him, it calmed him down a little and he felt the pleasant sensation of blood flowing smoothly through his body.

The voice that spoke in his head was sniggering and then started to slightly grunt in anger until it finally spoke sensible words, it was the voice of a man Lukeni had never heard, 'It's not your fault my son. You are more powerful than you think you know. There is a little I can do now but let me take over.' The words so reassuring that Lukeni immediately sighed surrendering to those words, that felt like hope. His face suddenly had a blank expression and he seemed to be looking through Wong, who had noticed the air of strangeness surrounding the boy. Stranger than that was Lukeni's eyes which went from being greenish and a bit brown to changing to a piercing light blue. 'His inside of him,' muttered Wong in astonishment. By this time, Lukeni stretched his hand, slightly pulling the wrist as currents of electricity violently sparked out and within a millisecond shot out towards Wong, who took the hit, gritting his teeth in pain. He closed his eyes sighing and imagined everything had hit the ground, including the unbearable pain. And then he felt something rise back up as his eyes shot open and Lukeni felt a sudden rebound of energy that knocked him meters back.

Wong knelt to the ground panting slightly before pulling himself back up and he strolled towards Lukeni, who now lay on the floor unconscious. 'You definitely are his son,' muttered Wong.

That incident was never spoken of again, Lukeni remembered it, yet he did not dwell on this over the years as he lived with Wong who trained him in the ways of the Tiger Claw. Lukeni struggled despite the episode that had occurred in his training in the beginning. The one thing he had that was astonishing was his latent brute strength. And regardless of the martial skill he later attained, Lukeni kept being his candid self a trait that Wong will tell him was uniquely Lukeni's and that not even his mom had this trait.

Wong would become to be the father Lukeni never had, he wished that Wong was his biological father.

Ten years had passed and Lukeni now a seven-teen-year-old young man was sturdy and strong in presence with the candid smile he always carried. He had grown to be tall and looked formidable in physique, his kind nature came like a shock of a surprise to people who first met him.

One day he caught a glimpse of a sad Wong deep and pondering in a pool of stressful thoughts. 'What is the matter, Uncle?' asked Lukeni. Instead, he got a wry smile as a response.

Wong then said sounding calm, 'I need to head out of Mbanza Laari to one of the small towns far from here...' Lukeni then interrupted, 'Where?' waiting with a mild frown for an answer he did not receive. Wong simply walked away and after four steps he turned around and muttered, 'if I am not back by the next day, head to you uncle Nzonzi. And do not hesitate, he will understand believe it or not.' Those were Wong's final words as he turned back and left.

Ten hours away from Mbanza Laari Wong met with two men at a diner, the sun was slowly setting. It was at a nameless smaller town then Mbanza Laari, with a population of a few hundred people.

They sat at a table covered in the ambience of the coffee smell that oozed out their cups. Each one drinking black coffee. 'So, we meet again Gringer,' began Wong after sipping his cup of coffee, 'So what is it you want?' Finishing his words, he gazed at Gringer's reddish hair and then turned to look at the other man who sat next to Gringer. 'Who is he one of your goons?' Wong added. Gringer leaned back sighing before replying, 'His one of my men.' 'I am Shadow, Shadow Chan but you can call me Mr Shadow or Mr S...or just S,' said the man calmly as he took a sip of his coffee, gently putting his cup down afterwards as he looked straight into Wong's eyes. 'Let's get straight to business where is the kid?' asked an impatient Gringer as he leaned forward.' 'I am not telling you anything, you cock sucker!' Wong stood up fuming and he continued, 'Years ago we eliminated the brotherhood and we were not saints, but we were putting order where there was chaos! But you were more obsessed with power!'

Sighing he continued his rant, 'What now! You really think you can gather the power of Fei by having the boy. You really were brainwashed by the remnants of the Brotherhood's propaganda, un-believable.' Gringer was silent for a few seconds slowly getting up and then his face glared back at Wong. Mr S stood up later as well both looking at Wong who glared back.

'This will only end in blood,' grunted Wong and in that sudden, his hand had gathered his cup splash-ing the bit of coffee that was left on the cup at Gringer. Then he lifted the table, knocking both men. In that space of a moment Wong dashed for the door, once he was out of the diner, an army of men in suits was waiting for him, they were armed and pointing their guns at him.

He turned around and saw an angry Gringer with

coffee stains on his chest and a calm Mr S by his side. A wry smile appeared on Wong's face as he gazed at them knowing Gringer would not take him on hand to hand combat. He turned back and charged at the suited-up men, as they all fired at him, the first few bullets only slowed his momentum, but he had managed to grab one of them ripping their throat with his tiger claw. And later he fell, bloodied and dead with a smile on his face as his eyes lowered to a close.

# CHAPTER TWENTY-FOUR- CONNECTED BY BLOOD

Nzonzi had visited Lukeni the day after Wong's death to Lukeni's astonishment. With a blank facial expression, he bluntly said, 'Wong has been killed, you are coming back to live with me. Pack your clothes let's go.' Lukeni felt a sinking sensation and that had been there the day of Wong's departure, however, it had completed its downward sensation with the news that Nzonzi had brought.

He did not resist nor argue or even ask to find out what happened. The questions were there rising with his blood as it boiled. A brief glare and sentiments of hatred flashed out of Lukeni's face. As he stared at Nzonzi for a few seconds. And in that silence, he sighed softly closing his eyes and managed to centre himself. He turned around and strolled to pack his things.

The silence between Nzonzi and Lukeni was broken by his uncle once they arrived at the Laari residence which was also in the family vineyard and not far from the inn. 'He was killed by a man called Gringer Solace,' he bluntly told his nephew. Lukeni absorbed the name and allowed it to float in his mind and then it made its way to the back and fell in the abyss of his thoughts.

Lukeni kept to himself and helped his uncle without his uncle asking for help. He was helping in the kitchen of the inn's restaurant. One day on his break Lukeni practised his Tiger Claw. Going through the style's form repetition after repetition. His body moved to pounce and he slightly grimaced when he struck out. The body was moving while the mind stood still, this shadowboxing session was paused, by the presence Dioko his eldest cousin who was about Lukeni's height. Both were tall and stared at each other for a second but Lukeni broke it off as he resumed training. He ignored the smirk his cousin had on his face and the sneering atmosphere Dioko had brought with him. Soon Nimi, Dioko's younger brother also appeared smirking as well. Lukeni sensed trouble was ahead but he had to repeat his form, he had to train, and the flow could not be ceased.

'Catclaw,' began Nimi as his brother chuckled at the comment. Since his arrival back at the Laari's,

Lukeni had done his best to ignore his cousins who did their best to not hide their dislike for him. Openly insulting their cousin even in front of Maria or Nzonzi. However, Lukeni to their surprise remained somewhat candid and joyful. He would remove himself from those altercations by simply walking away. However, that day was the first time they had seen him openly train.

'Get the drums!' barked Dioko at his brother and then he looked back at Lukeni excited as he clasped his hands and began to gently stretch drawing his body down and up slowly. Not far were the drums which Nimi began to play. They were traditional drums used for occasions such as the traditional occasion when "Ngolo" practitioners challenged each other to a duel.

Lukeni did not know much about the "Ngolo" however the beats of the drums he knew was a call to battle. He stopped and greeted his cousin with an open left hand and his right hand closed in a fist, the left hand was a on top of the right fight open with the thumb tucked and the rest of the fingers held together. This was an ancient martial Daoist way of greeting; the left hand represented the yin in nature and the right hand the yang. Together they formed a yin yang gesture, which represented "Taiji" yin and yang together, two complementary opposite forces.

Dioko sniggered at the gesture mocking it and

the drum beats stopped as Nimi joined him for a moment and resumed beating away. And then his older brother begun to move the next phase of his warm-up, side to side as he shifted switching his stance in sync with the beat. Ducking down as his hands touched the ground and a spinning kick went around. He was then immediately up, moving around Lukeni who stared back.

In a sudden, Dioko stepped in with a fake jab and then jerked back; a roundhouse kick was launched at Lukeni's thigh. Lukeni gently sighed as he simply squatted slightly down with a tucked in coccyx and Dioko's kick bounced back upon impact and he then fell. Both he and his cousin were shocked as Nimi stop playing the drum, both mouths wide open with eyes in awe.

Gritting his teeth Dioko quickly got up and grunted before charging at Lukeni. He tried to grab hold of his cousin but was thrown off Lukeni's back landing hard. He got up again grabbing hold of his lower back as he slightly grimaced.

'I give you a roof to live on and this is the shit you bring,' said Nzonzi appearing and glancing about as his eyes took in the situation making a few prejudice deductions. 'They wanted to challenge me and a challenge I gave them,' Lukeni immediately replied. His uncle simply nodded and made head movements to his sons who understood it to mean he wanted them to disappear. Dioko and

Nimi rushed away with Dioko adding, 'Now you will feel the real Ngolo...you bastard!' Lukeni simply sighed in response and then gazed at Nzonzi. Who was beginning to roll up his sleeve calmly and then said, 'I see that Wong's Tiger Claw is effective,' he paused for a few seconds and he then began to step forward his soft steps translated into thuds inside Lukeni. 'Your cousins are not a true manifestation of our family's martial art...Yes over the years we have had our Daoist's influences as well,' he said and greeted Lukeni in the yin yang gesture. 'The horse stance...*ma bu* as the ancient Daoists called it,' Nzonzi suddenly assumed the horse stance, crouching perfectly down. Ninety degrees off the ground with his back straight and his coccyx tucked in, 'We incorporated into our art as well standing like this connecting to the earth,' he continued and slowly got up. 'But Ngolo is sudden and unexpecting...' after those last words Nzonzi made a sudden move, and all Lukeni remembered was his uncle motioning his body one side and then he jumped hitting Lukeni on the head. All Lukeni could remember was seeing black and flashes of light as he fell. Stumbling to get up, he finally managed to shake the concussive sensations as he blinked a few times. Nzonzi chuckled and painted his face with a smirk and then he said, 'Tomorrow five in the morning I will begin teaching you our family art.' Lukeni rubbed his forehead still feeling slightly dazed and slowly nodded in agreement.

A year had passed leading to the current time; Charles Sobek and Mr S had stopped at a diner in a small town not so far from Mbanza Laari. Charles had Helga on his mind regardless of Mr S's words about her he could not push her out his mind. Gringer really had him tied this time he thought, coming to the Sud-West Republic raised many questions in his mind. His mission under the supervision of Mr S was to simply to head to Mbanza Laari to extract an individual. Once they were there was more only to be revealed. That is all he knew, he was not too nervous to mess up because he had done far harder things. Like taking the life away of criminal bosses on the behalf of Gringer, appearing like a demon and leaving with the souls of his victims as he killed them; only allowing them one last gasp of air.

Mr S was smiling to himself as he sipped his green tea and Charles who was gazing around the diner feeling how they were in the middle of nowhere muttered with an air of frustration, 'Wasteland'. Mr S glanced at him and his eyes moved away and then back towards Charles before he spoke, 'Like your life hmmm...a wasteland.' Charles snorted as he rolled his eyes replying, 'Yea whatever'.

'So why we stopped here!' snapped Charles a few seconds later after falling into momentary silence. Mr S calmly looked at him before responding, 'I wanted to relax, take it easy...' sighing he paused and then continued, 'you still have that bimbo in your mind?' Frowning slightly his stare cut through Charles who looked away and then violently got up shaking the table where they sat, he marched away towards the counter where the diner's waitress stood. A young woman in her mid-teens with short hair, and dark smooth ebony skin. She looked a bit anxious as she had caught a glimpse of Charles movements. And now nervously gazing at his rough outlines and leather black jacket, she felt her heart pound. Despite Charles transforming into a calm tiger as he tried his best to mimic some form of candidness with a slight smile. She did not buy it, however, he tried regardless, 'Sorry miss...' clearing his throat for a second he resumed and asked, 'what's your name?' 'Janice,' she quickly said. 'Do you have any music you can play? I got a flash drive with classics you can play,' said Charles. 'That wouldn't be a problem we have music, should have actually been playing. Usually it's around ten O'clock when we play music however that is not the case at the moment,' as she said those lost words Charles looked at clock that was behind Janice and then she added as he lowered his eyes back on her, 'I will quickly go at the back and set up the music will be a few minutes.' She then disappeared away and seemed to feel more comfortable around Charles.

Charles looked back where Mr S was still smirking to himself sipping his green tea, this bothered Charles and then he decided to ignore it as he murmured, 'Psycho.' The doors of the diner suddenly flung open and there walked in a familiar figure. A bald bearded black man who Charles suddenly recognised as his older cousin Felix.

Mr S had also caught a glimpse of Felix, and suddenly pulled out his phone calmly and quickly typed away sending a text. Nodding to himself he put his phone slowly away. And then slowly pulled something else, his gun as he adjusted the silencer with his eyes as a falcon fixed on Felix who suddenly walked towards Charles. Both cousins stared each other down, Charles showing mild signs of fury to his older cousin who seemed very calm. 'What the fuck do you want!?' snarled Charles. 'Charlie…It has been what…' Felix spoke walking towards Charles and his words were shot out to oblivion with a snappy response from Charles, 'Seven goddam years you shit!' Felix sighed and resumed speaking his facial expression between calmness and anger with a serious warning tone, 'Gringer is using you and that boy is our blood, do you even know what he would do once he gets his hands on Lukeni?' Charles looked away with a frown on his face and questioning everything he had just absorbed. 'Who is Lukeni? What demented shit are you spewing?' asked a puzzled Charles. 'We connected by blood! His Emperor Fei's Son!' Felix's patience had cracked as he raised his voice, to his younger cousin's surprise who suddenly felt a worrisome sensation sink in as he frowned at what he had just heard.

# CHAPTER TWENTY-FIVE- THE DARUMA PROGENY

'NO!!!' exclaimed Felix as he slapped Charles on his shoulder pushing him off his feet and right over the counter. He landed hard on the other side and while he was in the motion before landing, he heard the noise of a muzzled gunshot by a silencer. Immediately getting up with adrenaline his eyes shot wide open as he looked at Mr S pointing a gun with a silencer. And the gun was then pointed at him and a shot was fired. Charles ducked, however, he came back up, the grunting noises of who was Felix caught his attention and he naturally acted to peer up. His cousin was standing up and holding one hand straight out and the other hand was on his chest where he had been shot. Bits of blood leaked out of his mouth as he gritted his teeth. And floating in the air was the bullet standing dead still in its trajectory and it then fell on the ground. The same time Felix crumbled back to the floor, Charles then suddenly jumped to his cousin's assistance.

He stared briefly at his older cousin for a millisecond before turning back on Mr S with only rage in his eyes. Mr S simply looked calm with an air of prudence in his eyes as he fired another shot. And the bullet was stopped in mid-air again, by Felix who stuck his arm out and then snapped at Charles, 'Kill him you idiot!' His hand then slammed the ground and the bullet immediately fell. At the same time Charles obeyed his older cousin as he did in his younger days, he charged for Mr S who felt his gun aim up and a different direction messing around with his aim, frustrated he suddenly threw it away to prepare himself for the bull that rushed forth for him. Embracing Charles who tackled him, he did not resist going with it and only pushing his feet up with the motion once on the ground. Causing Charles to roll away, but Charles got up and charged again. Mr S deflected the first straight vertical punch thrown by Charles and countered with his punch moving from inches away. Charles flew away landing flat on his back and rolled up grimacing as he panted and felt a sharp pain in his abdomen. But what shook him was Mr S's movements, Charles was familiar with the movements.

'The Sobek or Subek bloodline, has sins it needs to pay for that are centuries old,' began Mr S as he spoke gathering a chair as he caught his breath and sat down, 'Sung Subek was the first to commit the greatest of crimes...not even caring for his sister's love for her husband, Daruma Chan. Daruma who gave him the greatest of presents his way of fighting, his way of breathing, his philosophy...Yes, you might be asking yourself how is it that I know what your family for thousands of years called, "*The Harmonious Fist*," I am a direct descendant of its original creator. Yes, Daruma is my great, great, great, great thousands of years ago great grandfather! And you can call me by my name, its Shadow Chan. Your ancestor poisoned Daruma before beginning his plans to rule the whole of the Sol Islands. Once Daruma was killed, he had set his eyes on Daruma's progeny and even his own sister. But they managed to escape and here I am.' Mr S or Shadow grinned and then chuckled before continuing, 'Felix what a name! You what? Felix the Second?' Shadow turned to Felix who laid on the floor slightly behind him and a few meters away. Charles still in pain grimacing gave it one more try as he grunted and eventually got to his feet panting for air as held his abdomen.

Shadow got up from the chair slowly, and then he and Charles heard the frightened plea of the crying Janice who had come out from hiding, 'Please don't kill me...' her words mixed in tears and struggling to come out. Charles seized the opportunity, calmly sighing as he raised his back and sunk his sternum a millimetre below. He felt a sinking sensation from down below the navel and then it went further down smoothly at a constant speed below to his feet and then out it into the earth. A sudden surge rose back up from his feet and out his stretched-out hands exiting out in the form of jolts of electricity zapping Shadow for a moment as he jumped meters away, landing unconsciously on the ground.

Charles was then surprised as he looked at his hands with his eyes widened and amazed at what he had just done; he did feel exhausted and the pain in his abdomen had disappeared. The grunts of Felix trying to get up immediately caught his attention and he glanced at Janice who stood there shaking in shock and then back at his older cousin. He helped him up and putting him on his shoulder as he lifted him and made his way out of the diner leaving Janice and Shadow.

# CHAPTER TWENTY-SIX- THE STEPPING OF NGOLO AND THE CLAWS OF A TIGER

Back in Mbanza Laari kilometres away from the diner and its events, hard at practice was Lukeni now eighteen years old moving to the drumming beats of Nzonzi who beat the drum and yet observed every movement his nephew did stepping to the beats while doing the Ngolo form. Kicks while maintaining one hand on the ground or simply kicking. Simulating a sweep, a takedown and a jab and then the hand's movements changed and an angry Nzonzi immediately stopped beating the drums. Drowning in a scowl that emerged on his face Nzonzi watched as his nephew's hand movements more and more resembled Wong's tiger claw.

'You disgrace me like this!' snarled Nzonzi and Lukeni then stopped not surprised by his uncle's comment. Nzonzi abruptly marched towards him and he did not budge in fear and kept looking at his uncle straight in the eyes, until a flashing slap spread across his face, turning his head to the side. He slowly looked back at this uncle and did not rub the burning pain that flowed up and down his cheek. Another slap came to his direction, and this time he grabbed Nzonzi's hand. The grip was tight, and the strength was incredible as Nzonzi sneeringly stared back at this nephew who let go as he pulled his hand away. And then Lukeni spoke as Nzonzi began to walk away, 'That is the Ngolo stepping mixed with the Tiger Claw!' Nzonzi responded immediately with, 'You now eighteen I want you out of the house and town. You are on your own now!'

Lukeni was neither shocked nor angry, he knew the time would come where he would need to leave. And calmly packed the little that he had and then he heard commotions which made him pause for a minute and then continued packing deciding to ignore it.

He left his room and the commotion suddenly made him pause as he heard the loud yell of Nzonzi. It seemed to come from the entrance of the restaurant. Lukeni stayed in a small cottage next to the restaurant and rushed out of the cottage with his small backpack. He ran to the entrance of Madia and there he saw a group of people.

The entrance to Madia was a courtyard with an ancient bronze statue of the Laari family's founding patriarch Kipura Laari, standing about two meters tall with glaring eyes and crossed arms. His glare shot down on the commotion from a crowd of men in black suits, some with shades with blazing guns pointed at a furious Nzonzi, who was lacking in any weapon and bravely standing his ground not backing down. Beside him was Maria concerned but yet also standing bravely as her two sons stood behind her looking frightened and feeding off their parent's courage.

Amongst the armed men in suits was a red-haired Gringer Solace, whose eyes had caught an immediate glimpse of Lukeni. And his face lit with instantaneous interest, Nzonzi noticed this as well and Lukeni gazed around slightly frowning as he looked overflowed with questions.

'RUN! LUKENI! RUN!' exclaimed Nzonzi, as he heard his uncle's loud words, Lukeni immediately darted off, his legs pumping with blood as they hit the ground propelling away with astonishing speed. He did not even look back but heard a second voice which happened to be Gringer's voice, 'GET HIM!'. And with that response, he could hear the footsteps of the men in suits following his movements.

Once Lukeni had disappeared out of sight with all Gringer's men chasing him like a tiger does its prey, Gringer suddenly found himself alone with the Laari family. Nzonzi gazed at him this time with a sneer, 'You alone mister, I do not think the odds favour you.' Gringer whose eyes where still focused at the direction which Lukeni ran from suddenly turned back to Nzonzi, he simply made a sniggering like grunt with an expression of disgust on his face, as he pulled out his handgun. And then darted off as well following his men. Nzonzi turned to Maria and his sons opening his arms and they all hugged each other.

Lukeni had made it out of the vineyard still sprinting for his life and was beginning to feel the strain as his muscles begin to announce their tiredness. This was nothing but a notification to him that a little fuel he had begun to deplete. It was then he decided to turn and see how close the men were, and some had kept up with him, the others were falling slightly behind. Sprinting in their suits, they were just a couple of meters away. They were about twenty of them, Lukeni controlled his breathing and picked up the pace, a few of the townsfolk who were outside the vineyard looked in bewilderment at the crowd following Lukeni.

He kept running and turned around again and noticed that they had given up and were significant distances away with a handful of diehards following him in strolling paces of fatigue. Lukeni laughed as he was simply pacing himself at this moment in a rhythmic jogging pace chuckling and smiling joyously as he felt victorious. Then he heard roaring engines rushing forth behind. He looked back and saw about five black big cars coming to his direction with one stopping to pick up the fatigued men that were still on his trail.

Relentless himself, Lukeni picked up his pace and a sudden voice screamed in his head, 'No son of mine runs!' the voice left him with a quick searing pain on his forehead, stopping Lukeni dead on his tracks as he rubbed his forehead. He sighed astonished, he knew the voice the last time he had heard it, it was when he was younger. Lukeni shook his head and the cars had caught up with him, with one riding past and stopping behind him and with the other stopping in front of him. They surrounded him and rushing out as the door flung open from one of the cars was Gringer.

'Lukeni,' begin Gringer calmly composing himself as he strolled towards Lukeni, 'I am Gringer Solace,' he said now that he was close enough and stretched out his hand. Lukeni simply glanced at it with distrust and remained silent. Sighing Gringer drew his hand back, by this time his henchmen had gotten out of the cars and encircled both Gringer and Lukeni.

'What do you want with me, and my family?' asked Lukeni breaking his silence and blankly staring at Gringer. 'I need you to come with me, I am sure you asking yourself questions? Like who you really are? I am sure they have held back a lot and not told you the truth?' responded Gringer and signs of confusion leaked out of Lukeni's face. 'Am I right or not?' Gringer pressed on and sighed before continuing, 'Come with me and I will reveal everything to you, I know who your father was...I am sure you want to know who your old man was right? Come with me...come,' Gringer placed his hand on Lukeni's shoulder with a look of concern.

'He did not know me! HA!' the voice in Lukeni's head began to speak, startling him as he slapped Gringer's hand away. And took a centimetre of a step back and the voice continued laughing madly at first, 'Don't be an idiot son, I am part of you, I am inside of you. This filth wants to harm you...I am taking over.' Lukeni felt his hands try moving without his volition and he resisted, and he yelled, 'NOOO!' Gringer looked at Lukeni in confusion sensing something bizarre was happening his men tried to make a move and he stopped them raising his hand as a gesture. They suddenly held back, frowning he scanned Lukeni who was looking at his hands anxiously as he shook.

'You are weak my son and I need to take over, stop fighting me! You CANNOT WIN!' Lukeni dropped on the ground rolling and moving violently in a fit of madness. Gringer surprised and frowning made a few hand gestures signalling his men move in. 'If he resists kill him, I only need his body,' he said coldly as his men swarmed in on Lukeni, drawing out their guns. None of them even dared to approach him as he growled and grunted moving and rolling on the ground, appearing possessed. They simply began firing and as the first bullet was shot in the air, Lukeni immediately stood up with sparks and jolts of electric current surging his body causing him to float in the air as the bullets were hit away by the electric currents. The sight of this sudden phenomenon stopped the men from firing their bullets and Gringer looked on frozen in awe at what he was seeing.

Lukeni's hair had changed to white and his eyes were light blue and piercing. And the surges of electricity stopped as he dropped back to the ground landing on his feet. He looked happily at his hands and then smiled. As he glanced around, the glee on his face was different, it had the ambience of a dark smile a killer would have before killing his victims. 'It's good to be back even for a moment,' he said. 'It's definitely not a myth he has Fei's blood, I need his essence...I need to have this power,' muttered Gringer staring in awe.

'How about a little warm up, you mortal cockroaches,' said Lukeni and then broke into erratic laughter and then started to growl as he greeted his teeth. 'Let me show you guys the ancient martial art of the Water School,' he said and stood up with a calmer demeanour this time and then in an abrupt moment he suddenly charged forth. Gringer's men resumed firing their guns but with each shot on their targe missing. Lukeni moved amongst them like a shadow of death. Dropping each one of them with deadly blows, as they fell like dead flies. Realising their futile attempt to gun him down, they drew their guns away and rushed for the cars with Gringer following. One remained brave or stupid with hands up as Lukeni smiled at him. He made the first move, throwing a left jab, which Lukeni welcomed with his left hand deflecting it as his right-hand made contact just above the man's elbow joint. With his hands being nimble and flexible they spiralled in motion. And the man was drawn in, Lukeni's left hand pulled one direction and his right the opposite direction, this was followed by loud cracking noise that snapped the man's elbow and as he screamed helplessly. Lukeni's face was painted with a sentiment of content.

As Gringer and what remained of his man rode away, he saw Lukeni's last move, a straight punch with his right hand hitting his henchman's head as it bobbed back and forth before the henchman hit the ground dead. Riding away Gringer looked forward, 'Sir what was that monster,' asked one of his men inside the car. 'That was power in its purest form and I want it,' replied Gringer.

# CHAPTER TWENTY-SEVEN- PLANTING A SEED

Eighteen years earlier, in Feiville and a few days after his inauguration and return an ecstatic Emperor Fei delighted in being back in his body, summoned an engineer from Gaia Corp after an urgent meeting with Union Guard generals. The engineer was a man who was responsible for the special construction of the life tank that had reconstructed his body. Daniel Faris the CEO of Gaia Corp was not aware of this meeting.

Fei thanked the nervous engineer who had become a member of the Brotherhood a year earlier. And was flabbergasted to be in front of what was ancient lore. This engineer was a bald young man at the time with a thin trimmed moustache and beady dark brown eyes. He was white and pale; looking like he was in his twenties and his name was Kepler Cloud.

'Get up!' said Fei as his voice rose in tone. Kepler had been kneeling being in the presence of the emperor. 'Sorry...' he nervously said. 'Do not apologise!' said Fei. They were in an office Fei had chosen for the meeting in the Union of Nations headquarters and Fei sat on a chair, getting up and walking closer to Kepler. His light blue eyes piercing every atom of Kepler's body. He could barely hold gaze looking straight at the emperor as he timidly glanced down. 'Kepler, I hate weakness and you are weak right now...you make me want to kill you! But do not worry I am joking after all the world need geniuses like you, that life tank version of yours was genius. Remember you are genius!' Fei pulled Kepler's chin up so the young man could look at him straight in the eyes and continued as he turned his back and paced about, 'Kepler my family's blood, my blood is the source of my power I do not know how to explain it! Sometimes I think if anyone managed to gather my essence, they would have my power...' Fei suddenly looked far away as he paused, and Kepler attentively looked at him intrigued at what he had just heard. 'Anyway, just a thought Kepler, my boy, do you know a girl that I could fornicate with...' pausing again a smirk appeared on his face as he tapped Kepler on his shoulder. 'I know a girl you will be delighted to meet,' begin Kepler this time at ease and sounding more enthusiastic. And Fei's eyes lit with desire he surrendered his ears completely to Kepler's words.

'Her name is Nzinga, she lives with me,' said Kepler. Fei slightly frowned pondering as held his chin and then said, 'Is she...' Kepler immediately interrupted him, 'No, no, she is well a friend she has been living with me and...' Kepler words drowned as he tried to explain himself and Fei then took the opportunity to speak, 'No more, present this woman to me, being in my original body has left me with an insatiable appetite for the fairer sex, besides the Sword Of Carnage being a vessel for my soul. I think I need to plant a seed...' Fei looked away in silence falling in his thoughts again. 'My emperor you want a child?' enquired Kepler. Fei's eyes suddenly glanced at Kepler and he felt his heart immediately sink in fear as he immediately looked away and slowly back at Fei. 'Never mind, get me the girl,' Fei coldly responded.

Afterwards, Kepler pounding with mild adrenaline left, a bit confused. As he had a heavy crush for Nzinga, a girl who had come from the small town of Mbanza Laari and had been staying with him for about six months. He had met her one day in Feiville stranded and homeless, it was her beauty that had captured his attention and her tears further entrapped him in her helpless web of distress. Wanting to help her, Kepler's attentions were never purely noble as the desire to sleep with her was great when he met her and boiled to great heights. Nzinga was not attracted to him and never gave in to his approaches telling him she saw him only as a friend or sort of a brother.

However, what broke Kepler's heart furthermore was when he found out she had been sleeping with some of Feiville's influential men. He never confronted her about it, even though once he had come back to the apartment where they both lived and heard her moans and groans with each thrust, coming from her room. And he would listen in as he cried with rage.

Kepler was still a virgin never having felt the warmth of women, he would masturbate feverishly to pornography while he glued his eyes to his cell phone or laptop. And then once he climaxed, he would fall into tears, crushing back into the realities of his life and feeling miserable with himself. He was lonely, horny and desperate. The day he met Nzinga, he thought his kindness and chivalry would make her spread her legs for him. Nonetheless, he still desired her and had come to the uncomfortable truth that she was not into him. Twisted in his thoughts he thought if he presented her to Emperor Fei, the emperor would reward him with something.

Once at the apartment he did not know how to break it down to her, however, he was excited and thought she would be too. Since she was into powerful men and within moments of her coming into his sight, he spewed out the words quickly, 'I met EMPEROR FEI...' he was loud she shook with fear and Kepler immediately realising this reduced his tone and recounted the story of him meeting Emperor Fei to Nzinga who listened passively until it came to the part where he revealed to her that he told Emperor Fei, she was willing to sleep with him the emperor. To Kepler's surprise she defiantly exploded to a, 'I will not do! SUCH A THING! KEPLER!' Shaken and further confused and mildly frowning he squeamishly said, 'But I thought that was what you were into?' Nzinga shook her head as she held her forehead and said, 'I have found someone.'

There was suddenly a moment of silence and Kepler stared back with a heavier frown and before he could ask who she was referring to, Nzinga then continued to speak, 'His name is Wong Claw and I have been seeing him for the last few weeks, Kepler his the one. Look I am sorry...I feel like I might have used you...' pausing she got close and placed her hand gently on Kepler's arm and her words continued flowing, 'look I am moving in with him soon. He's such a great guy, he is a union guard...' Nzinga continued talking about the man she had fallen for and with every word coming out her mouth, Kepler felt blows of pain crushing his heart further into the abyss of hurt he already felt towards Nzinga.

That evening he cried in his room, tears endlessly streaking down his cheeks, with periodic thoughts of storming Nzinga's room and raping her, to killing her and then killing himself. And then came the moment his eyes closed and then they opened with his sleep feeling like five minutes and the previous day a permanent stamp in his mind, he could recall everything that had occurred.

Kepler went about everything as if he was fine masquerading and appearing very happy when he met Wong Claw. Yet the more he faked his emotions the more hatred he felt for Nzinga increase. And the seething hate had reached further critical mass with the appearance of Wong Claw. Kepler had already thought of this, but his perverse clarity had been achieved. If he could not have Nzinga then neither could Wong Claw. Emperor Fei had not summoned him about meeting with Nzinga in the weeks that passed, Kepler understood that the emperor was too busy with more important matters and resistance from the Sol Islands, never mind the Separatist Movement who had increased their activities.

Sentiments of killing himself had drowned him in sorrow and he felt sluggish and depressed, spiralling in toxicity. Waking up he would catch a glance of a radiant smiling Nzinga in the kitchen of his apartment. This positive vibe which he had grown to loath would sometimes greet him in the evenings when he returned to work. Something somehow kept him going, Kepler's secret was that he was a member of the Brotherhood something he had surprisingly kept to himself and never had divulged to even Nzinga.

News that an evening ball was to be organised and even greater seemingly lifting his downed spirits was Emperor Fei bringing up, 'where is the girl you told me about?' they had briefly met. And Kepler's heart pumped and in his pathetic perverse mind, he had found a lifeline. He wanted to ruin Nzinga, he knew if he could get her in the sight of the emperor, her not wanting the interaction was irrelevant. He masturbated disturbingly on the thought of the emperor raping or ravaging Nzinga and then as him being the emperor ravaging her until he fell to a dark slumber feeling miserable the next day. He knew the emperor would get his way with her and most importantly he delighted in that Wong Claw will no longer be with her.

Nzinga ignorant of Kepler's ghastly plot accepted as he invited her to the ball, 'I promise I will not lie that you my girl, I will gladly say you, my friend,' he said lying like it was an ingrained reflex. Nzinga agreed with a smile.

On the evening she wore a spectacular white glittering dress that accentuated her already glowing beauty. Her dark skin complemented with the dress and her full lips was a distraction to the eyes of the males at the ball. Kepler was at ease during the evening, being someone who was naturally uneasy and timid. However, that time conversed around and chatted to the Brotherhood members with no social hurdle. It was Nzinga that felt a bit uneasy she was the only female at the ball but brushed it aside.

Kepler had lied to her it was a work function and that most of his work colleagues in his engineering unit of Gaia Corp were males. Besides, what made her feel uneasy was the molesting eyes that gawked as she moved around.

Following Kepler, she muttered to him, 'I'm really the only girl at this party,' a slight frown appeared on her face as she said this.

The room had been buzzing with noise and suddenly dropped to an abyss of silence. An announcement had been made causing this phenomenon and everybody silenced themselves. Strolling in the large hall where the ball took place was the intimidating presence of Emperor Fei. Quaking fear into each of the members of the brotherhood.

His eyes immediately fired like a falcon swooping on its prey at Nzinga. 'What is going on!' she grunted at Kepler whose betrayal glowed from his eyes and he seemed a bit uncomfortable as well, but in his perverse daring courage, he gently shoved her forward when she glanced back at Emperor Fei. His finger was gesturing her to come forward as he gleefully looked at his evening snack.

With each step she took her legs felt heavy and she wanted to run but she knew she could not. The emperor wasted no time in inviting her to another room where he got straight to the point. 'Take off your clothes!' he barked shaking her core. But the Laari bloodline kicked in and she was unyielding, and he continued, 'fighting me pointless woman, I am going to fuck you so hard right now...oooh.' Nzinga tried to run and the emperor pounced on her, excited, he ripped her dress and laying on her stomach, with her posterior bare, he inserted himself inside of her ravaging her hard with each thrust as tears trickled down her face.

After the horror she experienced, Nzinga had returned the next day in the wee hours of the morning of Feiville to the apartment. Shaken, and silent, Kepler had already returned and stood there waiting for her. He greeted her with a smile and then said, 'I am sorry.' He got no response but her traumatised silence. He caught a glimpse of her torn clothes and felt sentiments of guilt creep in and as this happened Nzinga held herself together as she strolled past him. She then came back from the kitchen with a sharp steak knife and pointed it at Kepler as she shook crying.

'Put that away!' Kepler anxiously said his words shivering, however, this angered her more as she yelled and charged for him. They struggled briefly and Nzinga managed to slash him across the face with the knife, cutting deep with blood splashing. Kepler yelled helplessly and was slashed again and then again and then he managed to shove her away as she fell. He rushed for the door screaming, 'You deserved it you whore!' opening it and then run away. Nzinga fell to her knees crying as she held the bloodied knife.

Wong Claw came over an hour later as he had been calling her and she did not pick up her cell phone. He felt that something was wrong, as he knew she had attended a ball, yet she had not texted him to recount how it was. When he arrived at the apartment, he was shocked. Nzinga told him everything as she sobbed, he could not believe what he was hearing even though the emperor's tyrannical tendencies were beginning to be known, what Wong found hard to believe or could not understand where the details. A ball filled only with men and Kepler. Also, the emperor being there, something was strange he thought. He remembered the Separatist propaganda recently mentioning a Brotherhood, an organisation that ran things under the veil of the Union of Nations, however, his mind was mixed with revenge and brewing questions. Wong listened to his woman's sobs and her story, asking less and listening more. Despite his mind fantasizing about ripping Kepler's vocal cords and although he dismissed the thought, he wanted to kill the emperor.

Hours later, Kepler had returned this time with an army of Union Guards, they had come to collect Nzinga an order issued by Emperor Fei. To Kepler's surprise and shock, he saw a seething angry Wong who glared at him. 'You VERMIN!' he bellowed moments into catching a glimpse of a bloodied Kepler whose cuts deep and fresh, still leaked with blood.

Before the return of Kepler and the Union Guards,

Wong had bathed Nzinga and then tucked her in. She had then later woken up by the commotion. Still dressed in a bathing gown, she was angry and in tears when she saw Kepler. Wong moved her behind him and glared at Kepler ignoring the guns aimed at him.

Another person was there, a white man with short blonde hair and piercing blue eyes. He was lean and dressed in black pants and a white shirt; the top button was unbuttoned, and its sleeves rolled up. He was not a Union Guard and presented himself as 'I am Eddy Sobek and Emperor Fei has requested an audience with the lady.' 'So, what the Separatists say must be true, you all part of the Brotherhood! I have been serving the wrong side this whole time!' The truth had finally shone on Wong and he then believed every single detail that Nzinga had recounted to him.

Eddy simply chuckled and then with a sneering expression on his face said, 'I am not going to deny anything, however, what are you going to do about it! Hey! What are you? Just another Union Guard soldier like these guys. What? You going to defend this whore and take on Emperor Fei!' Wong's immediate response was to charge towards Eddy who with an instant, snapped a front kick straight for Wong's abdomen repelling him backwards as he stumbled and re-gathered himself. Eddy motioned at the Union Guards to put their guns away and he returned his attention with a smile on his face towards Wong.

Wong positioned his hands like the claws of a tiger and Eddy carefully took note as he snorted, 'Tiger Claw you must be kidding me, that front kick is not even an introduction...' Wong did not have time to hear the rest as he furiously pounced at Eddy, slashing his hands around. Which Eddy deflected and then came a right vertical punch from Wong. This was deflected by Eddy's left hand as it deflected the blow spiralling and horizontally landed into a fist (with the palm and curled fingers facing up) hitting Wong on his body where the liver was located. He felt a sudden shock before the unbearable pain settled in. As he felt that for a split second, a sudden uppercut was launched throwing his head back and then all his saw was darkness.

A shocking sensation shook him unpleasantly awake from his coma after he had been knocked out by Eddy Sobek. The memories slowly trickled back in and then came a quick splash of cold icy water that sent his body into a shiver and then Wong realised that his hands were stretched and tied up while his feet dangled in the air.

'Wong Claw just promoted corporal in the Union Guard,' said a voice that came from Emperor Fei as he appeared forth. Wong glanced at the emperor and around struggling to widen his eyes, he was in some underground chamber dimly lit and two men who seemed to be elite union guards were there as well.

'Consider your freedom gone I will imprison you and for the remainder of your life you shall receive footage of me fucking Nzinga, I am going to impregnate her with my seed and make you watch all of it. Starting with every thrust...' pausing Fei chuckled and then cast a look of disgust at Wong who violently shook in anger, trying to free himself and was put out of his misery as one of the elite union guards shock him again with an electric baton, that had violent sparks of electric current zapping at its end. Wong yelled and in sync followed the roaring laughter of Emperor Fei.

Imprisoned in an underground cell, Wong's only torture was that he was made to watch footages of Fei repeatedly raping Nzinga as she screamed and hopelessly fought back. She did every time, however, then came the day she stopped and would instead grimace and then these grimaces became moans and groans that tore Wong's soul apart. They would tie him to a chair and drug him with a drug that paralysed him as he watched and experienced hell.

Nevertheless, Nzinga had it the worse, being penetrated like a sex slave, she was forced to live in a high-end whorehouse and Fei was her only client. Until she fell pregnant and the days before the Separatist Movement rid the world of Fei's menace. Nzinga managed to escape with the aid of Wong, who had managed to escape his imprisonment and he had joined the Separatist Movement. Darkness had fallen on Nzinga, even after Fei's fall, she had been put in a mental asylum because she heard voices. The voices were of Fei as he would say, 'I am alive, inside of you. I felt alive being inside of you...' then she would hear him pause and his mad sordid laughter would ring in her head leading to unbearable migraines and bouts of madness.

Kepler Cloud, after the offering of Nzinga to Emperor Fei, was promoted through the ranks of the Brotherhood. When the emperor fell, he went into hiding, and then reappeared strong, manipulative and cunning. He became the face of what was to be the remnants of the Brotherhood, the main goal was in retrieving and finding Fei's bloodline, his son and Nzinga's child. Fei was their god and Kepler deluded in madness, had the crazy idea of bringing back the emperor using Lukeni. A crazy procedure of bringing him back to life. However, this was what he preached into the heads of the Brotherhood members. What Kepler wanted was Fei's martial power, it was near impossible for Kepler to reach such power and so he thought based on what Fei had told him on their first meeting, *"Sometimes I think if anyone managed to gather my essence, they would have my power..."* Those words had implanted themselves in Kepler's memory.

Felix came to understand this when his unit hunted the remnants of the Brotherhood. His concern, however, was that if they ever found out the truth of Fei Yue, that he was of the Subek or Sobek bloodline. That the whole family would be in jeopardy from these crazy fanatics.

Gringer Solace was the man who had killed Kepler during a mission. He had managed to torture this truth out of Kepler, 'If you can get his son and gather his essence you will have Fei's power...imagine what you can accomplish...' those were Kepler lost words before Gringer bashed him repeatedly to his death as he punched his face.

Felix and Wong knew all of this was madness, and Felix already not trusting Gringer, did his utmost best to keep the whereabouts of Lukeni a secret.

# CHAPTER TWENTY-EIGHT- A TUMOUR OF IMMORTALITY

Lukeni woke up and the first thing he did was grab hold of his forehead as he felt the pain of a pounding headache. The pain then immediately disappeared, and he started to feel tingling sensations around his head, feet and arms. He was lying on a bed, while his head rested on a pillow.

The tingling sensations came from the acupuncture needles he realised where inserted inside of him. He remembered everything that had happened and how he lost control of his body. The blackness then crept up on him and now he was awake. He was wearing nothing but white shorts and lay half-naked.

Glancing around the room he recognised he was back in the cottage next to Madia and back in the vineyard.

A figure had come inside and Lukeni immediately recognised the figure which happened to be a man who was the doctor who had inserted the needles in his body. The doctor was followed by another man who happened to be Nzonzi.

'You awake,' beamed the doctor and Lukeni responded instantly with, 'how long was I gone for?' The doctor then glanced at Nzonzi who calmly nodded, and the doctor then looked back at Lukeni clearing his throat before responding, 'A few days...Seven days.' 'What!' said Lukeni surprised. 'Nephew,' begin Nzonzi as he proudly looked at Lukeni, something he had never done, 'I am proud of you, you did the family proud. The townspeople are cheering your name, saying you saved the town from those bandits. Everything is okay now.'

Lukeni did not understand if he was dreaming. He clearly remembered everything that had happened, however, what surprised him was Nzonzi's tone. His uncle was not good at expressing his emotions. Weird of all was the look, he had on his face, he smiled to the best of his capability and then looked at Lukeni like a father did with pride to a son who had achieved something great. Nzonzi had never given the same look to even his sons.

'What is going on, I sense you guys are hiding something from me?' A heavy frown covered Lukeni's face. 'You are dying,' Nzonzi bluntly said appearing sad for a second and then he beamed covering the emotion and the doctor cast Nzonzi a look of discomfort at the sudden bluntness. But Nzonzi Laari was not one to sugar coat things and he continued, 'You have a tumour my boy, he cannot explain what it is, the doctor here can sense it with his many years of experience. We may be wrong by calling it a tumour, but you are dying…' Nzonzi's words drowned into silence as he pulled himself together forcing a fake smile and then clearing his throat. 'I know a doctor who is familiar with these particular issues, she now lives in Wobbleton, her name is Dr Octavia Chan. Highly renowned for her research, it's our best shot in saving your life,' said the doctor. 'I hear voices, something is taking over me, it's been happening for years,' said Lukeni. Nzonzi sighed and then said, 'Felix Sobek and Wong spoke about this when they brought you and your mother over, I never believed them…' Nzonzi recounted the story about who Lukeni's real father was, Fei Yue. How he had raped Nzinga, and just as horrific the emperor had transmitted his consciousness during the conceiving of Lukeni and that besides sharing his genes like any father and son. Fei had gone beyond putting more than just genes but an actual part of his consciousness into Lukeni. Nzonzi went further telling the story of Nzinga hearing voices and that she had gone mentally ill during her pregnancy. Tears to Lukeni's amazement trickled down his uncle's eyes and they were immediately wiped away, as he told the story.

Nzonzi admitted how despite the madness Nzinga hearing Fei's voice tormenting her, she not once tried to kill herself. Fei would tell her to cut her womb to release him. Nzinga would say in small bouts of sanity that reverted that if she gave birth, the baby will be fine. However, if she had cut herself open not only will she die. But the thing or foetus or whatever it was would immediately manifest into Fei Yue. However, Nzonzi spoke about how she would say Fei would laugh and tell her inside her head that he would kill her and take over Lukeni once he was out that Lukeni was just a biological vessel for his survival.

Lukeni was shocked, his uncle revealing these truths made his heart pound. For starters, he now understood who was the man that was taking over his body. Other than that, he knew who Emperor Fei was and never would he have guessed that, would have been his father.

'This is why you need to see Dr Octavia Chan; Emperor Fei had achieved some form of a perverse form of immortality by entrapping his consciousness the first time in the Sword of Carnage. Immortality is something the Daoist sages of the past were obsessed with. Nonetheless, transmitting part of your consciousness is a darker skill that achieves this end. Trapping part of you so you do not experience the cycle of rebirth. Emperor Fei took his skill applied it in the sexual union of a male and female. Genius at its most evil state! I suspect he is the tumour you carry, I will make arrangements for you to meet up with Dr Octavia Chan, time is running out,' the doctor finished with a sigh as everybody looked at each other with great concern.

'Where is Shadow!' barked Gringer as he snapped, banging his table in his office and shook some his henchmen. 'I am here,' said Shadow calmly as he appeared just in time, strolling into the office and continued, 'I sent you the signal when I was in the diner as confirmation that Felix's appearance means that the son was at Mbanza Laari.' 'Yes, thank you,' said Gringer sounding calmer and then added by asking, 'What happened?' 'I did not get my revenge,' began Shadow, 'You know I never really cared about what happened in ancient times with my ancestor Daruma. However, my family has always lived in the dark because of it. The Subeks or Sobeks did force my family into hiding although it's an ancient story, the effects have echoed through time...' pausing he continued, 'So with your plan of flushing out Felix by showing up with Chuck; as I told you before if the opportunity is there to kill them both it would be better than just killing Chuck. Unfortunately, they were too much to handle or it's just that I did not suspect them to be that powerful.' 'Felix was the commander of my unit, his bloodline is powerful,' said Gringer. 'On the subject of bloodlines, I have information that will shock you and you would love to hear this.'

Shadow stopped and took his moment of silence to sit down the opposite side of Gringer's office table.

'I heard Felix tell Chuck that the kid...Fei's kid was of the same bloodline as them...' Shadow paused allowing the information to sink and Gringer's eyes mildly widened stopping short of being wider. He was trying to control the shocking surprise that erupted. Grabbing his chin, he responded with, 'Interesting,' and looked away before turning back to Shadow, 'Yes but I only need the kid's genes though.' 'Well it's still very interesting...I think you need to investigate that,' said Shadow. 'Me...I need to get that kid,' responded Gringer. Shadow simply smiled and then got up, as he turned his back to walk away, he added turning back, 'Chuck has become very powerful himself and for Felix...' pausing he chuckled with a wry smile on his face before continuing, 'He is a formidable force already,' with those lost words Shadow left. 'Round up the men!' barked Ginger as Shadow left the room.

Charles and Felix had left the diner by a car that Felix used to track down Charles and Shadow. As he always kept his eyes on Mbanza Laari and its surrounding areas. He revealed this to Charles and added that it was a mistake and trap for him showing up at the diner. He firmly believed Gringer planned to flush him out.

Felix had guided Charles to a safe house which

was a cottage out in the middle of nowhere about an hour's drive away from Mbanza Laari in the woods of a surrounding lush forest. There Felix first had Charles remove the bullet in his chest and he was inserted in a life tank to heal and rejuvenate.

His wounds had healed but Felix still felt a bit weak and time was running out he thought, if not it was too late, they had to head back to Mbanza Laari. Also, Charles then remembered that he had once accompanied Felix and Wong Claw to Mbanza Laari. Felix explained to him who Lukeni was and the whole story of the Sobeks or Subeks being related to Fei Yue. And then Felix drifted on a painful subject as he said, 'You might hate me for not avenging your uncle, my father...however, our family is to some degree responsible for the troubles of the world. From Sung Subek to Felix Subek the First, Fei Yue's father to Fei himself. A never-ending cycle of chaos...A vicious cycle...Letting go! Is me ending it!' Felix's voice rose in tone as he held back on his fury. His young cousin simply stared at him before sighing, 'Let's agree to disagree, however, forgive me for the way I have acted...thing is we are here, reunited,' said Charles as he beamed slightly, and Felix beamed back a little as well. 'We need to get to Mbanza Laari,' added Felix.

Within ten minutes the Sobek cousins were on the road, arriving an hour later to Mbanza Laari. They made their way to the Laari Vineyard and asked for Nzonzi at Madia waiting at the courtyard.

With Kipura's statue glaring with pride at them as they waited.

Nzonzi appeared within a few minutes greeting Felix and Charles with the yin yang gesture and they both responded in kind, he then told them immediately without wasting any time, 'Lukeni is not here...He left safely.' 'What do you mean?' a heavy frown covered Felix's face as he asked. Nzonzi told them about the appearance and the troubles that followed. Then mentioned the tumour, Felix was aware of Fei being inside Lukeni and the horrors Nzinga had gone through as he and Wong had informed Nzonzi of this. He believed Nzinga in that allowing the birth of Lukeni would prevent Fei from manifesting fully or buy them sometime time. However, he did not know that Fei being inside Lukeni had taken the form of a tumour.

Nzonzi revealed to them that Lukeni was heading to Wobbleton to meet up with Dr Octavia Chan. An expert that could help him in removing the tumour and ridding him of Fei. Felix had his doubts however he had heard of Dr Octavia being a brilliant acupuncturist and master in Daoist sciences and arts.

# CHAPTER TWENTY-NINE- THE HEALER AND THE FIGHTER

Felix and Charles immediately left Mbanza Laari heading straight for Wobbleton. They planned to simply head to Dr Octavia, as Lukeni had caught a flight to Wobbleton and was already there receiving treatment.

Dr Octavia Chan was a woman in her later twenties, single with alluring beauty. A healer and an accomplished martial artist. Deep in her subject with a raging passion, she was delighted to receive Lukeni. Everything was not revealed to her, all she knew was that Lukeni had an aggressive tumour and that he heard voices. They hoped she would figure out the rest given her expertise.

Her hair was black stopping at her shoulders with full lips and yellow wolf-like eyes. Her skin was soft, but the doctor was no dandelion.

She immediately examined Lukeni upon his arrival and she did not hesitate to begin inserting the needles. 'Well if time is not on our side! We better begin now!' she exclaimed and within minutes the needles were inserted. With most being inserted on Lukeni's head. Firing quick electrocutions as they were inserted, however as he lay face up everything settled and then he found himself go into an immediate slumbering sleep.

Dr Octavia's clinic was next to her house and despite her fame, it remained small, and she kept things simple. Lukeni's case had intrigued her, she immediately knew the tumour was more than something cancerous and she could feel it, however, she did not understand what was going on, that she fired off with some questions calling the doctor who had treated Lukeni earlier as she failed to reach Nzonzi, who could have been possibly avoiding her calls. The doctor revealed everything to her, and Dr Octavia could not believe it. She listened attentively in that stunned state after spending thirty minutes intimidating the doctor to speak the truth.

After the call she rushed back to one of the wards were Lukeni lay and he had disappeared. The receptionist who was also the assisting nurse said she had seen him get up and Dr Octavia simply sighed shaking her head. She could not get mad with the nurse because her patients were not prisoners. Then again

Lukeni had become a peculiar and very serious case, sighing one more time to root herself back down, she rushed out with the nurse following. 'His obviously by foot!' she barked as she sprinted with the nurse struggling to catch up. Lukeni appeared within view walking along the road at a slow pace. Not wasting time analysing the situation Dr Octavia stretched her hand out and sudden sparks of current sizzled around her hand and from a distant Lukeni dropped. 'Help me get him back to the clinic,' she said to the nurse who had finally caught up and was gasping for air.

He was hauled back to the clinic and it seemed he had been walking while in a vegetative state. His needles were still inserted and not removed. That is how Dr Octavia managed to track him down and neutralise him using her energy. The next day she had inserted new needles and this time had his hands and feet tied to a chair as he was made to seat, while he was out in a deep induced coma.

Alone she stood there pacing herself for minutes observing him and still digesting the truth that was revealed to her. She still could not believe it; the craziness was possible in theory and somewhat a myth you would have heard that happened in ancient times. She could not believe Fei was still alive or part of Lukeni's consciousness. It was consuming Lukeni ever so rapidly and the tumour was growing. The tumour was Fei, and his manifestation through Lukeni who was somehow of a host would kill Lukeni and out would come out a full Fei.

Dr Octavia pondered how she could save Lukeni or even if it was possible. One moment she looked away and then heard a grunt and she quickly glanced at Lukeni and saw that his hair had changed to white and was long. His eyes were open, and he glared at her, his eyes had become piercing and light blue. It was no longer Lukeni, but Fei Yue and Dr Octavia immediately recognised this.

'You fucking whore!' he snarled, grunting, even more, Dr Octavia had taken further precautions and the needles she had inserted prevented Lukeni from moving putting him in some paralysis, only his facial muscles could move if anything. 'I have neutralised your meridians, your energy flow, I am in control now,' Dr Octavia calmly responded as she crossed her arms and strolled towards him, 'I am the complete package...Not just a fighter, I am also a healer,' she added.

'Listen here woman! I know and seen ancient acupuncture you can only dream of experiencing!' snapped Fei and then chuckled before continuing, 'You good I will give you that, you lucky you have me bound, if I were free I will be having my way with you now,' he stared her up and down licking his lips. But the doctor blankly stared at him and she instead pointed her hand at him with the front of the palm looking at Fei slightly and zapping currents of electricity circuited around Lukeni's body zapping Fei. His scream was the combinations of two voices, proof that Lukeni was also feeling the pain. It immediately stopped as Dr Octavia dropped her hand down.

Fei then began to laugh hysterically, and Dr Octavia silenced him as she simply spoke, 'I could kill you both now and I do not think you understand. You value your life, that is why you find pervasive ways to stay in the world of the living. No, you cannot just be a memory or thing of history. You have become…no you are but a parasite, obsessed with power. Funny thing is true power, is mastering the self…We may never achieve it; however, we continue maintaining consistency however we can, you, however, fell off that wagon long ago. And have become a destructive force of nature, your type of immortality means you no longer human, you just chaos. Yes…I have studied antiquity and still do; I may not know the details. But one thing I can see is everything I have just said. The only student of the Water School, supposedly its only left master…you did not fail the world. You failed yourself.'

Her final words simply had Fei grunting, and then the eyes closed, and his face began to sweat, the changes of the face then took place. The hair suddenly changed colour and the eyes shot open no longer light blue, Lukeni was back. He was gasping for air, and then he looked at Dr Octavia with a look of hope, which then transformed to despair, 'I managed to fight him, inside…while you guys spoke

I sneaked up behind...I hit him, we were in a white space or room,' Lukeni spoke with a look of exhaustion and bewilderment.

A spark of epiphany hit Dr Octavia and she said, 'A dimension has been created in your mind an arena for you to challenge him. This may be the only way, only you can defeat him. You have lived this long you have the strength, now go get him.' Lukeni sighed nodding slightly and Dr Octavia then pointed her hand at him and with this gesture, he closed his eyes going back into the induced coma.

He found himself opening his eyes again this time in the room he spoke of, stretching for miles there was nothing but white. Looking down was a white bright surface and his feet were supported by it and he could feel the gravity as he felt grounded. It was all generated by his mind. He then looked ahead about a few meters away and there he saw Fei glaring back at him with piercing blue eyes. He wore ancient armour of his time, with his long white hair stopping at his shoulders.

'My son!' he snapped in disgust. Lukeni preparing himself, simply bent his knees tucking in his coccyx gently as he rooted himself further. Fei Yue then began to snigger and then sneered, 'You really think you can take me on.' Lukeni had heard enough and charged for Fei fearlessly.

331

# CHAPTER THIRTY- SINS OF THE FATHERS

Felix and Charles had managed to arrive in Wobbleton hours later after Dr Octavia's witnessing of Fei's manifestation. They had managed to find out where the doctor lived and rushed to the location. Speaking to the receptionist at the clinic they desperately asked for an audience with Dr Octavia. She finally met them in the reception area.

Felix and Charles were both taken aback by her beauty, as she stood before them in splendour with an air of seriousness. She greeted them with the yin-yang gesture, and they glanced at each other before responding the same way. She knew they were martial artists by doing so and Felix having heard of her before knew she was considered an expert in martial arts but did not know of which style.

'I am Felix Sobek and here is my cousin Charlie Sobek,' said Felix. 'You can call me Charles or

Chuck,' responded Charles as he beamed at Dr Octavia. 'I will go with Chuck,' she said and then continued, 'So what can I do for you gentlemen?' Felix then began explaining to her exactly why they were there and about Lukeni and finished with, 'You can check with Nzonzi.' He sensed a little mistrust in Dr Octavia's eyes.

'Call Mr Laari,' Dr Octavia said turning to the receptionist and once the number was dialled and the line was ringing on the other side, she headed to the phone holding it by the ear waiting for Nzonzi Laari to pick up. 'Morning Mr Laari, I have two gentlemen over here…' when she was done with the call, Nzonzi confirmed that he knew of Felix and that was indeed him that told them to head to the clinic. Once she was done, she gently put down the phone and then said, 'follow me.' She took them to the ward were Lukeni remained to seat with his hands and feet tied.

Charles and Felix looked at Lukeni and back at the doctor with frowns on their faces. And she explained to them why it was necessary and what had happened. Dr Octavia also informed them the short time they had before Lukeni died and Fei Yue would take over.

'The state I have put him in has allowed or created a dimension in his mind, sort of an arena for him to battle Fei Yue only he can destroy and defeat Fei. I believe he has the strength if that fails. With the aid of the needles I can kill Fei or whatever is left, I hope. I can sense the ongoing battle right now.' Once Dr Octavia finished her words, Charles immediately asked, 'Who is winning now?' 'Fei,' Dr Octavia coldly answered. 'Allow Lukeni the time though,' she added. 'On another subject, I must ask…' pausing Dr Octavia looked at both Felix and Charles straight in their eyes as if she was trying to read their souls. 'You two are the Sobeks of Sobeks right?' she then asked. 'Yes, and proudly so,' said Charles. 'Well I am a Chan, probably means nothing to you too…' Dr Octavia's words were cut by Felix as him and Charles had immediately figured out who she was. 'Shadow Chan would be your brother? Father? Uncle? You part of the Daruma bloodline?' asked Felix.

'Shadow is my older brother and yes I am, your family…' Felix cut the doctor again, 'Look we know the story and it's the sins of our fathers. We cannot change the past only the future by living in the present,' Felix ended his words trying to douse down his frustration. 'I agree,' Dr Octavia calmly said and then asked, 'so how did you meet Shadow?' 'That scum bag works for Gringer Solace,' said Charles not holding back, 'he tried to kill me and thy holy over here,' he added beaming teasingly at Felix who did not dance in the amusement and remained calm. 'I took the bullet for you…you…' Felix sighed again controlling himself. He then told Dr Octavia everything, the whole story of how he was Commander of a unit in the Union Guards Elite Force responsible in eradicating the remnants of the brotherhood and how Gringer Solace wanted Lukeni's essence to attain the power of Fei Yue.

She listened carefully and then once he was done, she responded with, 'Knowing my brother he did not want to let pass the opportunity of killing two Sobeks to avenge our ancestor Daruma. One thing our families share is a long memory and a tendency for vengeance, an ancient tradition and trait from the Sol Islands.' 'However, I sense there is more, especially with you Felix, why do put so much importance in caring for Lukeni?' she asked. 'It's another long story, Fei Yue's father was Felix Subek the First of the Sol Islands,' answered Felix. 'Fei had revealed this to me...' he added. 'It's a really fucked up...' Dr Octavia chuckled with a wry smile, 'I do not know what else to say,' she added.

Thousands of years earlier, a small boat with a makeshift sail landed on the coast of the Sol Islands. Back then populated by different clans. Coming off the boat was a man now thirty years of age, his name was Daruma. Unlike most people of the Sol Islands, Daruma had wider eyes than the average Solese. His eyebrows were thick and black and so was his beard. He had wolf-like yellow eyes and a permanent hawkish gaze, dressed in dirty robes, Daruma Chan had returned from his odyssey around the world.

He had left in armour, sword and splendour, with a chest filled with some gold and silver coins, enough fortune to set up elsewhere. Departing on a small Solese boat, which could take on the seas; a warrior of high nobility is what he left as. And on his return, he looked ragtag; he was thought long dead, and nor did he bring stories of conquest. The small fortune he had left with he could have used to hire a band of armed men and then grow that gradually into an army, however, none of this occurred. But, despite the rat tag look, physically he looked strong and mentally, sharp. His hawkish gaze pierced the soul and rattled it with natural intimidation.

Daruma Chan had left his clan which stayed in the main island of the Sol Islands, his father was the chief of the clan. And Daruma was the youngest of all the children, the fifth child and all the children were boys. His first four brothers died honourably in battle fighting the other clans around the islands and the fourth one from raiding far coastal cities in the continents. Daruma, the last son, wanted more and did not like the traditions, he decided to leave the island and promised to come back a conqueror.

Upon his return, his father Kam Chan, chief of the Chan clan was still alive and in his death bed, stubbornly believing his son to be alive and promising to only give up his last breath when he laid his eyes on his son again.

Most in the clan did not recognise Daruma, and those who did saw him as a failure and hid their loathing sentiments as the chief was still alive. Kam was overjoyed and mustering the last bits of his life force he said, 'Daruma! My son you back!' Daruma beamed at his father amazed how his once-powerful warrior chief of a father was now weak on his death bed. 'He grew weaker from missing his son, you know...' said an old woman who stood by the bed, looking at Daruma disappointed. 'Close your mouth Teki!' exclaimed Kam and then coughed. 'I am sorry,' Daruma said. 'Ignore your mother she is crazy...Our son is back and this all you can say,' said Kam looking at his wife Teki who looked annoyed.

He then turned to Daruma beaming and said, 'I can see you have returned more powerful than before. You were weak when you left and have returned a man! Wish your brothers were here so they can feel what I am feeling. I am not disappointed with my son. You did not conquer cities, or come back an emperor, you did what most warriors fail to do, you conquered yourself, the inner enemy. Even I did not manage to come to this level. Regardless I have no regret. Look at me, I longed for more in my younger days and rightfully so, it's natural, yet with the months of your departure. The only thing I wished for was to see you alive. Nothing else mattered. Yes, my health has deteriorated, but at least you came back and are alive. I will not stress any of the traditions on you. I just wish you a peaceful life and that you bare grandchildren, beautiful boys or girls,' chuckling Kam grabbed Daruma tightly, and Daruma could feel the last remaining strength of his father, he still had some power. The grip loosened his eyes closed and there went his last breath. Teki cried placing her head on her husband's abdomen as she sobbed. Daruma felt a tear trickle down and he gently rubbed it away.

Leaving the chief's dwelling, the bigger hut in the clan, he suddenly encountered the clan's warriors waiting outside armed and ready. Daruma knew what was coming next.

'You will not let me at least weep my father's death?' he asked them kindly. 'You fool!' snapped one of them. As they drew out their swords from their sheaths and one retorted, 'Your travels have weakened you! You cannot be the next chief! Once we kill you, we will kill what is left of the Chan name.'

Daruma simply stood there silent and both his hands spiralled out with the fingers down and the front of the palms out facing forward. The warrior charged for him, each one brandishing a sword, ready to cut Daruma down. When they got close to slash him, his sudden movements surprised them. One moment he was in front of them and the next behind them. They stopped flabbergasted and stared at each other in disbelief. 'What sorcery is this?' anxiously asked one of them. 'Sorcery?' sneered Daruma and then continued, 'This is the result of years of consistent training, years of refining the mind, the essence and the energy. This is harmonising the body and the mind.'

The warrior glanced at each other again with uncertainty creeping in with fear and then they were suddenly overwhelmed with it that they bowed down to their knees immediately seeking forgiveness. 'Get up!' barked Daruma, 'all I ask for is peace,' he added setting himself down in a calmer tone and the warriors immediately dispersed.

The event caused a ripple of rumours spreading and soon before Daruma knew it warriors from the clan and afar from the other islands wanted to challenge him. And he did not decline their challenges, welcoming it. He never killed any of his adversaries and with more victories within the following months, his name travelled to all corners of the islands.

Daruma did not formally become the chief of the Chan Clan, the elder council kept order and his mother Teki was part of the council and headed it. However, Daruma was somewhat of the de facto chief and he decided to keep it that way.

One of Chan clan's main allies the Subek Clan which occupied most of the Northern parts of the main Island of Sol Islands was led by the young chief, Sung Subek. He was five years younger than Daruma and ambitious. He was fascinated by Daruma's skill and had coined the martial art style, "The Harmonious Fist".

Sung became a disciple of Daruma learning everything he could and training arduously. Daruma fell in love with Sung's sister and she fell in love with him, that they married and had children. They had two boys, the firstborn was named Kam Chan and the other one, born five years later was named Darum Chan. The alliance between the Chans and the Subeks could have not been firmer.

With this firm alliance, Sung pleaded to his ally and master that they unify all the clans and with Daruma's knowledge, conqueror the world. However, Daruma would calmly decline each time. 'I have travelled the world with that pursuit and discovered I need to conqueror myself first,' he would say. And Sung will stubbornly respond with, 'Well lets at least unify the clans here.' Daruma would then chuckle instead of replying, it was his way of responding to the idea that he found it ridiculous.

Sung was too ambitious and had already begun spreading his influence, having taught the "Harmonious Fist" to his cousins and the rest in his clan. The warriors of the Subek Clan had conquered smaller clans absorbing them and Daruma stopped his disciple when other clan chiefs fearing Sung pleaded for peace by going to Daruma. This immediately halted Sung's plans. Growing with frustration he did the unthinkable, knowing he could not take on his master who was beyond his ability, he poisoned Daruma one day during a banquet.

Daruma found himself choking on his blood as his life drifted away and he struggled, he cast a look at

Sung, knowing that he was behind it. Sung brushed aside the guilt and held a huge funeral to pay homage to Daruma his master. There were seven days of mourning and at this time Daruma's firstborn, Kam was thirteen years of age and very proficient in the "Harmonious Fist" and his younger brother Darum was but eight years old and not a threat to Sung. Lizek, Sung's sister who was Daruma's wife. Could not believe her husband's sudden death. After the mourning, Sung's used Daruma's death as an opportunity and blamed the poisoning as a plot from all the other chiefs in the Sol Islands. Mobilising his army, he began his conquest and met no major resistance. The warriors of the Chan clan were united behind this cause. Nevertheless, Lizek started to suspect her older brother and Sung sensing that his sister could be a threat, including Kam Chan plotted for their murder. Nothing could get in his way; nothing could stop his lust for conquest.

Using some of the Harmonious Fist she knew Lizek managed to escape one early morning before sunrise. Packing a little, her and Kam managed to defeat guards set to protect them, however, who Lizek knew were awaiting the order from Sung to murder her and her children. She escaped by sailing on a boat and received refuge at the Loham Temple. A place where Daruma had spent some of his years and introduced the monks there to certain chi kung exercises and martial arts. The Loham Temple monks welcomed her and her children.

Back in the island, the Chan clan was eventually absorbed into the Subek clan and within the grasps of achieving his dream of unification, Sung Subek died in battle from a random fever, received after he stubbornly refused to receive immediate medical care from a battle wound. Instead, he wanted to the press on. He was replaced by his son Lik Fa, who stopped the conquest of the Sol Islands and a peace treaty was signed amongst what remained of the other clans. It was Sung's grandson, Felix Subek the First. Determined, unrestrained and craftier than his grandfather before him, who poisoned his father, Lik Fa and blamed the murder on the other chiefs resuming the war and within two years the whole Sol Islands were conquered. With Felix Subek the First as its king, consolidating his power and crushing whatever remained of resistance, his eyes were now set on the continents of the world.

Felix Subek was tall, slightly darker of complexion than the average Solese inhabitant. He had thick furious eyebrows and a heavy black beard with short black hair. Built like a rock, he was an intimidating figure, notoriously known to head into battle half-naked with nothing but his sword which he wielded in one hand. His iron body from his chi kung training could not be pierced nor cut from the swords that slashed at it or the arrows that tried piercing through, all were bounced back before he struck with a counter.

Setting his light blue eyes like a falcon does his prey, he peered at the sea and he set out to conquer the lands beyond the Sol Islands after his coronation as king. Sailing with a handful of men, they were to conquer first the small coastal villages. After crushing two villages, the third did not fight back and the chief even offered one of his daughters for marriage, she was the prettiest of his daughters. A luring beauty, she had long light blonde hair and fair skin like none of the women in the Sol Islands. Her eyes were blue but darker in comparison to Felix Subek's. She was fifteen years at the time, and had no choice in the matter, scared and repulsed by Subek she did her best to not offend her father and clan who counted their survival on her.

Felix wasted no time in ravishing her the night after the wedding, his subjects were surprised as he waited days. Telling them, 'My loins are on fire, and shall let the flames grow bigger because when I penetrate the virginity out of her, she shall not forget.' The girl gave some resistance, as Felix smiled at this resistance delighted, he forced himself on her and took rounds after rounds of thrusting her and manhandling her in positions he found pleasurable.

Her name was Helena, this young girl would be part of his collection of wives and she had become his youngest. He obsessed over her, to the point his generals and subjects if found to look at her in a manner Felix Subek found suspicious, he who would order for their instant death. He was a cruel king that was feared and Helena detesting him, she would cry till her eyes were dry as he would force himself on her. When she fell pregnant, she started plotting her escape out of the Sol Islands.

The other wives who saw her pain and were jealous Felix Subek spent most nights with her, plotted her escape hoping that Felix Subek would spend more time with them. They aided her in her escape on a trading fishing boat. The boat headed to the coast of one of the continents, that would be the city of Feiville in modern times, on that continent further inland, was a village not far from the mountainous Dragon's Lair. There Helena found refuge in a very small village and would give birth to a son she would name Fei and she took the name Yue, which became the new family name.

Hell had broken loose and Felix Subek's insanity was triggered to higher levels. His conquest of the coastal villages had stopped. The escape of Helena had occurred during one of his campaigns, the wives then began betraying each other. Hoping they would be favoured and have Felix Subek all to themselves. But this vile man had other plans, insidious in thought and action, for his generals to prove their loyalty to him, he ordered each one to all rape his wives and then kill them. An order they all obeyed and then made his children who were all mostly boys watch as they burned the dead bodies of their mothers. Felix Subek did this as a display to his own that he did not accept betrayal. Now crazier than ever, he no longer focused on the conquest of foreign lands. In his megalomaniac nature, he amassed an armada that sailed the seas in search of Helena, raping and pillaging when it hit the shores. The Sol Islands had extended its kingdom to just a few conquered territories, from the nearest continent and then because of the madness of Felix the First they resumed to just pillaging, including rapes and bringing women and bounty back to the Sol Islands. However, the Sol Islands despite Felix Subek's tyranny amassed plenty of wealth during this period of pillaging.

Obsessed and relentless, one day he found the village not far from the Dragon's Lair and like a rampant raging fire. Felix Subek and his men raped all the women and murdered everything that moved, he raped and killed Helena. Angry she was still beautiful from all these years and she never told him where his son was, 'His name is Fei and you will never meet him nor know him. I told him of you and that he should never be like you,' was her lost words when he pierced her body with the traditional short sword, he had wielded in all his battles. And this was the last time he would use the sword as he abandoned it there. It was a massacre of catastrophic proportions.

Felix Subek was swarmed by his sins, as they came in the form of horrific nightmares, however, what made him fall in an abyss of sorrow, was that he knew those nightmares or the unidentifiable voices that tormented him, was nothing compared to his appalling actions on his victims.

Despite ailing mental health, the tyranny somehow seized, and the raiding of coastal villagers or towns gradually stopped, he then founded the Council of Masters in his last days and commissioned for the building of statues of Daruma, hailed the creator of the "Harmonious Fist".

Word then spread from the continents to the seas and then to the Sol Islands of men conquering territories from the newly established Fei Kingdom. When Felix Subek's subjects told him of this, he smiled beaming and excited, his subjects were surprised at this they had never seen him in such a state. Felix Subek ordered the immediate preparations of ships as he was going to meet this Fei. Knowing it was his son and knowing this was the only part of Helena that was still alive, Felix Subek was willing to abdicate to see his son.

However, the news of Fei's growing power came from one of the few parties that still raided the coasts, who came in contact with Fei and his army and were crushed. Only one's life was spared, and they sent him back with some of the body parts of his comrades. Therefore, the Council of master's saw this as a declaration of war and were amazed at the glee in Felix Subek's face as he ordered the preparations of the ships.

The Council of Masters, which at the time only

consisted of Subeks, plotted the murder and abdication of Felix Subek the First. But before the plotters could get a hand on the king, he was found dead in his royal chamber. He had stabbed himself through the heart. It was said he was heard talking to himself as if he spoke to someone else. He spoke to Helena who was long dead, and his last words were apologies to his late wife before he fell silent.

With his death came the end of his reign over the Sol Islands, now unified and ruled by the Subek Clan. During the Fei terrors, the Sol Islands aligned themselves with what would later become the Sud Empire. Fei wanted to conquer the Sol Islands and defile what remained of his father, however, he got caught up in his power.

# CHAPTER THIRTY-ONE-DAMSEL IN DISTRESS

Charles had left Felix with Dr Octavia and Lukeni, he told Felix he had unfinished business in Feiville. They knew Gringer Solace had his men out looking for Lukeni. But also, for Charles and Felix. Charles was planning on saving Helga Jones from the hands of Otto Von, he did not care about her past or Shadow's warning. He could see that Otto was obsessed with Helga and rescuing her would enrage Otto he thought. Despite Shadow's warning ringing in his mind, *"Her charms, her beauty that is her weapon, if you do not cure yourself of her poison you will end up one of her victims."* He ignored those thoughts walking around the mega-metropolis that was Feiville, he had missed the city.

From his arrival he had sensed people were following him, it could not be his paranoia and he knew it would be a matter of time before they tried something.

However, it seemed his followers who Charles thought were Gringer's men seemed to only be gathering information. Charles found this a strange thing for Gringer's men to do and decided he would strike out first.

Arriving at Feiville he did not dare visit the high-end bar in the city's affluent area. Doing his best to be unpredictable, he did not visit any brothels nor frequent any bars for a week. He would walk in the city's parks for exercise and could sometimes see the confusion on his follower's faces without them knowing. And visit a dog shelter, where he had volunteered to assist in the feeding and caring of the city's abused dogs, who were rescued from dogfighting pits. This unpredictable behaviour followed to the following week, throwing his followers further astray.

Charles then struck, one day a man who wore a blue shirt had appeared where Charles was. What gave him away was the fact that he was present in different locations across the city. Although well covered in appearing to mind his own business. His shirt and him being at the park and passing by cycling outside the dog shelter to other locations that were far apart from each other was more than a coincidence.

The man was riding his bike and as he rode past Charles, in a sudden moment, Charles closed lined him. Stretching hand out and hitting the men on the chest. The men immediately fell off the bike and landed on his back. Charles was on him like a predator on its prey, he knelt over and grabbed the man by his collar, glaring with all fury.

'Fuck face…hey!' exclaiming as people glanced around, surprised and confused, Charles did not care and shook the man by the collar that he banged the back of the head a few times against the ground. Then he lifted the man still holding on to his collar, 'Speak! Who sent you?' he snapped. 'Otto Von…' said the man, struggling to speak and once he spoke his words. Charles immediately shoved him away, he stumbled a few meters back and then fell. Charles had heard enough and walked away.

He had thought something was strange and it made sense because Gringer's men would have made a move already. He did not need to ponder further and that evening under a full bright moon he made his move, by heading straight to the high-end bar.

The bouncers outside immediately recognised him and warned him to turn back. 'As far as I see it you guys have a few choices, either you let me in or I break a few of your bones and I let myself in,' said Charles with a sneer on his face. The bouncers cleared the way remembering too well what happened the last time.

Bright lights and crystal chandeliers and a crowd dressed in the latest of fashions, and like the last time, he was there, with his bushy wild hair and a leather jacket. He stuck out like a sore thumb;

Charles immediately glanced around for Otto, trying to keep calm as he felt doses of adrenaline being released into his blood.

Then he heard the voice that sunk his heart and massaged his body with warmth, that of Helga as she appeared on stage speaking and after a few claps of applaud, she began to sing. She had not caught a glimpse of Charles who stared at her in awe. She looked like she was in her element singing and casting her charms on the crowd and Charles. After a deep sigh, he regained his focus and moved around, finding a spot where he would be out of sight while everybody was glued on Helga's figure and voice.

Once she was done singing and had headed backstage to her change room. She was welcomed with fear momentarily gripping her at the presence of Charles, who had sneaked in her changing room waiting for her impatiently. And before she could yell for help. He covered her mouth; she felt his strong grip and did not bother fighting back. Removing his hand, he then launched his lips on her forcing a kiss. Helga resisted shutting her mouth and pushed him off and then slapped him suddenly. 'Stop it!' she grunted.

Charles chuckled, 'Its fine if you do not want me, but why Otto? Any men but him!' exhaling Charles realised he was allowing his frustration to control him, and he lowered his tone, 'I am not going to apologise for forcing that kiss, now we can confirm you not attracted to me. That's fine. However, I have come to rescue you. Give you your freedom, and I clearly will have nothing in return,' said Charles. Helga gathering herself, cast away the fearful look she had on her face, and this was replaced with one that was strong and confident. This caught Charles off guard as he just stared at her.

She strolled past him, and he stared struck by her sudden air of confidence, she sat on the chair which stood in front of the mirror she used when she put some make up on, and this was next to a wardrobe.

Seating down she gazed at Charles like a fussy cat with the same cool and arrogant elegance. 'You will have something in return,' begin Helga and continued, 'it will destroy Otto and you know it. I am an independent woman, I promised I will get the bar back in my father's name and that is what I intend to do. Him forcing his way means nothing to me. For a martial artist, you clearly not familiar with the concept of yin-yang, or taiji…' pausing she laughed a bit and sighed, 'Where your martial skills end, my charm begins, do you really think Otto would kill me if Gringer ordered it?... Even if he did, I am ready to die. He plays tough but his all soft inside… the little rich boy cries when he orgasms after going at it for thirty seconds…pathetic…even you…all tough…But I am sure you also weak…' Her final words made Charles dig deep sending signals of confusion he looked down and exhaled. He was far from weak, nonetheless, he now saw what Shadow saw in her and understood. He found honour in Helga, she was ready to fight tooth and nail for the bar which originally belonged to her father. And this Charles admired, he looked at her with respect and could not help but fall further because of this. 'You wrong about me, I have my demons but they real ones...Subek or Sobek we are born fighters and then learn the Harmonious Fist, my life has real darkness. And so, does yours, but whether it's your beauty or your current display of honour. You one of the few things that shed the light I need,' falling in silence he beamed at Helga, who giggled and rolled her eyes in rejection. 'Chuck, its better you leave,' she said as she slowly got up and looked back at the mirror.

Charles felt his heart sink with the stabbing of a thousand knives, somebody needed him at this moment his cousin Felix. Even more the world, Fei could manifest himself out of Lukeni's body and re-incarnate back bringing his terror at any time. And here he was obsessed and loving a woman who did not feel an ounce of the equivalent emotion. These thoughts raged in his mind at a sudden with each heartbeat as he felt a mixture of despair and adrenaline.

The doors flung open nearly going off their hinges and charging through was Otto followed by an army of bouncers all armed to the teeth. Guns blazing, cocked and ready to shoot, Charles simply looked with his eyes widened a little. He was trapped just when he was about to say goodbye to Helga and wish to never see her again. 'Now you fucked,' she said, and he glanced back at her and then gazed back at Otto and his men.

'You cockroach! What are you doing in my establishment!' yelled Otto as his face reddened with rage. 'I was just leaving,' Charles brazenly responded, he did not care, if death was going to come there and then, so be it he thought. And then he began to calm and drop everything down. Just below his navel, he felt a sudden sparking surge. That was flowing first from his feet; he then added, 'And this is a message for you and Gringer.' With those final words, he lifted his hand and slightly bent his wrist and surging currents of electricity zapped one of Otto's men. Quick, sudden and instantaneous, it was no longer than three seconds of which after the man hit the ground. His clothes burned to a crisp and his body was unrecognisable as smoke and the smell of burned corpse permeated the room. Everybody stood in shock and confusion, Otto's rage was replaced with fear as he gazed at the now-dead bouncer and then back at Charles in awe with his mouth wide open. Behind Charles, Helga covered her mouth in shock and the room stood silent, Charles then cleared his throat as he looked at the dead bouncer he had incinerated.

'Well, I suggest you drop your weapons if you do not want to join him,' said Charles beaming. Slowly Otto and his men lowered their guns and then all knelt to the floor, to place their weapons on the ground. Charles then strolled out not turning his back to say bye at Helga, he had to head back to Wobbleton.

# CHAPTER THIRTY-TWO-THE LAST FLAME

Charles was back in Wobbleton within two days, immediately visiting Dr Octavia to see how Lukeni was doing. He was joined by Felix who had been visiting occasionally.

The progress on Lukeni was in dire straits, with no improvements. 'He has been fighting Fei inside the last few days and it's clear he's losing the battle,' said Dr Octavia as she sighed crossing her arms and resumed scanning Lukeni who lay on a bed no longer chained. His forehead was covered in sweat and he shivered with his eyes closed as if he was experiencing the deepest of nightmares.

'I managed to speak to him when he was awake… the tumour or Fei is moving around his body, trying to reach his energy centre…' Dr Octavia was interrupted by Felix who said, 'His dan tien.' 'Yes,' agreed Dr Octavia and then continued, 'I have told Lukeni he would need to eject the tumour out, if he manages to defeat Fei, he can then eject the tumour out. I do not know how he will do this, or even if he will still be alive after doing so, however, it's the only way Fei can be put to bed forever...oh one more thing,' pausing she held her chin. Slightly impatient Charles asked, 'What?' 'We need something to destroy the tumour once it's ejected out of Lukeni's body, or if all fails as well...We need the Last Flame.' Felix and Charles glanced at each other with heavy frowns and Dr Octavia immediately begin explaining what the Last Flame was, 'The Last Flame is a thing of legends, a blue flame burning for eternity, what it is, is the energy of dragons gathered and issued usually as a dragon's last move in a fight when all is lost. It's a very powerful source of power, if projected like a flame it burns for eternity.' 'And it can only be doused by the calmest of minds, which represents the needed water,' added Felix. 'Yes, but the point is we need its strong yang energy to destroy Fei,' responded Dr Octavia. 'Great, we really out of luck, there is no longer any dragons and we will need to head to the Dragons' Lair to find this Last Flame, it would really be a waste time. Time, we do not have,' said Felix. 'Well? Do you have anything else in mind?' Dr Octavia asked.

'Yes,' Felix confidently begin and continued, 'I have an old friend James Stockhorn, I will contact him immediately his bloodline is of dragon handlers who were dwellers who once wondered the Dragon's Lair before the appearance of Daoists there. His uncle Drasul Stockhorn once displayed this power, the Last Flame ability. James has the ability now.' A smile painted itself wide on Dr Octavia's face and she hugged Felix and then said excitedly, 'There is hope, after all, please contact your friend!'

Felix got to it straight contacting James and in the meantime deep in the depth of Lukeni's mind. In the white terrain where he faced Fei, the two were at it like two wolves battling for dominance. Lukeni was the weaker one and this was evident as he found himself up in the air after an uppercut to the chin. He landed hard on the white bright ground. Feeling dizzy, he stumbled to get up, the blow feeling real with the added pain. And strolling towards him was Fei diabolically laughing as he then he said, 'Your tiger claw is weak, and I am done playing. Time to show you my true power son!' with his last words and his hand outstretched sparks of current shot out in a sudden like lightning zapping Lukeni who yelled from the top of his lungs. The pain excruciating and the electrical thunder-like current paralysed his body as it surged.

This was the end he could not bear it anymore and then began to close his eyes, and Fei seeing this began to gleefully laugh. 'This is the power of the Harmonious Fist son!' exclaimed Fei as he began to get closer to finish off the job. Thoughts of Wong Claw, his Uncle Nzonzi Laari and most importantly

Nzinga Laari his mother who he had never met came to mind. Lukeni then shot his eyes back open before they fully closed and got in a horse stance. Welcoming the pain and suffering, he stretched his hands out, his thumb curled, and index finger pointed straight. The rest of his fingers were curled, and he pulled both hands back in, in line with his sternum as he began to absorb the surge of energy issued by Fei allowing all of it to seek into the ground.

Frustrated by this action Fei increased the impact tenfold. Dropping his hand as surges of lighting like currents exploded off his body hitting Lukeni. 'I may not have the power to issue, but I can absorb and give it all back to you,' said Lukeni sensing it was now time. He felt a surge go up to his spine and stretched his hands out both forming tiger claws. The surge shot out, giving Fei back what he had issued into Lukeni. It hit Fei with immediate effect sending him up and away as he landed three metres from his original position.

Lukeni looked at his hands surprised he did not feel drained, and he noticed he was not burned by Fei's attack. He then glanced at his father who struggled to get up and bellowed, 'I WANT YOU OUT OF MY BODY!' Bolts of thunder appeared out of nowhere, hitting Fei from all directions as he screamed.

Lukeni felt himself wake up as he rolled out of the bed and fell, he then got up. Catching a glimpse of

Felix, Dr Octavia and Charles. A few days had passed, but the time inside his mind when he fought Fei felt like minutes ago. They tried to assist him, and he snarled, 'No!' grabbing his head and then below his navel, it seemed a lump was moving about his body and Lukeni begin to scream and grimace as the lump seemed to be moving up, he was preparing to vomit it out.

'So, here is the kid,' said another voice, it came from an old man with short black hair with streaks of silver hair on both sides. He was white, with hazel eyes and had a short silver goatee. The man was James Stockhorn. Everybody ignored his statement as their eyes remained glued on Lukeni, who had begun vomiting something slimy and dark, he struggled for few more seconds and then it was out completely hitting the ground of the clinic. It began to move around like a slug, it looked like it had a face, with what looked like light blue eyes and bits of white hair. It was what remained of Fei. It made weird noises and small sparks of currents began surging around it. 'JAMES QUICK!' yelled Felix as he stared at the thing that was supposed to be Fei.

Silent, James stepped forth, and gently stretched out his hand and his hazel eyes lit up to bright blinding light as he issued his energy out in a sudden. The room got hot and a blue light streamed from his hand onto the thing suddenly setting it light into a blue flame. It began screaming helplessly as everybody stared at it. Lukeni, who looked completely worn out looked in disbelief as the thing rapidly burned.

Nothing but black ash was left, and James then said, 'It's over now.' 'Thank you,' said Dr Octavia as she turned to James and then looked at the black ashes on the burned floor with a frown on her face. 'Where is the blue flame?' she asked James. 'I took it back, it does burn for eternity after all,' he responded with a smile. 'Well the worst is over,' said Felix. 'No, it's not,' begin Charles, 'We need to get rid of Gringer and Shadow,' finishing his words he glanced at Dr Octavia and simply shrugged his shoulders. 'There is no need for that my cousin, Gringer will meet his end soon and as for Shadow his no match for us. You see that is the perfect example of the curse or vicious cycle we have had in this Sobek Legacy,' said Felix as he looked at the ashes of Fei. 'You mean Subek Legacy,' said James as he beamed. Charles chuckled, and Felix simply smiled and then everybody turned to look at Lukeni who had fainted hitting the ground with a thud.

Lukeni was thrown into a Life tank to rejuvenate rapidly for two days and then he was rehabilitated by Dr Octavia through heavy acupuncture sessions for few more days before being released. He joined Felix and Charles who had decided to head to the Sol Islands for some training and they wanted to introduce Lukeni to his other roots.

Gringer Solace's power and influence had begun

361

to show cracks of weakness and his men had grown restless. His obsession with finding Lukeni had caused this decay and so was his obsession for power. Shadow Chan his trusted lieutenant had disappeared in an unknown abyss. And in complete disarray, Gringer had resorted to hard liquor. One evening, alone in his office, the noise of gunshots startled him, and he grabbed hold of his handgun and downed what was left of his liquor, as he stared at the door wearily pointing his gun as he heard footsteps. He fired shots anxiously at the door each round leaving gaping holes on the door. This was done until he was out of bullets, desperate he threw his gun at the door, and then moments later the door flung open off its hinges and landed on the ground.

A few men dressed in black with masked faces stormed in, they did not point their guns at Gringer and once in, one more person who was also dressed in black strolled in unmasking himself. His hair was mostly black and curly, with streaks of silver. He was clean-shaven and white; he still had an off-air of youth on his face and the silver streaks were testament that he was becoming an old man.

'Who you!' snapped Gringer in his drunken state. The man beamed and chuckled a bit before responding, 'I was an upstart who challenged the Baron, bless his soul. He even sent his men to kill me, they took me to a dungeon tortured me and they fired a bullet at the back of my head. Dumping my body, and like most gangster stories I was lucky enough to still be alive. I am Smokey and I have been in the shadows ever since. I never dared to seek revenge, because Carl Sobek was the father of a dear friend of mine Felix Sobek. The underworld of crime is riddled with wolves and I sense weakness, so I made a move to take over that is why I am here. However, it funny how you pretended to make it look like it was one of your men who was running things in Wobbleton, that decided to kill the Baron. No, it was you and you wanted to flush out Felix and instead, you had his cousin Charles showing up, you then manipulated him all these years to flush out Felix...Yes, I am also here on Felix's account as well. Now, do you have any last words?'

Gringer grunting charged forth, and with each step, he could make, bullets hailed down on him piercing every part of his body; stopping him in a sudden as he dropped to the ground. Streams of blood leaked out onto the office floor as his body lay dead.

# THE END

Printed in France by Amazon
Brétigny-sur-Orge, FR

13616954R00210